KV-033-860

3 8014 05150 7181

The Toll of the Sea

The Toll of the Sea

Theresa Murphy

ROBERT HALE · LONDON

© Theresa Murphy 2013
First published in Great Britain 2013

ISBN: 978-0-7198-0793-0

Robert Hale Limited
Clerkenwell House
Clerkenwell Green
London EC1R 0HT

www.halebooks.com

2 4 6 8 10 9 7 5 3 1

Typeset in 11/15.2pt Palatino
Printed in the UK by the MPG Books Group

Prologue

Anxiety on her face, the woman was kneading dough on a rough wooden table. Years of poverty and hardship had eroded her prettiness but an indelible sensuality remained. Her dark auburn hair was tousled and concentration caused her heavy bottom lip to droop a little. Lean arms dusted with flour up to the elbows, she kept her eyes nervously averted from the man standing in the corner of the crude kitchen. He was a big man in an obese way. Expensively dressed, he had a bulging stomach covered and supported by a gaudy chequered waistcoat more suited to a bookmaker than an insurance agent. His black hair was parted in the middle and greased flat to the skull on each side. A heavily jowled, florid face had as a centre-piece a bulbous nose criss-crossed with blue veins. His breathing caused a purring rattle in his throat, and he had an aura of sour perspiration that extended six feet from his gross body. As he made a display of opening a thick book with a glossy black cover, the small girl sitting on the floor studied him with the ego-absent scrutiny of an infant.

Placing a finger on a page of the book, he pursed his fat blue lips in an expression of concern. His loud voice broke an uncomfortably lengthening silence, startling the woman. She cowered, reacting to each of his words as if they were physical blows.

'I hadn't realized how sorry a state you are in, Mrs Willard.' The man shook a large, despairing head. 'It says here that the last payment you made was on the 23rd of September. That is coming up to four months ago, Mrs Willard. I am sure you appreciate that it can't be allowed to go on like this.'

Though her lips moved, the woman had no reply to make. The impoverished could only hope to evade issues such as this. They certainly didn't argue them.

From somewhere high and distant outside came the mournful and repetitive cry of a wheeling seagull. Closer then, so near that it seemed to be a threat to the stone house that had been built without mortar, came the pebble-scraping roar of a wave building up to smash against the beach with an impact that shook the dirt floor beneath their feet.

A chicken, its dark-red feathers caked with mud, walked in uninvited to do a pointlessly circular tour of the kitchen in its peculiar neck and leg stretching gait. Both the man and the woman watched the chicken intently as if it was right then the most important thing in the world. As it went back out of the door the child waved the arm of a rag doll at the hen and giggled a farewell.

Regretting that the diversion was over, the woman turned her gaze back to the dough in front of her. Watching her keenly for a moment, the man suddenly clutched jerkily at the book he was holding in both hands, giving the impression he was struggling against some action the book had decided to take independently.

'It's only a matter of pence, Mrs Willard,' he used a reasonable tone to point out.

'Pennies don't come easy to the likes of we, sir,' she said.

As she spoke she turned her face to him. It had a strength, something of a masculinity that was, conversely, exciting in a woman. Yet she seemed to have been frightened by her own temerity, and was using long white teeth to hold a moist bottom lip to prevent herself from saying more.

The rattle of the man's breathing increased in volume. It no longer resembled a feline sound of contentment. There was a threat to it before a noisy clearing of his throat cured the wheezing, but only temporarily. Soon the rasping was louder than before as he seemed to be fighting to retrieve a lost voice.

'I do understand that these are hard times, Mrs Willard, but as a good wife and mother, an admirably intelligent woman if I may be so bold, you will recognize the security that these few pennies buy you.' Pausing, he tilted his large head to one side in a listening attitude, the excess flesh on his face dangling lopsidedly in rounded folds. Another wave had crashed against the shore, and he waited. The violent crescendo eased to an angry hissing as the shattered breaker died. Then he went on, 'There's a huge swell out there this morning that makes hauling in those nets dangerous. Is your man trawling with them, Mrs Willard?'

She nodded, putting more effort into her kneading, pounding her knuckles into the dough as if it represented all the deprivations in her life. From under long lashes she covertly watched him bend to run fat white fingers through the copper-coloured ringlets of her tiny daughter. His smile displayed artificial teeth and bogus sincerity. The woman was hurt by the way the man energetically wiped the hand with which he had touched the child.

Then, taking a sudden step towards her, he seemed to fill the room so that she felt a claustrophobic suffocation. He laid the open book on the table in front of her. Repeatedly tapping the relevant page with a forefinger, he again made his lips bell-shaped to produce a sighing sound to let her know this was the part of his job that he didn't like.

He coaxingly enquired, 'Perhaps you could manage this week's payment and a little off the arrears, Mrs Willard?' When she gave a rapid, negative shake of her head, he added in a less pleasant tone, 'Otherwise I will have no option but to cancel the policy. Sad to say, it won't end there. My superiors will take immediate action to recover your debt to date.'

Under pressure, the woman started to cry. It wasn't a self-pitying sobbing, but the weary weeping of someone who'd fought too many unequal battles against overpowering odds. A small tear leaked from each of her closed lids. She cringed as he moved closer to her. Using a crudely suggestive middle finger he ran it up through flour dust from the wrist to the elbow of her right arm, leaving a temporary track on her skin while inflicting an eternal mark on her soul.

'It has to be paid,' he told her hoarsely. 'One way or another ... Lucy.'

For a few seconds her body went as rigid as steel. Then she slumped forwards in defeat, grasping the thick edges of the table with both hands to support herself. After a little while she straightened up to walk zombie-like across the kitchen. Being one of the poorer houses in that part of Devon, it had only one other room. She stooped to sit on her heels beside her tiny daughter. Reaching out with both hands to clasp the chubby little shoulders, she whispered falteringly, 'Be a good girl for Mama, Bella,' she urged, using a swift movement of her hand to knock away a falling tear before it could land on the small girl. 'Stay here and play with your dolly. Mama will be back soon.'

Standing up, the woman carried on to go through the doorway into the adjoining room, avoiding the lustfully clutching hands of the man until they were both out of the child's sight.

The fact that she kept her eyes closed saved the woman from witnessing the grimace of distaste the man gave on seeing sacking masquerading as bedclothes. He glanced up disdainfully at the black-edged hole in the ceiling that served in the absence of an unaffordable chimney. But his needs overcame his repugnance and he reached for her.

Twenty minutes later it was the man who came back into the kitchen first. The red/blue hue of his face had gained a purple depth from exertion, and there were beads of sweat linking up with each other on his brow. His top lip was wet either with perspiration or smeared dribble. Picking up his book from the table he closed it with a thud that frightened the child. Permitting himself a brief, lip-smacking leer of satisfaction, he fed his book under his right arm, the shoulder doing a practised lift to accommodate it. Then he walked out of the house without glancing at the smiling child who was waving the arm of her doll at him.

Less than a minute later the mother returned to run across the room and drop to her knees beside her daughter. Tilting back her head of shining ringlets, the child's face came alight with a loving smile. Putting out her hands to the little girl, the mother then snatched them back violently before they could actually touch the child.

Dismayed at being deprived of an anticipated embrace, the girl began to cry. Making comforting sounds, the mother dashed to where a basin of water rested on a rickety chair. Stooping over, she washed her hands over and over again.

Becoming aware of a commotion outside of the house, she swiftly dried her hands and lifted the child from the floor. Taking the weight of her little daughter on a thrust-out right hip, she walked out into the grey winter's air that was filled with the sorrowful wailing of women.

Instinctively, she knew. As she inwardly collapsed she outwardly tried to deny her usually reliable intuition. Surely a sin didn't attract instant punishment! Trying to convince herself she had wrongly surmised what was happening, she failed miserably as the parade of shouting, sobbing women advanced on her.

The majority of them were old, with toothless gums and wrinkled faces. The young were among them, wailing and howling just as loudly as their elders. Wheeling seagulls joined in the lament with their loud cries. Josephine Heelan, a woman of her own age, cried out tearfully, 'Ooooh, Lucy. It's your man, Lucy! It's your man.'

Parting without an order having been given, the women moved with the precision of military drill. Four men came forward between them, ghostlike in the white flannel suits the fishermen wore for warmth in winter. They moved towards her in an awkward, shuffling gait, each of them holding one corner of an improvised stretcher fashioned out of a blanket. Not being in step, they caused a constant jolting that performed a pseudo-resurrection of the body they carried. Covered by sacking, the corpse was more animated with each step the bearers took.

It was a parody of a cortège. The screeching women were the mourners, the unshaven fishermen impromptu pallbearers, while the rhythmic pounding of the sea provided a background of funereal music.

An elderly man, so weak that he clasped his corner of the blanket with both hands, called out an explanation. 'He didn't have no chance, Mistress Willard. A great wave hit us when we was a-pulling the nets. Ned got caughted in the rope and was draggeded over the side. He drownded long afore we could get to 'im.'

With tiredness preventing them from showing reverence, the four men lowered the body on to the ground before her. The sackcloth shroud made the dead man comfortingly anonymous. Dry-eyed and in the grip of shock that allowed her face no expression of any kind, Lucy Willard looked down numbly. The taste of salt spray on her lips was welcome after the wetness of the unwanted kisses she had just endured. She couldn't connect this inert, silent homecoming with the laughing, loving, living man she had expected to stride up from the sea to embrace her daughter and herself.

All around her the women fell silent. They had led lives that were too harsh, too cruel, and, in many cases, too long, but not one of them had ever seen a new widow react with such indifference.

With a bemused expression on her face now, seemingly at a loss to know why they were staring at her or what they expected of her, Lucy Willard looked back at them steadily. She behaved like they and not she were the recently bereaved.

There was some muttering among the crowd. Several of them were ready to criticize what they regarded as a heartless young woman. Others, the more sensitive, were sadly aware that something was terribly amiss. They neither knew what it was nor what they could do about it.

After a considerable spell of quiet that only the restless sea had the courage to disturb, Josephine Heelan broke away from the crowd and made her hesitant, slow way towards where Lucy Willard stood unmoving, as lifeless as a stone statue.

Josephine was a tall woman whose height and thinness had disguised her many pregnancies so that each of the six children she had given birth to had taken the village, and most probably her, by surprise. She was three months gone now, and was aware of her condition. But her hardworking fisherman husband, Jacob was already terribly worried over having so many mouths to feed, so she would allow him to remain bliss-fully ignorant for a few months yet.

Lucy Willard made no protest when Josephine took her daughter from her arms, bouncing the bewildered child up and down as it started to cry. An older woman, encouraged by Josephine's intervention, shuffled forward in frayed boots. Bent over permanently from gutting fish, she peered worriedly up into Lucy Willard's face. The old one stank of fish, and the breath she puffed at the new widow reeked in a way that defied description, but Lucy Willard neither cringed nor flinched.

'Did you pay into the club for your man, dearie?' the fishwife enquired in a whining, wheedling way. 'Was he insured, dearie?'

For quite a time Lucy Willard remained motionless and silent. Then she moved slowly. Reaching into her bodice she pulled out a crumpled piece of paper. When she did speak her voice was flat and dispirited.

'Oh yes, my Ned was insured.'

This brought a variety of sounds and comments from the crowd. Some were pleased that the young widow and her baby would not have to struggle to live; while others would selfishly feel better about their own battle for a bare existence had they learned that Lucy Willard would be worse off than they were.

Suddenly switching from immobility into convulsive movement, the widow waved a piece of paper above her head, a little document so recent that the ink was smudging under her fingers.

'Fully paid up!' she shouted, her voice cracking partway through the sentence.

Then everyone there, men as well as women, pulled back a little in horror as Lucy Willard, standing over the body of her newly dead husband, shrieked out in peal after peal of hysterical laughter.

It went on and on, causing people to clap their hands over their ears and turn away. It was Josephine Heelan who once more made a constructive move.

Passing Lucy Willard's daughter to the woman beside her, Josephine went to her friend, who was still rocking backwards and forwards as she screamed out insane laughter.

As Josephine's arms went round her, the young widow's laughter became interspersed with sobs. By the time her friend was leading her slowly away towards her home, Lucy Willard was no longer laughing. Bent over, her steps dragging, she wept.

After glancing at each other to come to a tacit agreement, the four fishermen picked up the stretcher. Josephine guided the widow in through the door of her house, and the men bearing her husband's corpse followed them.

Ned Willard was home from the sea.

One

RABELLA SAT BESIDE the bed on which her sick mother lay. She pushed her mass of copper-coloured hair away from her ears in a worried attempt at trying to identify one of the many sounds going on outside. It was a horrific din. A wind that had howled earlier in the evening was now an ear-splitting screech. Occasionally there was a mighty rumble as yet another chimneystack toppled, while a continual shattering of glass recorded the breaking of windows as displaced tiles and slates flew like missiles. She was glad that her mother slept the deep and infrequently disturbed sleep of the very ill, even though it left Arabella feeling very much alone.

She had wished over the years that she and her mother could share life. Lucy Willard had always been remote, as if she wanted to avoid the reality of living. Josie Heelan, Lionel's mother, said this was due to shock when the father Arabella couldn't remember had been drowned.

According to the older villagers the young Lucy had been a vivacious beauty. Arabella could not fit that description with the poor sunken creature that slept on the bed.

A loud bang outside brought Arabella into alertness. Although expected, the storm had struck Adamslee with a devastating fury that had caught even the village fishermen unawares. Since it had begun, Arabella had been praying that Lionel Heelan would call to check that her mother and she were safe. Lionel and Arabella were 'walking out', if that quaint term could apply in their circumstances. They spent most of their time together at opposite sides of her mother's bed. Yet he never complained. He was a caring lad who took care of his widowed mother and younger sister with what he earned by occasionally doing menial work. The first-born of the Heelan family, Esther, had married a clergyman and lived on the far side of Exeter.

Between them, Lionel and Arabella constantly nurtured an idea that they would one day improve their lot dramatically, to rise far above the line of poverty. But it was a yearning not a plan – a dream that she believed would never permit itself to be dreamt. Generation after generation in Adamslee had spent a lifetime fighting the sea in order to survive. They had died, most of them prematurely, having succeeded only in turning the impoverishment of their birth into the destitution of their death.

Though recognizing it was a futile hope, Arabella didn't want Lionel to find permanent work on the boats. The sea had claimed her father, leaving her mother alone with a family of only one child and long years of neediness and aching empti-ness ahead of her. Although Arabella loved her deeply, she had never been able to get to know her the way a girl should know her mother.

She leapt up from where she was sitting then, in the grip of terror as the outside door in the kitchen imploded. Assuming that someone had lifted the latch and the wind had done the rest, Arabella heard the door strike the inner wall so hard that it reverberated. Swiftly the gale came into the room, lifting the bedcovers and disturbing her mother a little before extin-guishing the smoking lamp to leave Arabella in an inky blackness that disorientated her.

Then her frantic worry subsided together with the wind that had been buffeting around the room. The door was being closed, and she could see a flickering yellow light in the kitchen.

Making her way carefully to the doorway, Arabella saw two

heavily garbed figures straining to secure the door. Both were wearing oilskins, but she easily identified Lionel Heelan, who was tall and thin like his mother. A hurricane lamp had been placed on the floor, and with the door closed, Lionel bent to pick it up. As the shorter figure turned she saw the rain-dripping face of Ruth, Lionel's crippled sister, peering owl-like out at her through a protective hood.

Lionel opened his mouth to speak but had to wait until a mighty wind that shook the house from top to bottom had subsided.

'Are you and your mamma all right, Bella?' he asked, having to shout to be heard.

Arabella nodded. 'We're fine.'

When Ruth hobbled her way over to him on her club-foot, Lionel moved closer to Arabella, his lean and sensitive face anxious, the face of a man who would have been a scholar under the patronage of a more kindly fate.

'I tried to get here before, Bella,' Lionel explained, 'but there is so much damage out there. I've been helping board up shattered windows and doors. We've been fixing walls, too, Arabella. Even the thickest of them have been breached. A tree fell on the Philpots' house. It demolished half of it and we had to rescue young Tommy from underneath.'

'Is he dead?' Arabella enquired – wondering people expect the worst.

Shaking his head, Lionel's facial expression told Arabella that he was excited about something even before he announced enthusiastically, 'There's a ship aground, Bella! She's a big 'un, and there'll be lots of things to be had. We'll get stuff to keep all of us through the rest of this winter and beyond. Get your waterproofs on and come with me.'

'But Mamma!' Arabella heard herself protesting, as she caught Lionel's excitement.

'Ruth's come to sit with your mamma.' Lionel used one hand

on his sister's back to move her forwards. Ruth gave Arabella a smile that lit up her plain, broad-nosed face.

'But …' Arabella attempted to find another objection but there wasn't one.

It was clear that she could do much more for her mother that night by pulling luxuries from the sea rather than sitting beside her bed as usual. She wouldn't be abandoning or neglecting her in any way, for Ruth was an able person. Overcoming her handicap through sheer courage, Ruth Heelan brought in some money for her family with an arduous one-girl business collecting seaweed as manure.

'If Mamma awakens,' Arabella instructed Ruth, 'it will only be for a drink. There's water here. Are you sure you can manage?'

'Trust me, Bella,' Ruth said, looking up at Arabella with soft brown eyes that had a loveliness totally wasted in the round, bland face.

Bending to kiss her friend on the forehead, a kiss of thanks as well as an unspoken plea that her mother was taken good care of, Arabella joined Lionel.

The night outside was as wild as Arabella had anticipated. But it was much less dark than she had expected. There was only an occasional patch of stars in the sky where the wind would tear the clouds temporarily apart, but all the rushing movement seemed to have generated some kind of illumination so that it was possible for her to see the semi-ruined buildings all around.

Clinging together, sometimes forced backwards by the wind, they made steady progress through dust-laden air. The debris from smashed tiles and slates made walking hazardous. Past experience told Arabella that the occupants of the storm-besieged houses would have been busy stashing away treasured possessions such as grandfather clocks, patterned plates, and china tea sets in places where they would be in least danger of being broken. Lights glowed orange inside the still intact windows that they passed. There would be no sleep this night in Adamslee. Arabella, born and raised in the West Country village, could not recall a previous storm in which Adamslee had been so drastically battered.

Reaching the beach, they screwed up their faces against the stinging rain as they took a place in the line of watching villagers. It was a 1500 ton, three-masted, fully rigged ship that was in trouble. There would be spoils: items that the people of Adamslee could never afford to buy, to be gathered like an illicit harvest from the turbulent sea. But Arabella was starkly aware that Adamslee's good fortune would be paid for in the lives of the seafarers aboard the stricken ship. There would be yet many more unmarked graves in the cemetery up on the hill behind the village.

Recognizing them as new arrivals, a man yelled above the storm to identify the ship. 'She's the *Paloma*. She's a trooper bringing the 38th Regiment of Foot back home!'

This information warned that they could be looking at the start of a disaster of epic proportions in the loss of life. The winds had driven the ship hard into the Bluewater sandbank offshore. She had heeled over on impact and the decks were alarmingly aslant. Everything loose on deck was sliding into the raging sea. Arabella could see figures trying desperately to scramble up the angled deck, clinging to anything that might offer a fragile chance of safety. Looking away as a monstrous wave washed over the ship, Arabella forced herself to look again, to shudder when she saw there was not even one of the tiny figures to be seen on the deck.

In the vain hope of being able to 'claw off', pull his ship back from the bank, the captain kept her under full sail. Experienced men among the Adamslee crowd said that this was a mistake. They were proved right when a thrusting wind pushed the ship further into the bank.

A sad Arabella reached for Lionel's hand and clung to it tightly. She prayed that there were no women and children on board. She had a terrible memory of a decade ago when the *Sea Horse* had foundered on the rocks that sided Adamslee's beach and ran up jaggedly against the lofty cliffs. On that occasion it had been curiosity that had brought the young Arabella down to the shore. Half-believing it was a large doll she saw floating face down, Arabella had waded a little way into the water to discover that it was the body of a girl aged about five. She was wearing a nightdress, and Arabella watched as a man reached out to grasp the long skirt of this garment.

Drawn by the horrific, and not old enough to realize she should protect herself from the harsher things of life, Arabella had continued to watch as the man lifted the little body from the water, its long fair hair drooping wetly over his arms. As the little girl was turned, Arabella, who had anticipated seeing a pretty face, saw that there was nothing but a bloodied red and blue pulp left. Turning away swiftly, Arabella had vomited. Ever since then that pitiful, faceless little creature had visited her in dreams on winter nights.

She was seeing the vision again now, but it faded as a mighty cheer went up. Due to what had to be a miracle, a heavy swell rolled in to lift the ship clear of the sandbank and set it down safely and upright on the shore side. This time the captain's error was the fatal one of ordering the anchors put out. Had he left well alone, then the sea would have brought his ship on into the beach with little or no further loss of life. But now one of the two anchors gripped before the other, causing the ship to slew in the wind and head for the rocks at the east end of the beach, both anchors dragging.

Aboard the ship emergency plans were put into action under atrocious conditions. First a sea anchor constructed from a boom and several gun carriages was tried, but it failed to slow the ship's movement towards the rocks. The two proper anchors and the makeshift one were all let go in the hope that the ship would move towards the beach, but the wind had her now and drove the vessel on relentlessly in the direction of the rocks.

As she pitched and tossed, heroic sailors took in all the canvas. When she did strike the jagged stones it was at a point opposite to an immense cliff that was close to being perpendicular. The sea ran too high for boats to be launched, and the sheer cliff was within an oar's length of the ship. Had it been possible to launch the boats they would have been instantly smashed to pieces.

'Look, they could make it!' Lionel shouted in Arabella's ear as an ensign staff was laid across from the ship's side to the opening of a cave in the cliff.

But the ship heaved, breaking the staff in two. Even so, those on board were determined not to give up. A more substantial spar then replaced the ensign staff. This was left in position to test it while the ship rolled several times. The spar remained intact, and those on shore held their breath as a man worked his way out from the ship along the bar, a line coiled over one shoulder.

The courageous fellow moved on steadily. If he could make it then many on the ship would have a hope of reaching the cave before she broke up. Arabella clung tightly to Lionel. Around her she could hear prayers being said aloud.

Then a rogue wave, squeezed to an astounding height between the ship and the cliff, plucked the man from the spar, carrying him along in its foamy crest, spinning his body round and round, rolling the doomed fellow head over heels before he was sucked down.

The ship moved, its keel grating loudly on the fangs of rocks jutting out of the breakers all around it. In another try at easing the ship the mizzen-mast was cut away, but without any useful effect. Those on board were crowding onto the poop deck, the highest part of the wreck above water. But then a creaking and groaning told folk ashore that the stout hull of the *Paloma* was breaking up.

The foretop-mast come crashing down as the ship snapped in two amidships, and the people ashore realized that this was the end. The stern section was held fast on the rocks while pounding waves split away the bow part. Crates and casks were washed out of the middle of the broken ship and thrown around in the waves.

Relief came then for the sensitive in the guise of a sudden and violent squall that closed off all light from the heavens. It became so dark that Lionel was for Arabella just a blurred silhouette even though he was standing close beside her. The rain that had been uncomfortable as it beat against their faces was now replaced by hailstones so large and painful that the line of people protected themselves by kneeling and doubling over so that the hail could do no more than attack their bent backs. This turn for the worse in the weather continued for more than an hour before the squall eventually eased off. They were able to stand and watch it go twisting and writhing like a grey wraith wandering away.

Most of the ship was still there, but it was being smashed relentlessly asunder by a sea that had scarcely abated. Some fluke of nature had altered the earlier violently chaotic scene into something approaching an eerie semi-calm. Puncheons of rums, kegs, and crates were bobbing in a raggedy but compact formation in the bay out from the beach, while bodies, in such a great number that they jostled each other like people on a busy street, were floating in among the rocks.

At first light of day a second separation began on the beach, with the greedy forming human chains to go into the still restless water in pursuit of floating booty, while the caring made their way to the rocks where the first of the bodies neared the shore.

For a moment Arabella was disconcerted by Lionel's apparent hesitation, but then she saw that he was studying John Nichol, the Customs man who lodged at the Ship Inn in the village. With utter contempt on his face, Nichol watched men shouting excitedly as they waded into the sea, often pushing a floating corpse to one side in their eagerness to reach the treasure-trove that was carried on the waves. Although his duty was combating the smuggling that was prevalent in the area, Nichol had no real jurisdiction over shipwrecks, and the looting already going on was too large-scale for one man to deal with. Nevertheless, it was obvious to Arabella that John Nichol shared her feelings about the avaricious scum who were grabbing everything they could from the sea.

She knew that she shouldn't have doubted Lionel, even for a fraction of a second. The armada of bodies were beyond mortal aid, but the dead had no rights and it was up to the living to provide the respect that they deserved. Ready to go down to the rocks, Lionel shouted to her above the wind.

'Are you up to helping, Bella?'

Nodding vigorously, but uncertain deep down if she could stand the sights she was about to see, Arabella took the hand proffered by Lionel and allowed him to lead her down the beach to where high-rolling waves shattered themselves into fountains of spray against the rocks. Neither of them would be taking the gifts from the sea home to those waiting there expectantly, but neither Lionel nor she was capable of profiting in tragic circumstances such as this.

From earlier, smaller shipwrecks, Arabella had learned the system. First the bodies would be pulled from the sea and laid on the beach to await being taken to the boathouse. From there they would be transported to the cemetery for Christian burial. This time it would be different. A mass grave would be needed. Those who had been known, had been loved, who'd had names and status, would be forever anonymous in a crowded grave.

Nearer to the rocks, Arabella weakened momentarily. Men, nowhere near as many as those dragging goods from the sea, were carrying bodies ashore. Still holding her hand, Lionel was taking them into the sea, heading for the nearest body. Bracing herself, Arabella reasoned that she would feel better once she had met her first corpse.

Soon they were waist deep, stumbling against slippery rocks as they were knocked about by waves that were both powerful and persistent. She looked at the body they were closing in on, and had to stifle a cry of relief as she saw it was a soldier with one uniformed arm round a rock, making jerky attempts to pull himself out of the water.

Overjoyed at having found someone alive, Arabella released Lionel's hand, wedged her feet at painful angles between rocks, and bent to grasp the booted ankles of the soldier as Lionel slipped his hands under the man's armpits. They lifted together, turning the soldier on his back ready to carry him ashore.

It was then that a stunned Arabella found she was looking into the face of a dead man. The pulling of the arm against the rock had been an illusion created by the movement of the sea. A dropped jaw had opened the soldier's mouth so that both ends of a drooping moustache had been swallowed. The hooded eyes stared past her into the mystery that is death.

Pulling herself together, she aided Lionel in getting the dead man on to the beach. Ludicrously, although earthly comforts no longer interested him, they made him comfortable when laying him out on the pebbles. Yet it had seemed the right thing to do, and Lionel was as guilty as she in this bit of crass stupidity.

Then they were wading back into the sea together, hand-in-hand, arms stretched wide as they negotiated limpet-encrusted rocks that scratched and bruised them as each heavy wave rolled in to knock them off balance. She saw Lionel turn his back on a heavy wave then continue to stoop until he could grasp the bare arm of a woman with a small-featured, pretty face who was floating on her back. Her long hair was entangled in the seaweed that grew profusely among the rocks. The dead woman wore a scarlet dress that was unaffected by immersion in the water. It gave the appearance of elegance that belonged in a ballroom and Arabella couldn't equate it with drowning in a stormy sea.

This time it was Lionel who took the ankles. It was as if the two of them had agreed this was the fitting thing to do. Lionel was a decent fellow, but still it didn't seem right for a man to place his hands where the woman would have strongly objected to being touched when alive.

With the body suspended between them, and with Lionel doing a precarious backwards walk towards the beach, stumbling against the rocks, a mountainous wave came in unnoticed. Roaring and hissing it knocked them both off their feet.

Landing with her back across a sharp rock, Arabella didn't initially realize how deep under water she was. Looking up, she could see daylight playing on the surface far above her. All she could do was hold her breath until the giant wave had subsided. With her lungs beginning to burn as they were put under pressure, she was thankful that she was still holding the body of the woman, although the legs now floated free. Lionel had been pushed away by the force of the wave, and Arabella peered unsuccessfully through the dark-green translucency of the sea in the hope of seeing him.

Then the swirling motion of the water was wrenching her around. Head pounding, arms aching, she clung on to the body as the motion of the water threatened to snatch it from her. Moving her right arm with difficulty, Arabella encircled the woman with it. Having gone through so much already she didn't intend to lose her.

But the exertion to secure the corpse had caused her to blow bubbles, and Arabella had to discipline herself not to ease her distress and clear the blackness that was growing inside of her head by breathing out. Even though she knew it would be the end of her, the temptation to attempt to breathe was powerful. It was possible that the urge to find relief came from the knowledge that she couldn't stay under water for much longer anyway. A split second and the choice of whether or not to breathe would be lost.

Something began to happen, giving Arabella the resolve to hold her breath just a little longer. The wave was receding, but in doing so it had set up a whirlpool that rotated her body as it dragged her painfully along a rock-strewn route. At long last there was no water above her. Lying flat on her back, eyes sore, Arabella pulled in a deep breath. It hurt; hurt her chest terribly, but it was welcome.

As more deep breaths cleared her head and brought her back to full consciousness, she discovered to her absolute horror that the body she was holding had been turned by the turmoil in the water. It was lying on top of her and Arabella found herself looking into a pair of unseeing blue eyes. The woman's cold face was pressed against hers. They were as close as a pair of lovers.

Struggling to push the corpse off, Arabella opened her mouth to release a piercing scream just as another wave rolled in. This was nowhere near as high or as forceful as its predecessor, but it filled her mouth with sea water, causing her to gag in a frantic effort to clear her lungs. A choking Arabella thought she could feel a pair of legs pressing against her, but then she experienced a terrible feeling of suffocation that mercifully ended in unconsciousness.

When she came round she was on the beach, lying on her side. Something seemed to have awoken her as if she had been sleeping. At first at a loss as to what it could be, she then recognized it was her own retching and spewing out of seawater. Holding her as her stomach tightened and slackened alternately as it acted as a pump, Lionel then gently moved her into a sitting position. He kept himself close in front of her, using his body as a shield against the still raging gale.

'I'll take you home, Bella,' he shouted, concern for her on his face. To her right was the body of the woman in the scarlet dress. Lionel had laid the body beside that of the soldier. For Arabella there was poignancy in them being companions in death, even though it was not of their choosing.

Men were still moving in among the rocks on Arabella's left. They judged the movement of the waves as they went in search of more bodies. She saw that some twenty-five had already been laid out. Most were soldiers, but there were a few women and some smaller bodies that a sorrowful Arabella had to accept were those of children.

'Come along, Bella,' Lionel urged her, reaching out clasping both her hands and easing her up onto her feet.

Aware that he was anxious to get her home as quickly as possible, Arabella tried to object verbally, but no sound would come out of a throat she discovered was agonizingly sore.

She made gestures, pointing to her throat to indicate why she couldn't speak, then conveying her determination to stay to help on the beach. Both of them were chilled to the bone, their sodden clothing as heavy on them as suits of armour, but they exchanged weak smiles, so close that they could communicate without speaking. Then they made their weary-legged way down to where the angry sea was as ready as ever to fight to keep its victims.

There were so many of them that momentarily Arabella wilted. Scornful of herself for her own flash of weakness, she put out a hand to clutch Lionel's, and they waded back in among the rocks.

Close to them, wedged in under a large, flat rock, was a middle-aged woman with a round face and chubby cheeks. Her hair was held in a bun, and there was a smile frozen on her lips that Arabella found perturbing. Nevertheless, she took up a position opposite Lionel, each of them taking a plump shoulder and pulling. But their effort had no effect because something was trapping the body in under the rock. They were about to try once more when a loud shout stopped them.

Retaining the hold they had on the body, both Arabella and Lionel turned to where the man who had shouted was entering the water. Although the person approaching was clad from head to foot in oilskin as a protection against the weather, Arabella recognized Gray Sawtell, a hard-faced fisherman who was rumoured to be the leader of Adamslee's smuggling gang. Aged around forty, the taciturn Sawtell lived a semi-reclusive life in a small cottage that was precariously perched on the precipitous cliff on the eastern side of the village.

Sawtell's shout had been directed at her, and she clutched at a rock as she moved away to allow the two men to bend and gradually free the body of the woman from under the rock. Glancing over his shoulder to see Arabella watching the grim proceedings, the fishermen shouted at her again, 'Look away, woman! For God's sake turn your eyes from this!'

The commanding way in which the order was shouted made Arabella instinctively obey. But then a spark of annoyance ignited anger in her. All her life she had been afraid of Gray Sawtell, seeing his difference from other more sociable men as a threat. But now, after the traumatic hours she had already spent in the water with Lionel, she wasn't prepared to let Sawtell order her around.

Turning defiantly, she watched as the overweight body of the woman was pulled clear of the rock by Lionel and Sawtell. Then she saw a sight that made her fervently wish that she had complied with Sawtell's order. Having to fight to stifle a scream, she couldn't avert her eyes from a dreadful scene. Clinging to the woman, making sure that they would be with their mother through the tunnel into the unknown, were three small children. Lionel was standing upright, and Arabella could tell that he was swaying because of emotion rather than the waves that were breaking over his shoulders. Seeing Sawtell bend and tenderly prise the fingers of the children from their mother's dress, Arabella felt guilty when she realized that the tough fisherman had known what was attached to the woman before he had first shouted, having tried hard to spare her the distress she was now feeling.

It took a tremendous effort to recover but then Arabella was wading towards the two men, her tears unnoticed as they joined rain and seawater to flow down her face. She stooped to pick up the first little body. It was a boy. His face, which should have been young and happy, was aged by an expression of terror that was fixed upon it. Carrying the lad ashore, it seemed to Arabella that she was holding an old man who had been squeezed into the body of a child.

Lionel and Sawtell brought the other two children to the beach with their mother. They were girls, pretty children who gave the impression of being twins until Arabella judged that at least two years must separate them. Not that age now mattered to them.

She was astonished and shamed by her formed-from-a-distance opinion of Sawtell when she saw him smooth the hair of the girls into place as he stretched them out beside their mother. His face, ruggedly handsome, betrayed the sorrow he was feeling.

Unable to continue looking at the tragic family, Arabella turned her gaze back to the sea. A man's body was in close, rising and falling in the water, occasionally colliding jarringly with a rock. Steeling herself, she made her way slowly to the water, determined to secure this body while Lionel and Sawtell finished laying out the mother and children.

The body was that of a young man, but he was not in uniform. Floating on his back, he had long yellow hair that flowed out from his head to form a poorly shaped halo. She stepped into the water then held back until a wave at the end of its long run broke up around her on the shore. Then, lying on her stomach across a rock, she reached out to the body. The nearest part of it was a hand, and Arabella felt that there was something creepy about touching it. She preferred the dead to offer a much less personal arm, shoulder, or leg. But she had no option. Forcing herself to keep her eyes open, Arabella took the heavy, long-fingered hand of the young man in hers.

For one moment she felt a strange, fearful elation in the certainty that she had felt a fleeting tightening of the fingers she was holding. The trauma of it all was getting to her, she scolded herself. What she had detected in the hand could be no more than a post-death reflex action. Yet the shock of it cleared the apprehension she had been feeling. She was relieved to find that the eyes of the dead no longer disturbed her. His were startling blue. As it had been with the previous corpses it was easy to accept that he was staring at her.

Pulling the body closer to the rock, finding that she still didn't want to be alone with the dead, she looked over her shoulder to see if either Lionel or Sawtell were about to join her. They weren't. The two men were standing side-by-side, each with a hand up to shield his eyes as they peered out to where the sound of a sharp cracking signalled that the ship was disintegrating further.

Pushing up a little from the rock that was painful against her ribs, Arabella kept hold of the hand. She shuddered as she looked into the blue eyes that were now closer to her. There was something peculiar about them. The eyes of the dead had no depth. It was as if a door had been closed at the back of them. This pair of blue eyes was different in some indefinable sense. Accepting that she was fooling herself, dismissing what she thought she was seeing, Arabella suddenly changed her mind. Now she was aware beyond all doubt. She could not be mistaken! The man in the water was definitely looking up at her.

Arabella discovered that her voice had returned. She could shout, but it would cause her throat excruciating agony to do so. Her voice was working, but the two men on the beach wouldn't hear her. So she waved her arm wildly and Lionel saw her. He touched Sawtell on the shoulder and the two of them came running towards her.

'This man is alive!' Arabella yelled at them.

'Impossible,' Lionel shouted back, as he and Sawtell came into the sea, the face of the latter showing his unspoken disbelief.

Sawtell bent to look down at the yellow-haired man, ignoring Lionel's shouted warning as an extra-large wave came in at them. Holding tightly to each other, Arabella and Lionel, though battered by the sea, managed to keep on their feet. The unprepared Sawtell fared less well. After being tossed between two overhanging rocks he disappeared under the swirling water.

Making sure that Arabella was safely holding onto a rock, Lionel waded to where he expected the fisherman to surface, ready to help him out of the sea. But Sawtell came up out of the water a little way off. He was holding the yellow-haired man and his chisel-featured face was animated as he shouted to Arabella and Lionel, 'This man *is* alive, by God!'

Two

ADAMSLEE HOUSE WAS a large and imposing porticoed white building set back cautiously some seventy yards from the edge of the sheer cliff west of the village. The original house had been built on 600 acres of Devon land given to Francis Adams by James I of England. Since that time the Adamses had been the predominant family in the district, with the males successively being the squires. In deference to the gentry, the villagers stayed clear of the Adams' home in daylight, while only the drunk or the nerveless went near the reputedly haunted house at night. The present house was the second built on the site. A century earlier the incumbent Oliver Adams had been crazy enough to deliberately set fire to his home, and stupid enough to perish in the conflagration of his own making. The second house constructed round the surviving chimney of the earlier building was a feeble parody of its rebirth.

Yet now the Adams dynasty was without a male heir, and doomed to extinction, as the voluptuous Sarai Adams was the last in the long line. Should she, as was eminently possible, have issue out of wedlock, then the family name would survive, but with the brand of bastardy.

As dawn broke to bring the night of the great storm to a close, Sarai stood looking out of a window on the upper floor of the three-storey house. Rain still splashed heavily against the glass and the wind still blew but not so fiercely. The cliff cut off her view at an angle, but she could see about one-third of what was left of the *Paloma*.

In the courtyard below she could see the diminutive figure of Ben Morely, her conscientious groom. He was exercising the horses in a sheltered section of the yard. Caesar, her stallion, was easily distinguishable in the gloomy light of that miserable morning.

Looking down at the seething sea around the rocks and what remained of the ship, she sadly assumed that the night had claimed many lives. She pondered on what the events of the night had meant. She felt that it had brought her dead parents closer to her. Not in an otherworldly way, but as a hint of what family life could have been had they not drowned in the Irish Sea during a similar storm. Sarai had been but a child then, and she was frustrated by not knowing whether she had a true memory of her mother and father or if what she believed was recall owing everything to the portraits of them hanging in the hall in Adamslee House.

They had both possessed the sophistication and respectability expected in a squire and his lady. This often caused Sarai to puzzle as to how she had come by her near immorality and outright rebelliousness. The old changeling myth of a passing gypsy exchanging her baby for an aristocratic child couldn't apply in Sarai's case, as she had inherited her father's lean, strong jaw.

Nonetheless, Sarai wasn't complaining, as she was arrogantly proud to acknowledge, about what it took to drive just about every man she met wild. In addition she had a singing voice that, though below classical standard, meant she was in demand at aristocratic social functions. During her six months in Paris, which had ended the previous autumn, she had lived in the Rue de Lille and had gained many admirers when performing at some grand house where she had gone for the evening. Sarai basked in the applause her singing promoted.

Dragging her mind away from the much-enjoyed acclaim of last year and back to the present, she thought of how the storm had prevented a small fortune in contraband being brought to the cellars below her house. Yet it had only postponed that exercise. Once the wind had died away and a fresh-born moon had grown to a quarter, then a caravan of small, fully laden ponies would wind its way up the smugglers' paths from the caves at the foot of the cliffs.

This would be a closing stage in an operation that had begun out at sea in Gray Sawtell's ketch, the *Dark Rose*. From Adamslee House the smuggled goods would be carried, usually concealed in haycarts, to the City of Exeter and the developing towns of the area.

With an inheritance that included property in Ireland, Sarai had no financial interest in the smuggling. All she looked for was the excitement of the contradictory thrill she achieved from cheating a system that she, as a member of the upper class, was a part of.

Another attraction, which waxed and waned for Sarai according to her mood, was the rough and ready, habitually silent Gray Sawtell. Widely separated by class, the two of them were drawn together by lust. Neither she nor he had any illusions about their relationship. Aware that Sawtell expected their loving to end when she tired of him, Sarai had to admit, to herself but not Sawtell, that he probably had it about right. What was likely to keep them together was her enjoyment at being involved in smuggling. That would end one day, too. The Revenue officers now had specially designed pursuit craft and orders to shoot on sight.

In what she recognized as her saner moments, when her all wasn't throbbing with excitement as she gave herself and the cellars of her house to the smuggling cause, Sarai clearly saw that she was risking her liberty, perhaps even her life. But the game was addictive and she found it impossible to pull out.

Believing that she could see a figure making its way along the 'Brandy Pad', as the smugglers called the clifftop path, she quickly used a hand to wipe away the mist her breath had painted on the windowpane, and she saw that she had been right. When he was close enough, Sarai recognized him as he stepped out of a veil of rain. Worry replaced the light-hearted curiosity with which she had watched the man advance. It was John Nichol, the Customs man who was stationed permanently in the village.

Sarai had two conflicting theories, one comforting, the other slightly perturbing. Right now her cellars were totally empty, so even if Nichol had been informed that she was involved with the smuggling then he would find nothing to incriminate her. But weighed against that was the fact that the Customs man had walked all the way up from the village in such atrocious weather. That meant that whatever his purpose it was of significant importance.

Sarai had met John Nichol just once, when he had been among her guests at the New Year's ball she had held at Adamslee House. He was a stocky, balding fellow with a round, plain face that at first suggested unintelligence. But Sarai had learned that her impression was mistaken when she danced with him, just as she had danced with other guests such as the Sheriff of Devon, and found that the Customs man had a razor-sharp mind.

Remembrance of that ball came back now. She had escaped the limp-wristed grasp of overly polite dancers to go out of the french-windows into the energetically muscular embrace of Gray Sawtell. An erotic delight for her out under the stars, as a dalliance with the rough fisherman in the ballroom would have caused an acute embarrassment.

So hopelessly lost had Sarai become in the smuggler's arms that night that she had misjudged the time. Dashing into the house, she had managed to run to her bedroom and change out of the dress Sawtell had ruined, and then rejoin her guests, smiling with a fake serenity, to see the old year out and the New Year in. She'd had to pretend enjoyment when the champagne corks had popped, streamers had been sent spiralling across the room, and kisses exchanged, because that night had earlier climaxed for her in the wonderland she had shared with Sawtell.

A sudden realization moved Sarai back from the window. She was starkly aware that she couldn't allow Elsa, her maid, to answer the door and then innocently reply to any cunning questions put by Nichol.

Running down the curved staircase that was surmounted by a magnificent glass dome, she passed the portraits of her curious ancestors peering out of their yesterdays into her today. As she went by a bewigged Oliver Adams, she communicated silently with the lunatic arsonist. Sarai silently pleaded: if you are haunting this place, Oliver dear, then frighten this man from my door.

On opening the door she had to cling to it as the wind took charge. Unable to wait for a polite invitation to enter, Nichol leapt across the threshold, to take the door from her and close it. Taking a handkerchief from his pocket, he wiped his wet face with it before honkingly blowing his nose, then giving her a half smile in which the right side of his face didn't participate. His cheek remained still, a drooping to it noticeable by the dragging down of the corner of his mouth.

Seeing the semi-lifeless face jogged Sarai's memory. She had been told Nichol had been seriously injured when single-handedly tackling a notorious family of smugglers at Beer in the east of the county. Bravery was a factor that Sarai looked for in a man, and remembering the story of Nichol's courage raised him in her estimation.

'Forgive the somewhat ungentlemanly entrance, Miss Adams,' he apologized with a stiff little bow.

'It isn't exactly a day for protocol to be observed, Mr Nichol,' she replied, 'so an apology is unnecessary.'

He gave a second small bow. 'You are most gracious. Indeed, Miss Adams, it's a terribly sad day.'

'I have heard nothing, nothing of what took place in the night,' Sarai explained.

Having difficulty in finding words, he looked at her long and dolefully before saying, 'Oh dear, oh dear. Then I have to give you the terrible news, Miss Adams, and I fear that it will mightily distress you.'

'Was there considerable loss of life?' Sarai asked, moved by the incipient tears in his eyes and the catch in his voice.

'May the Lord help and succour us all, Miss Adams,' Nichol said hoarsely, 'for they are counting the dead in hundreds, literally hundreds, Miss Adams. I have seen the long lines of the poor wretches lying on the beach. She was a troopship, but there are many women and dear little children among those who perished.'

'Oh my God!' Sarai exclaimed, naming herself as a coward for being glad that she had not known the extent of the disaster during the long night. 'Were there survivors, Mr Nichol?'

He shook a head that was pink where the hairline had deserted. There was a white scar, long and jagged, tracking its way through the pinkness. Some said that a metal plate had been put inside of Nichol's head to support the skull that had been shattered in the assault, but others claimed this wasn't true. The possibility of this and the surgery that would have been involved intrigued Sarai, but she wasn't about to ask the Customs man if it was a fact that he had been trepanned.

'I've heard a rumour that there was one survivor, Miss Adams, but that is so unlikely that I have dismissed it. I think, to my immense sorrow, that it is safe to say that no one from that ship was saved.'

'What a terrible disaster,' Sarai sighed.

'It is my regret that I am the one to tell you of it,' a grave-faced Nichol told her, going on. 'In addition, Miss Adams, I ask your forgiveness for not having immediately stated my purpose in calling on you.'

Heart missing a beat, Sarai desperately wanted him to explain why he was there, while at the same time dreaded what he might say. It didn't help to consider that he was faultlessly civil. Some of the most serious of sins and the most heinous cruelties are committed politely.

'I would imagine that your reason for being here on such a day is an important one, Mr Nichol,' Sarai said, surprised by the steadiness of her own voice. She was so pleased that she ventured further. 'Yet, having regard to your profession, sir, I am at a loss as to how I may help you.'

Giving her one of his lopsided smiles, Nichol said, 'Ordinarily I would agree that a lady like yourself and lawlessness would never come within a million miles of each other, Miss Adams, but please permit me to explain.'

'Of course,' Sarai said, liking the way that his smile, although made into something of a grimace by paralysis, reached his pale grey eyes. So many people were sickenly insincere, but not John Nichol.

'You may or may not be aware that Revenue officers along the coasts of Dorset, and in parts of Devon, now have observation towers.'

'I didn't know that,' Sarai lied, instantly ashamed of how easily the untruth came to her.

Nichol gave an emphatic nod. 'They have indeed, and one day we may have one here at Adamslee. Until that time comes I have my orders to improvise.'

Sarai got it then, and a minor panic started churning inside of her. Adamslee House stood on a high vantage point, but how could she allow a Customs man to set up a look-out there? Gray Sawtell would be the first to walk into the trap, and then as others were netted, one of them would be sure to implicate Sarai. Yet the second question, how could she refuse to permit it was equally as impossible to answer. There was no way of avoiding the issue, but Sarai tried to gain a little time by changing the subject.

'You must live a lonely life, Mr Nichol. Living in lodgings can't be pleasant, but no doubt a single man is more able to cope with the situation.'

'I thought my haggard look would preclude such a mistake, Miss Adams,' he said with rueful good humour. 'My bachelor days ended more than twenty years ago.'

Cheeks flushing hotly, Sarai murmured, 'I'm sorry. I didn't mean to pry.'

'Not at all, not at all.' He gave her a smile that was as reassuring as the effort of half a face could manage. 'I have a wife and two daughters at home in Dorchester, Miss Adams. I am able to spend every Saturday and Sunday with them.'

He spoke fondly of his family, and Sarai chided herself. Of late she had been assessing every man she met for one reason only. Wealth and a grand house didn't provide a guarantee against becoming a whore. The only preventative was self-discipline, something that Sarai found difficult, often impossible, to implement. Having a purpose in life, like getting involved in smuggling, hadn't helped. Quite the reverse, in fact, because it had led to Gray Sawtell becoming her lover. Whatever pursuit she had followed in the past, at home or abroad, had inevitably included a man at some stage.

'You must be very proud of your family,' she said, because it was the right thing to say in this situation.

'Indeed,' he said, his eyes showing that he had gone inwards to mentally visit his family.

Then he became his sharp self once more as he looked at Sarai. 'To return to the point, Miss Adams. I am sure that you are as keen as every other respectable citizen to see this illicit trade stopped. Smuggling is not just a local activity. It eats away at the economic fabric of the whole country. It would be rude of me to presume, but I have a feeling that you would be very willing to co-operate.'

'Of course,' she confirmed, noticing that her lie had come even more readily than before. 'I take it that you wish to use my house, Mr Nichol?'

'No more than for one month,' he said, quickly becoming more relaxed and confident now that she had agreed. 'I promise that I will not inconvenience you in any way.'

A month! Sarai groaned inwardly. She had worked out a system to keep the servants fooled and ignorant about her part in local smuggling and her clandestine meetings with the rugged Sawtell; it wouldn't be possible to hoodwink this alert, intelligent man.

'I do believe the wind is slacking,' Nichol commented, and she had to agree, as the door and windows of Adamslee House were rattling and banging far less.

But the storm, even the immense tragedy of which Nichol had informed her, had lost prominence in Sarai's mind. With no alternative but to assent to Nichol's request, she now had to ride out to find Sawtell and warn him of the turn events had taken. If he wasn't cautioned, then John Nichol's mission would swiftly be successful.

When Nichol left her, and if the storm was truly abating, she would ride Caesar on a search for her smuggler lover. Needing more information, she enquired of Nichol, 'When would you wish to start, Mr Nichol?'

Needing time, she tried to will him by thought transfer – next week, next month, next year, or, better still, never!

His answer disappointed Sarai, coming as a shock that temporarily put much of her nervous system out of action.

'Ideally, Miss Adams, I would very much like to be established here today.'

*

In a village preoccupied with clearing debris and repairing damaged houses, the yellow-haired man was a sensation that took people away from their vital work. On all different kinds of pretext they came to Arabella's door hoping to get a glimpse of him. Being young and of superb physique, he had quickly recovered. A benefit for Arabella in having the rescued man in the house, was that her mother had left her bed for the first time in many weeks. Though wan and weary, Lucy Willard sat with them, enjoying being part of a small, elite circle that had the miracle of the stormy night at its centre. The rescued man had thanked them, and had given his name as Joby Lancer, while offering no further details about himself. Ruth had stayed to cook a meal for them all, and Lionel was there. To Arabella's amazement, the usually taciturn Gray Sawtell had stayed to eat with them, astonishingly often saying a few words. Sitting beside him was Willie Brickell, the tousled haired young boy who was employed by Sawtell but was more than a worker on the ketch. Arabella was aware that Sawtell had all but adopted Willie as a son, making sure that the boy, who lived up at the Hamoon workhouse with a mother crippled by arthritis, never went without.

All of them were helped by the relieved and relaxed atmosphere that comes in the wake of a time of great danger. They mourned the huge loss of life just as all Adamslee did, but the harshness of their existence, and previous shipwrecks had inured them to some extent. The village's physician Reverend Lionel Worther had applied for permission to hold a mass burial in a communal grave close to the shore but out of the reach of the highest of tides.

'If you's thinking o' biding round 'ere,' Willie was telling Joby Lancer, 'you won't find no work. Lionel there,' – he indicated Lionel Heelan with a jerk of his head – 'is one of the best workers 'ereabouts, but he cain't get no regular job.'

Awaiting Lancer's response, Arabella looked to where he sat on the dirt floor, his knees pulled up and his arms wrapped round them. His hair was swept back now, remarkable by its startling colour and extraordinary length. The young man's face was thoughtful, as was to be expected, Arabella reasoned, for he must be wondering what 412, for that was the total number of dead from the *Paloma*, to one chance had been in his favour, and why. Outwardly he had casually dismissed his good fortune, saying that he would have drowned had not Arabella and the others reached him in time. This was no answer. None of the others had been washed in alive.

'I will be moving on, Willie,' he said at last, giving the boy a smile.

'Not until you are fit to travel,' Arabella said quickly, then felt herself blushing as the others looked at her, surprised by her vehemence.

'Going home, Joby?'

It was Arabella's mother who had asked the question. This was the first time for ages that the sick woman had showed interest in anything or anyone. It prompted Arabella to go over to where her mother sat and put a loving arm round her thin shoulders.

'Something like that, Mrs Willard,' Joby Lancer said softly. Arabella could sense that it wasn't a real answer, and guessed that he had avoided telling her mother a lie.

'Where's your home?' Willie asked with juvenile brashness.

'Far away, son,' Lancer gave one of his answers that said nothing.

Getting the impression that Joby Lancer was having difficulty in not continually looking at her, Arabella was thrilled. There was something about the stranger that she found fascinating, perhaps even exciting if she was prepared to admit it. But this made her feel disloyal to Lionel. On the evening of last Christmas Day, he had told Arabella and her mother that he was determined to earn enough money to break through the poverty barrier that had kept generations of Adamslee folk oppressed through long years. He had ended up by stammeringly asking Arabella's mother if, when the time was right, he could marry Arabella.

Lucy Willard, who was very fond of Lionel, readily gave consent. Where any other male was concerned, Arabella's mother was fearful for her to the point of distraction. But she had total faith in Lionel. Although she had given her consent, both the mother and daughter knew that they were dealing with a time a long way off, or most probably one that would never come. Determination wasn't enough to let a poor man become wealthy. They both were aware that Lionel's pride wouldn't allow him to ask her to be his wife if he had not achieved his ambition.

In a way, though she appreciated what a good man Lionel was, Arabella often wondered if she really did love him. Who could define what love was? How should she feel? Many times she had been tempted to broach the subject to her mother but realized it would be pointless to discuss her problem with someone not fully in tune with life.

Arabella had no doubts that her uncertainty over Lionel stemmed from a recurring dream that had been with her over the years. It was a waking dream, a daydream that happened when she was fully conscious but lulled into a restful state of tranquillity while sitting all alone in her favourite place on the hill behind the house.

From there, physically close to the village but mentally distant, she would experience what she would only presume to be a peep into a misty future. The same young man was always there. Unable to see him anything like clearly, she knew that he was an exciting stranger who had come to take her away from Adamslee. This had to be the romantic self-delusion of a village girl. But she now found that her romantic streak was seduc-

tively offering to turn the good-looking Joby Lancer into the
stranger in her daydream. She pushed these alluring thoughts
from her head, dread filling her as she heard Lionel directly
address Gray Sawtell, which was a dangerous exercise few if
any in Adamslee were brave enough to undertake.

'I'm seeking regular work,' Lionel was saying in a way that
made it plain he was asking for a job. 'The occasional work
don't come along like it did.'

There was tension in the atmosphere, with only Joby Lancer
being unaffected because he didn't know what was going on.
Gray Sawtell gave little of himself. The wise didn't venture into
the private space with which he surrounded himself.

But Arabella was surprised and relieved when he replied
affably, actually complimenting Lionel, by referring to his part
in the rescue. 'You did well last night, friend, and I was pleased
to be at your side. But the fishing doesn't do more than just
about keep Willie and me.'

Hearing Lionel's intake of breath had Arabella silently plead
with him to leave it at that, to say no more. But Lionel had
gained self-confidence during the dramatic night on the beach,
and Sawtell's praise had boosted this. Arabella's feelings for
Lionel made her fear a rebuff from Sawtell that would wound
her sensitive friend deeply.

'I wasn't meaning with the fishing,' Lionel told Sawtell.
Everything went silent. Ruth, who had been cleaning a
saucepan, stopped partway through the chore, stood as still as
a statue, worrying over her brother. Fiddling with the frayed
edges of the blanket she had round her, Arabella's mother kept
her white face down, but Arabella could sense her anxiety.
Everyone in the village, although in no doubt that Sawtell led
the local gang of smugglers, had the good sense not to even hint
at it. Now Lionel, by implication, had made it clear in front of
others that he knew Sawtell was involved with contraband.

Still leaning relaxed with his back against a wall, Sawtell said nothing. But his level stare was on Lionel, and Arabella saw her friend wilt under it, his resolve slipping as the full force of Gray Sawtell's tough personality showed through.

Ever so slowly, Sawtell used the muscles of his back to push himself away from the wall. When he spoke it was in a quiet, reasonable tone that no one there had expected. 'I'm leaving now. Perhaps you'll walk with me, friend.'

As surprised as anyone there, it took Lionel a few moments to understand the invitation. Sawtell had reached the door by the time Lionel had pulled himself together and caught up with him.

At the door he turned to give Arabella a quick smile. She smiled back, weakly, far from certain that what she was witnessing was a good thing, despite the enthusiasm Lionel exhibited as he went out of the door with the smuggler.

Three

'STAY STILL AND stay quiet!'
Gray Sawtell's hissed warning reached Lionel at the same time as the fisherman's restraining hand gripped his shoulder. The hand moved him back against the high wall by the quay. Even after several weeks Lionel still found there was a delay in finding his sea legs when they put out in the ketch. He had the same problem getting the use of his land legs when they came ashore, and he was glad of the support afforded by the wall. He could hear Willie Brickell breathing close beside him, but couldn't see the lad in the shadows.

When the three of them had fished a long way out earlier it had been a black, moonless night. A fast learner, he no longer had to puzzle over what Sawtell was doing when he peered over the bow of the ketch searching for the phosphorescence, the light created by shoaling fish. Once hesitant and awkward compared to Sawtell and Willie as they had played out the net, Lionel could now work with them as one of a team. When Sawtell used admirable skill to bring the boat round in a full circle to fill the net, Willie and he had moved with practised ease to ensure that the net was pulled tightly to make a bag or purse with the fish securely inside. Even after having performed the task many times since joining Sawtell, Lionel still got a pleasant feeling of achievement when the fish were scooped up to cascade into the boat like a glistening silver cataract.

There remained a sense of the unusual in it all for Lionel, which he thought, or rather fervently hoped, would fade in time. They had stopped fishing when a young moon had crept nervously into the sky. Lionel had felt easier when the weak moonlight thinned the density of the night and stitched a million sparkling sequins onto the surface of the gently moving water.

He had been paid little for his fishing work, which was only a cover for the activities that had in a short time rewarded his pocket handsomely. Even more remote and detached at sea than he was on land, Sawtell, with time, tides, and the points of the compass somehow innately a part of him, would steer them unerringly to ships that would suddenly loom up out of the night as hulking silhouettes. With hardly a word spoken, goods would then be transferred. Following that the contraband would be brought ashore and stored in a cave.

That cave was packed now. Lionel had not been informed, but he gathered that this was because John Nichol had set up some kind of observation post somewhere on high. Obviously there was another place of storage to where the illicit goods would have been moved from the cave had it not been for the Customs man, but Lionel had not been told where this secret place was.

Life had taken a decided turn for the better since he had summoned the nerve necessary to ask Sawtell for work. Although the taciturn fisherman wasn't one to show emotion, he had definitely taken to Lionel. Sawtell was even interested in his relationship with Arabella, which was at last progressing because he was earning good money. It seemed to Lionel that the reclusive Sawtell, denied romantic liaisons by his way of life, was enjoying the experience vicariously. It pleased Lionel that Arabella was gradually – and the process was speeding up – losing her fear of Sawtell and the reserve she had shown towards the fisherman.

In keeping with the change in their financial fortune, the health of Arabella's mother had continued to improve since the night of the great storm.

As they waited now, backs against the wall, Lionel was relieved that they had nothing to hide that night. There had been no rendezvous, no smuggling, but he accepted that, with John Nichol constantly on watch, Sawtell could not take any chances whatsoever. But impatience was growing inside of Lionel. Of late this had been an increasing feeling; wanting to get on with things, to build his finances further. It pleased him to remember that Joby Lancer, now fully recovered, was moving on in the morning. He hadn't said where he was heading; neither did they know anything more about him now than when he had arrived. Though he had grown to like the stranger, and although he trusted Arabella completely, Lionel feared that she and Lancer were attracted to each other. He had no evidence to support this, it being more of a hunch than a belief.

Something or someone had moved up ahead. It was no more than a flitting shadow, but anger, an emotion he was experiencing more of late when any threat to his new prosperity emerged, had Lionel break free of the hand Sawtell had kept on his shoulder. Leaping forward in the dark, an instinct that he hadn't known he possessed guiding him, Lionel reached into a crevice formed partly by the end of the wall. Using both hands, his fingers finding clothing and getting a grip on it, he pulled a man out of hiding.

It was an undersized fellow but an enraged Lionel felt no guilt as he put a hand round the man's throat and slammed him back hard against the wall, the skull making a dull thudding as it was knocked back. He could see now that it was Ben Morley, the groom from Adamslee House.

Beside Lionel now, Sawtell issued a terse order. 'Let go of him, Heelan!'

'He was spying on us,' Lionel protested, keeping his grip on Morley's throat, half-throttling him.

Moving fast, Sawtell drove an elbow hard into Lionel's side. Knocked off balance and winded by the blow that could have stoved in his ribs, Lionel's fingers were slipping from the groom's throat when Sawtell's right fist caught him on the jaw and he knew no more.

When he regained consciousness, he was lying on the quay. Lionel saw that Morley was standing with Sawtell and Willie, all three of them looking down on him. As his head cleared he recalled that it had been Ben Morley who, the first time Lionel had joined Sawtell, had brought a warning that John Nichol was waiting and watching for when they moved the smuggled goods from the cave.

Putting down a hand, which Lionel clasped, Sawtell pulled him to his feet, keeping hold of the hand as he spoke so low that only Lionel could hear, telling him. 'We've worked together well, friend, and I want it to go on that way, but that won't happen if you can't learn to control this mad temper of yours. When I give an order I want it obeyed at once, understand?'

Feeling his bottom lip puffing up and what he took to be blood trickling from his mouth, Lionel nodded.

'I need to know that I can trust you to do as I say,' Sawtell went on.

'You can,' Lionel promised. He realized now that he had completely lost control when he had attacked Morley. Lionel hadn't known that he was capable of such an explosion of temper, but then accepted that he never before had anything worth getting angry about.

'Good,' Sawtell was satisfied. 'Now, John Nichol has given up his lookout. We move the stuff out of the cave tonight.'

Morley had moved away but he returned now, coming out of the darkness, having produced a string of ponies, complete with packs, as if by magic. Lionel wondered how Morley could supply ponies that were the property of his employer, the arrogant, stand-offish Sarai Adams, without arousing her suspicions.

Then he had no more time to consider this issue. The four of them, Morley leading the ponies, were heading for the cave. They went in single file, walking along the beach and passing the rocks from which Arabella, Sawtell and he had pulled the bodies on a night that seemed a million years ago on this still night in the pale moonlight that illuminated a calm sea.

A cold tingling sent itself up and down the length of Lionel's spine as they went by the single, long and wide mound that was the final resting-place of the many dead from the *Paloma*. The day of the burial had been a moving experience that would stay with each and every villager until they went to their own graves. Looking, and no doubt feeling, strangely out of place among the local folk, Joby Lancer had stood a little apart, hands behind his back, head bowed. He must have known at least some of those over whom the Reverend Worther was saying prayers, but he had never mentioned them. If anyone near and dear to him had perished in the shipwreck, then Joby Lancer showed no grief. The face that his long hair framed that had fallen forwards as he'd bowed his head, had been completely expressionless.

They had sung hymns together, and then the choir from Worther's church had sung a final, haunting tribute, their voices becoming disembodied in a mist of drizzling rain so that it was as if the angels were singing in the cloudy sky over a sorrowing Adamslee.

Lionel welcomed reaching the cave, where work would keep his body busy and slow down the thinking that was causing his problems. Recall of the burial prayers and the sweet singing reminded him that he was breaking the law: he was sinning.

Then his ambition came pushing through, and he was glad that it had when he heard Ben Morley tell Sawtell, 'My mistress said not to get to the house afore two o'clock.'

At first Lionel found it impossible to believe. Sarai Adams, whom every man in the village desired because of her stunning looks, and every man, woman and child in Adamslee feared due to her great wealth and power, was part of Gray Sawtell's smuggling ring.

Somehow this knowledge eased Lionel's conscience. Knowing that the lady of the manor was involved made his own participation seem minor and justified by comparison. Sarai Adams couldn't claim grinding poverty as a motive for her criminal activities, but Lionel Heelan most certainly could.

Pausing on the shoulder of a small knoll, Joby Lancer looked down to the cove where a raging sea had tossed him ashore. Now it was a peaceful scene. Small waves rippled in close together to gently and lingeringly kiss the beach. Backlit by the golden glow of a new day's sun, two ageing fishermen were bent over nets they were repairing, and Lancer could see Ruth Heelan standing waist deep in the water. Her wading awkward from the crippled foot, Ruth had a huge basket on her back that was held in place by a leather strap across her forehead. Using a long pole with a hook at the end, Ruth was laboriously pulling seaweed to her before tossing it over her shoulder into the basket.

Apart from the industry shown by the lame girl, it was a desolate, indolent picture that was a reminder for Lancer that Adamslee held nothing for him. There was no work available in the village, but that didn't prevent him from feeling a wrench at walking away. While his head was urging him to go, his heart begged him to stay with Arabella. The girl and he had become close. Perhaps their relationship had moved near to the mystical borders of love. But it had been unspoken. Lancer felt that words would dissolve the magic between them.

Neither of them, Arabella in particular, would have betrayed the trust of devoted, good-hearted Lionel Heelan. The local boy had a prior claim on the girl, and he could offer her total honesty. Arabella knew everything there was to know about Lionel, whereas Lancer had not told her one thing about himself, why he avoided any real mention of his past, and why he had been aboard the *Paloma*.

Someone other than he would be required to answer that question. As an army captain, Lancer had received many decorations for bravery, and had been mentioned in dispatches twice. Although he maintained an aloofness that his rank demanded, his men had liked and trusted him. Most of them had regarded him as a friend, albeit within the framework of a disciplined force. But was all that, an auspicious record, enough to balance out his desertion? It had been tough in the Crimea, but that hadn't worried Captain Lancer, whose leadership and bravery had earned him the respect of both friend and foe.

It had happened outside of Sebastopol a little over a year ago. At the beginning of January, an unexpected and heavy thaw had set in so that the trenches were canals of mud on that cold, wet, and damp winter's night.

To Lancer's soldier's mind, everything had been wrong about that night. With the French to the south of the British lines, Lancer and his men had lain in the lonely position in front of the advance trench. With muskets loaded and capped, they had been keeping a watching eye on every embrasure in front of them. But in the town the Russians had proved they were more intent on celebrating their New Year than they were fighting. They had lighted watchfires on the north side of Sebastopol, and illuminated the heights over the Tehernaya with rows of lights in the form of a cross that shone through the darkness with a pseudo-divine brilliance. At midnight the church bells in the city had begun to ring.

Able to sense the unease of his men, Lancer hadn't been unnerved himself, but this unusual background to a battle area was off-putting, and he had since wondered if this had contributed to what had later happened.

Runners had come with warnings to be on the alert, and the advance posts had been strengthened accordingly, but the Russians were playing a game of nerves, a ploy to unsettle the British and French troops. At about one o'clock in the morning, after the people had come out of their churches, a mighty cheer had gone up. Lancer and those with him had guessed that something was about to happen, and it did!

The Russians had started the fiercest cannonade along their positions that the British had yet faced. The batteries had vomited forth floods of flame that came through the dense smoke like lightning breaking through thunderclouds. Night had been turned into day so that Lancer could see distinctly the batteries crowded with soldiers and the buildings in the city behind them. The round shot came in rapidly, ploughing up the ground behind them into furrows, or thudding as they struck the parapets. With the sandbags, gabions, parapets and fascines being knocked down, the British artillery had been forced under cover and could barely reply to the volleys.

Lying twelve paces apart, Lancer and his men were largely untouched as their position had been fifty yards in front of the trench on which the Russians were accurately laying their guns.

Under cover of the firing, a strong body had come pushing up the hill towards Lancer's position. He had passed the word along the line: wait for his signal to fire, then retreat to the trench to rejoin their main force. The enemy had come on in strength, so Lancer had sent a man back to alert the field officer in charge to send up reinforcements from the other parallels at the rear.

On Lancer's order his men had fired, cutting down a row of Russians. But they were sacrifices the enemy was prepared to make, and the enemy had come on, braving the fire, many of them dying. They had come over the escarpment as Lancer and his men had retreated into the darkness. But Lancer had halted his men when they had dropped back a short distance.

They had all been in bad shape. Their uniforms that had saturated during the thaw had frozen stiff again to become desperately cold and uncomfortable. He had realized that to retreat in an attempt to join their comrades in the trench would mean they would be cut down by Russian artillery before they reached their lines. Aware that it would be taking a chance, but it was the only move open to them, he had known that they had to go forward.

He had explained to his men that they must advance by going round the advancing enemy's flank to take out at least one of their batteries. This would cause confusion in the other batteries that could well produce a lull in the cannonade that would allow the British and French troops to advance.

Having taken the Russians by surprise, they captured the first bunker without suffering any casualties. Under his instructions his men were disabling the cannon when disaster struck in what he later discovered was a direct hit by a French round shot.

On regaining consciousness, Lancer discovered that he had been taken to the French trenches. His injuries had been treated, and the French soldiers had given him coffee as soon as they realized that he was conscious. They had cooked some biscuits for him in pork fat; the smell had left Lancer in no doubt as to how hungry he was. Grateful, he had eaten and drunk feeling some of the exhaustion lifted from him as he had waited for his own soldiers to arrive to take him back to his own lines.

When they had arrived it was as an escort. Shaken to the core, he had found himself charged with desertion and cowardice in the face of the enemy. At first he had judged it to be a mistake and he had been amused. He had lost no time in asking for the men who had entered the Russian battery with him. They were his witnesses, and their testimony would see the charges dropped and an apology tendered.

But every one of them had died from the round shot that had been fired by the French allies who had not known that he and his men had moved ahead. Back in his own lines he was stripped of his rank and confined to await court martial.

It was totally unjust, but by the time he had voyaged under guard towards home on the *Paloma*, Lancer had resigned himself to a lifetime's imprisonment at best, and execution at worst.

Sorrow over so many losing their lives in the shipwreck kept him from a selfish theory that his miraculous escape had been a righting of the wrongs that had been done to him. But he had seized the opportunity of an unorthodox reprieve and another chance at life. That was why he could not tell the villagers anything about himself. It was a matter of great regret that even Arabella had to remain ignorant. Until he studied the lay of the land, established some kind of new life, even a remark made in innocence could jeopardize his welcome but unexpected freedom.

Feeling bad about not confiding, at least in part, in the girl who had saved his life and with her mother had taken care of him, Lancer had no alternative but to leave Adamslee and start walking inland.

The town of Footehill was his destination. He had been told that work could be had at the town's hiring fair. Lancer wanted to earn money to first recompense Arabella and her mother, and then to finance some kind of new life for himself. It pleased him to imagine that once he was solvent again he would be a free spirit able to walk the other way should the wind be blowing in his face. But he doubted that this would be a reality: Arabella Willard was already someone who would influence any decision he would make in the future.

A well-worn track uncoiled in front of him, winding its way

like a drab-coloured ribbon through the rolling, treeless countryside. Spring had a tight enough hold on the day to warm him so that when he came upon a stream bubbling crystal clear from between rocks, he knelt beside it to splash the cool, invigorating water over his face. With his ablutions over, and not knowing when he would again find water, he drank deeply before moving on.

There was a vastness to the terrain that was green, pleasant, and offered a solitude that he was keen to embrace. It was his first opportunity to be alone since being rescued, and he welcomed the chance to do some deep thinking. But his spirits sank as he rounded a spur of chalky stone to find that he was about to share his newfound world of peace and quiet.

Up ahead a horse stood listlessly, its head drooping. A woman stood beside the animal, her head high, looking at him steadily without any trace of fear at being alone with a stranger in what was virtually a wilderness.

Having travelled the world as a soldier, Lancer had met many women, but none as stunning as the one who was coolly surveying him as she leaned one shoulder against the magnificent stallion. It would be an error to describe her as lovely or beautiful. In fact, an apt description eluded him. All that betrayed what was perhaps an underlying uncertainty in her was the way she tossed a whip from one hand to the other as he approached her.

'He went lame,' she said by way of greeting, and as an explanation of how she came to be standing there.

Nodding, Lancer sat on his heels to lift each of the stallion's hoofs in turn. Still holding a back leg, which had a loose shoe that required the attention of a farrier, he was about to look up to tell her so when he felt something cool against his chin.

It was her whip, and she applied pressure to bring his face up so that she was looking down into it. A small smile put long white teeth on display, as she said, with the inflection of someone solving a perplexing puzzle, 'You are the man from the sea – the only survivor.'

This was something that he would once have readily responded to, but there were too many problems in his immediate past and too much uncertainty in his near future for him to do so now. Not that he wasn't interested: no man alive could fail to be fully aroused in her presence.

'I've heard of you, of course,' she was saying, still keeping the whip firmly against his chin. 'But I don't know your name.'

'Joby Lancer, miss,' he told her, raising a hand to move the whip away from his face so that he could straighten up.

She had been looking at him as if he was some kind of animal she was considering purchasing at a market. Lancer took exception to her attitude. It may be that she exuded class and breeding, but in his day he had danced with the wives of generals and brigadiers, and had bedded more than a few of them. This self-assessment generated arrogance in Lancer, and he locked gazes with her. Maybe she was accustomed to addressing country yokels, but he wasn't going to permit her to talk down to him.

'That is my house up there.' She pointed with her whip to a large house standing high on a cliff. 'You have probably heard them speak of me in the village. I am Sarai Adams. My name is not spelt S a r a h, but S a r a i.'

'The same as Abraham's wife in the Bible,' Lancer said, enjoying the fact that his knowledge rocked her off balance.

She quickly recovered her poise. 'You are a rarity in these parts, Lancer, being able to read when most around here can do no more than make their mark.'

'I can make my mark, Miss Adams,' he told her with bold ambiguity.

Averting her gaze, she murmured something in such a low voice that Lancer had to strain his ears, and even then he couldn't be sure. But it seemed to him she had complimented him by saying to herself in a whisper. 'I'll wager that you can'.

'Where are you off to now to make your mark?' she asked in a normal tone.

'I'm heading for the hiring fair at Footehill. I am told there is always work to be had there.'

'Oh yes, that's true,' Sarai Adams said scornfully. 'You'll find work mucking out the cowshed of some blockheaded, cider contaminated farmer, Lancer. A man like you can do better than that. What were you before they pulled you from the water?'

'Very, very wet,' he told her, neither liking her attitude nor the kind of questions she was asking.

'You give nothing of yourself, Lancer,' she complained, a touch of temper in her evident by the way she rhythmically beat the whip against her thigh.

'What do you give of yourself, Sarai?' he enquired, watching her anger register in her large eyes.

'You are most impertinent,' she rebuked him. 'Now, can you do anything with that horseshoe?'

'No, miss,' Lancer slapped the stallion on its flank. 'He will need walking home.'

'Then you may walk with me,' she said, her conceit assuming that he would welcome the opportunity.

'Am I to feel privileged?' Lancer raised a cynical eyebrow.

'You may feel how you wish to feel, Lancer,' she snapped, her heavy lips thinning a little as she rebuked him angrily. 'The fact of the matter is I was considering offering you a position at Adamslee House.'

'Which will make my walk to Footehill unnecessary?' he enquired, interested now and regretting his earlier flippancy towards her. She had begun to walk. Lancer fell in beside her, the horse pacing along with them, its partially detached shoe making a regular clinking sound.

'Not exactly,' she replied, head down, biting at her bottom lip as she gave his question some thought. 'You see, Alfred Gribble, my estate manager, retires this coming August. Which means that you would need to make a living until then.'

An incredulous Lancer croaked, 'Are you offering me a position as estate manager, Miss Adams?'

'Come now, Lancer,' she chided him, a curl of amusement on her lips. 'What I have just said was absolutely fundamental. You have gone out of your way to impress upon me that you are intellectually superior to the dullards I have to tolerate in the village, so surely you can grasp the meaning?'

'I am perfectly able to understand your offer, but can't believe that you are prepared to give such an important job to a total stranger!'

'No one remains a stranger to me for long.' She lifted her head and turned to look directly at him as they walked. 'I read your arrogance as self-confidence, which tells me that you can ably manage my estate. Your way with words assures me that I will not be bored, as I now am. In the final analysis, your physique is reassuringly powerful so that I will not have to fear poachers nor any kind of intruder.'

'And my impertinence?' he couldn't resist asking cheekily, although aware that it could cost him the job before he even got it.

Head down again, watching her own feet as they paced along, she stayed silent for a moment. Then she said slowly, 'Your impertinence informs me that you are accustomed to having whatever woman you choose. Consequently, I will teach you a lesson by proving that there is at least one female who is perfectly capable of putting you in your place.'

'Was that one of your considerations when offering me the post?' Lancer asked.

'Not at all, Lancer, but it is a side issue that I anticipate with relish,' Sarai Adams said quietly, but in a way that Lancer presumed was a warning.

For Lancer there was a deep mystical sensation in walking

with a woman like Sarai Adams that struck him as being primeval. It was as if they had stepped together, naked but for animal-skin loincloths, out of the first ever dawn.

The idyllic setting was suddenly enchanced when a skylark disturbed by their approach came up out of its nest. Climbing vertically into a clear blue sky, its song had the sound of angels in it. They both watched it until the bird was no more than a speck, and its delightful song had to be imagined more than listened to. Neither of them said a word, but it was a shared moment so profound that it would live on in each of them forever.

Still unspeaking, they came to a brook that bubbled as melodiously in a different way, to the bird that so recently had serenaded them. Stepping over the water, Lancer reached out a hand to her as she led the stallion across. The feel of her slim, cool hand in his was more powerfully sensual for him than the full intimacy he had experienced with lesser women. Close to him for too brief a moment, the growing warmth of the day had coaxed a natural fragrance from her that he breathed in eagerly.

It encouraged Lancer that she left the hand in his longer than was needed. But then she withdrew it, saying, 'That was a mistake.'

Lancer was uncertain whether she was referring solely to the hand contact, or the whole magical, mystical thrill of their momentary closeness. To enquire would be to ruin everything, so he stayed quiet as they rounded a low hill to enter a miniature valley, the rocky sides of which announced that the sea was just up ahead.

Stopping, pulling the horse to a halt, Sarai stared straight ahead.

Following her gaze, Lancer saw a man sitting on a rock, obviously expecting Sarai to come along this track. There was a familiarity to the figure, but Lancer found that he had to cancel out men he had known before coming to Adamslee while running through his mind the few acquaintances, he had made here. Then he had it: the man up ahead was the enigmatic Gray Sawtell.

'Go now, Joby Lancer,' Sarai was telling him while still looking to where Sawtell was sliding lithely down off the rock onto his feet. 'Go to find your work at Footehill, but be sure that you come back to me in August.'

Noticing the change that had come over her since seeing Sawtell waiting up ahead, Lancer paused for a moment, looking at her strong, almost Mediterranean profile. Eventually turning back the way they had come, he was astounded at how difficult it was to walk away from her.

As he went, discovering an acute loneliness for the first time in his previously self-sufficient life, he felt a stab of guilt at the realization that he hadn't given Arabella Willard a single thought since meeting Sarai.

He walked on towards Footehill, somehow as a very different man to the one who had left Adamslee earlier that morning.

'Are you funning me, Reverend?'

A flustered Arabella stammered out her question as she reached for the hand of her mother. The two local dignitaries, Reverend Worther and Dr Rupert Mawby had come to the house at noon to announce that the May Day committee had elected Arabella to be Adamslee's May Queen. She just couldn't believe it, and though she could tell that her happily smiling mother had accepted what the clergyman had said, Arabella found herself protesting.

'It can't be. There are much prettier girls than me in the village.'

'Not the way we and the committee see it, me dear.' Mawby frowned at her. He was a short, chubby man who wore a constant severe, almost angry expression on his moustachioed face that belied his kindly, generous nature. 'Not only was it decided that there is none fairer than thee, Arabella, it was also taken into account that you are an inspiration to all in the way that you take care of your good mother. In addition, your participation in the *Paloma* incident was praised most highly.'

Aware of the tears of joy running down her mother's lined cheeks, and seeing that the two visitors were serious, Arabella felt elation as she at last knew that it was true. How could everything suddenly be going so right? Throughout her life fate had conspired against her, but her mother was now in better health than she had been for years, Lionel was a happy man, becoming happier by the day as his fortunes continued to improve, and now, to top it all, this honour being bestowed upon her heightened her happiness immensely.

Suddenly filled with a conviction that it would mean she could make a complete fool of herself, Arabella asked fearfully, 'What will I have to do?'

'Just be your sweet self.' The Reverend Worther gave a smile that was magnified by protruding top teeth. 'Miss Adams has graciously put the grounds of her house at our disposal for the big day, as she has so kindly done in previous years.'

Mawby came in then. 'You will be at the centre of the celebrations here in the village on the eve, and then on May Day itself you will lead the grand parade up to Adamslee House, where you will hold a position of honour throughout the day's events.'

It all sounded so good that a great excitement began to well up in Arabella. Never one to put herself before others, she was nevertheless proud to have been chosen, and had quickly accepted that it would do no harm to have her one day of glory.

'You won't be alone, of course,' the clergyman told her reassuringly. 'An attendant will be chosen for you.'

Without thinking, Arabella, who would never ask anything of anybody, was so moved by love for the good-natured, crippled Ruth Heelan, that she blurted out, 'Could Ruth be my attendant, please?'

The magistrate and the clergyman exchanged amused glances before the latter turned back to Arabella to ask. 'You mean Ruth Heelan?'

'Yes!'

'Well, well, isn't that strange.' Doctor Mawby shook his round head in disbelief. 'You will find this difficult to believe, Arabella, but young Ruth has already been provisionally chosen. All that remained was for you to give your consent to her being your attendant.'

That was enough to convince Arabella that the whole thing was fated, so it would go well. The only blot on her near horizon was that she would have to leave her mother for the day. This was the first subject she broached when the two men had left the house, but her mother soon put her mind at rest.

'My only regret is that I won't be able to see it all happening,' Lucy Willard said. 'You must not worry about me: Josephine will come and sit with me. She will be as proud as I am of you, Arabella. This is to be your big day, and I want you to enjoy it to the full.'

'I will bring something home for you, Mama,' Arabella promised, as she kissed her mother's cheek. 'I will make sure that you have a memento so that you, too, will remember the day.'

Four

OOTEHILL WAS A collection of houses and buildings that
flanked a wide street of considerable length. Lacking the
intrigue of the towns that have side streets and passage-
ways to be explored, it struck Lancer as being so bland that it
was totally characterless. Cow dung was liberally splattered
over the street, the unmistakable and not unpleasant odour of it
heavy on the air. The cattle fair was over for the day, and to Joby
Lancer's chagrin the hiring fair didn't seem to have ever begun.
There were just two girls and himself, a trio to whom passers-
by paid scant attention. His hope of employment was dying in
advance of a sun that was slowly dropping towards a western
horizon of cloud-crowned, purple hills. He was aware of a
growing urge in him to walk towards those distant hills. Yet
logic cautioned him that though there was nothing here for him,
it was likely that there was just as little awaiting him on what
was to him the far side of nowhere.

'It ain't never been like this, mister, honest it ain't,' one of the
girls told him, as if the absence of potential employers was her
fault.

As thin as a rail, she had a narrow face and crossed-eyes that
wrongly, Lancer was to discover, gave an impression of slyness.
The neck of her cheap frock was low cut. Where breasts should
have been there were just bones that looked sharp enough to cut
through the tightly stretched skin. Her companion was, in
contrast, a buxom, rosy-cheeked wench with a heavy bosom as

full as that of a nursing mother. She looked at Lancer through piggy eyes as she supported what her friend had said.

'I've been 'ere when there's been twenty of us all taken on of a morning,' the big girl recalled better times.

'Are you sisters?' Lancer asked, not in the least interested but making an attempt at polite conversation in return for their friendly overtures.

His question made the cross-eyed girl giggle, while the large girl parted her fat cheeks to smile as she replied, 'We bain't sisters. More like cousins, I allow, but we ain't in no way related, really. Until two years ago, Hett and me had worked up at Moor Farm since we was both twelve. Then old Mr Matthews passed away.'

'Gertrude and me bin in service at two other houses since,' Hett added. 'We've been together all the time and we was hoping to get work for the two of us this day.'

Looking Lancer up and down, her small eyes squeezed tighter by the fat of her face, Gertrude questioned him. 'What manner of work do 'ee be seeking?'

'Anything.' He gave a shrug, hope having him cut off any further conversation as a wizened old man rode slowly towards them in a trap.

Reining up, the old fellow climbed stiffly to the ground, his body no thicker than wire, the clothes he wore hanging baggily on it. As he came walking up on legs so bent that he rolled with each step, the two girls tidied their threadbare clothes in antici-pation. But Lancer found that the ancient man was watching him through eyes that leaked tears that owed everything to age and nothing to sadness. This encouraged Lancer to believe that he was the one the oldster was interested in, but it was then he realized that he was being watched cautiously by the old man, who stopped in front of the two girls.

Flicking another wary glance sideways at Lancer, he enquired, 'Can ye keep house?'

Opening his mouth to speak had caused the old face to implode, leaving on display a toothless upper gum and a row of black and brown, snaggly teeth in a lower jaw. His sunken eyes watered profusely as he looked to one and the other of the girls.

'Indeed we can keep house, sir,' Gertrude dropped one knee in a half curtsy. 'Have you work for the two of us, sir?'

Shaking his head, lined face screwing up as if this was the most difficult question he had ever been asked, and it was causing him pain, the old man looked at Hett critically before commenting, 'You look more than a mite sickly, wench.'

'She's strong and wiry, sir,' Hett's friend came loyally to her defence.

The old man studied Gertrude intently. 'You do seem to be the picture of health, girl.'

'I am so, sir.' The big girl did another little bobbing curtsy.

'What about in the winter?' the old man asked as he reached out a skeletal hand that was sheathed in horny, discoloured skin. 'Don't get cold in these, lass, do 'ee?' he continued, cupping the girl's big left breast, first taking the weight and then caressing it.

Aware that Gertrude's face had paled and that she was shrinking back from the lecherous old man, and with Hett's cross-eyes begging him to intervene, Lancer took a step in the direction of the oldster. But he was halted by a discreet signal from the big girl. Gertrude was desperate for work for Hett and herself, and she was confident that she could handle the old man. A perturbed Lancer was far from sure about this, but his attention was drawn to a farmer who had walked up to him unnoticed.

'Do ye seek work, Ted?'

The question came from a squat man who had shoulders like an ox. His short, bull-like neck kept his head down close to his chest. Lancer at once recognized the build as that of a fighting man. This farmer, whose thick, black, wavy hair was brushed back from a forehead so low that just a narrow strip of skin separated the hair from the bushing eyebrows, would be a formidable battler with his fists. Lancer had known the type in the army. Often they were bullies who loved violence behind the lines but became cowards when called upon to face the enemy from a trench.

'I do need work,' he replied.

'What can you do, Ted?' asked the farmer. He had an aggressive face that was beard-stubbled. The slit of a wide mouth opened and closed like a trap when he spoke.

'Anything that is asked of me,' Lancer replied.

He looked past the farmer to where the two girls were walking with the old man to the trap. Gertrude's head was held high, but Lancer assessed that it was bravado and not confidence that was motivating her. A quaking Hett looked over her shoulder at him, her fear showing in her out-of-line eyes. Wanting to interfere, aware that he had no right to do so, Lancer tried to shut the girls and their possible fate out of his mind as he brought his attention back to the farmer.

'Full of yourself, are ye?' the farmer said cynically, his voice a deep rumble as was to be expected from a barrel chest. 'I don't go for boasting, Ted. If I wants to 'ear that sort of thing I do listen to the ducks fart back at my place. Never ye mind, though, I am in bad need of help, so I has work for ye if ye wants it. I suppose you know that the hirings here are for six months?'

'So I understand,' Lancer said, though he had never heard of the rule. There was no point in arguing over something that meant nothing to him.

'Well,' the farmer said, becoming furtive, his voice coming from higher up in his body, squeaking a little as his confidence leaked away from him, 'things ain't too rosy right now. I cain't offer ye six months right off, Ted, but there's two months' work out at my place if ye wants it.'

'I'll take it,' Lancer said without hesitation.

'You've made a good decision, Ted, as any bugger aroun' 'ere'll tell ye. Ye'll get a fair deal from Euart Owens,' the farmer told him. 'Ye'll get two-shillin' a week and your keep.'

'That will do me,' Lancer nodded. 'And I go by the name of Joby Lancer.'

'I'll remember that, Ted,' Owens told him pointlessly. 'I've some buying to do 'ere in town. What's say I pick ye up in an hour? Do you know Maxwell's Lane?'

'No, but I'll find it,' Lancer assured him.

Less than an hour later, after having slaked his thirst at a well he had located in the town, Lancer discovered that Maxwell's Lane was what the lower section of the main street of the town was called. It was the thoroughfare along which he had arrived from Adamslee. He stood there for close to two hours before Owens arrived in a creaking cart drawn by a pony that was in a worse condition than the vehicle.

Pulling up beside Lancer, Owens clambered down to kick one of the axle pins with the toe of a boot. Taking this to be mechanical maintenance, Lancer assumed that, without the kick, the wheel would have come off somewhere along the track. Owens was a little unsteady on his feet, and when they both climbed up onto the seat of the cart, the farmer blew out bitterly foul fumes that Lancer identified as the cider that flowed freely in Adamslee but which he had avoided.

They left the town in the direction of Adamslee, which Lancer found pleased him greatly. Not only was he going back towards the sweet Arabella and the provocative Sarai, but also he found that Adamslee had a pull for him. This came, he felt sure, from him having been in a sense reborn in the small fishing village.

'Ye'll get your money at the end of two months,' Owens told him round a rattling belch. Stomach gas formed from fermenting apples wafted sickeningly past Lancer's nostrils as the cart trundled along. Turning his head, keen to breathe in the air that was pleasantly fresh, he heard Owens going on, 'That's if ye works hard. Ye'll get good grub, Ted, and a comfortable bed of straw. After dinner every Sunday the rest of the day be yours. Ye'll find me a good man to be working for.'

There was no need for an answer, and they carried on along the track, unspeaking, although Lancer was aware that Owens had turned his head to study him.

'Ye look like ye might have an eye for the ladies!' the farmer suddenly commented.

'No more than the next man.' Lancer gave a meaningless answer that seemed to satisfy the farmer's low intelligence.

Whipping the pony for no apparent reason – there was certainly no prospect of getting one more ounce of speed out of the ruin of an animal – Owens kept his eyes front as he warned Lancer, 'Make sure ye stay that way, Ted. Had a fella work for me one time, skinny little bit of a thing he were. I comes back from haymaking one day to find him apeeping at my woman while she was taking a wash. I stomped on 'is guts, Ted, so ye's best keep that in mind.'

'Don't threaten me, Owens,' Lancer said tersely. 'I don't need to peep at women, and you're a fool if you think you're capable of stomping on my guts!'

Face flushing dark red with rage for a moment, Owens then gave a laugh that sprayed frothy saliva far and wide. 'It's ye that's the fool, Ted. There ain't a man in this district that could stand up to Euart Owens, and there ain't one of 'em that would risk trying.'

Lancer let it drop. They journeyed on, with him amused by trying to imagine himself wanting anything to do with a woman who would marry some uncouth lout like Owens. He wanted no trouble with the farmer. Having done more than his fair share of fighting, Lancer rejected completely the hypothetical skirmish that Owens had just involved him in.

They veered slightly to the north, but had travelled far

enough east to satisfy Lancer that he would not be far from
Adamslee when they eventually reached Owens' farm. He saw
a cart heading slowly their way, the young man up on the seat
waving a hand and smiling as he pulled his empty cart to one
side so that Owens could pass with his loaded one.

'It's a fine day, Euart,' the man up on the other cart called.

'It is that, it is that, Ted,' Owens agreed in a shout, before
turning to Lancer to inform him, 'That's young Peter Wright
who's got the place near to mine, Ted.'

When they topped a rise, Owens halted the cart to sit looking
ahead, pride on his moronic face as he looked down upon what
Lancer saw as an example of neglect and decay.

In an otherwise pleasant hollow there stood three ramshackle
buildings. Two were crumbling barns and the third a semi-
derelict house that had at one time held pretensions for a
veranda. This had never been completed, and was in evidence
now only through some weed-strangled wooden planks and a
collapsing rail that was tangled in brambles. All that saved the
scene from absolute desolation were two conifer trees standing
together liked bored sentinels at one end of the house.

'There she is!' Owens gave a cider-laden sigh of satisfaction. 'I've got a dozen calves in that shed to our right, Ted. We
does all right. I grows some hay meself, and I've two fine
horses that I do use to mow meadows for other folks 'ereabouts. Besides that I regularly draws meal from a place up in
Newton Arris and hauls it down to Footehill. Some days ye'll
be takin' care of the calves, Ted, others ye'll be haymaking,
and then there'll be times when ye'll be 'elpin' me out with
the hauling.'

Having imparted this information, Owens moved the cart
creakingly on towards the buildings, where Lancer saw a
woman stood bending over a large wooden tub of washing.
Hearing their approach she stood up, using a soapy hand to lift
a mass of curly dark hair away from her face. She looked

towards them for no more than a second or two, then bent back to her task.

They pulled into the debris-strewn yard, sitting up on the cart as a snarling, snapping, teeth-baring, half-starved cur circled it. Owens appeared to be afraid to get down from the cart because of the dog. He shouted a one-word command. 'Woman!'

Straightening her back, the woman shook both her arms vigorously to free them of soapsuds. Then she walked their way. She had a natural swing to her hips that was attractive, but the rest of her had the used, abused, defeated and dejected look that Lancer had expected to see in a woman married to Euart Owens. Her profusion of curly hair, which was streaked with grey, tumbled over her face so that it was impossible to see what she looked like.

As she neared the cart it was apparent to Lancer that there was some kind of affinity between the woman and the dog that had ribs sticking out so that it looked more like a skeleton than it did a living animal. Staying close to the heels of the woman, it desisted in its snarling and snapping.

Stopping in front of the cart, she tilted her head back and used one hand to push hair away from her face. Properly fed and decently treated, she would have been a good-looking woman. Not pretty, but with an individual kind of face that Lancer, who had become something of an expert during his army days, was aware had much sensual potential. She gave him a hurriedly nervous glance with eyes so black that they could have been all pupils and no iris. Then she stood in front of her husband like an obedient slave, eyes down.

'Get us a meal, Nancy,' Owens ordered gruffly, climbing down from the cart with an uncertainty of movement caused by the cider he had drunk. Waiting until its master had both feet on the ground, the cur leapt savagely, mouth open wide as it went for Owens' ankles.

Cursing, Owens kicked out viciously, his boot catching the

dog where its left back leg joined the side of its body, sending it hurtling through the air, crying out shrilly in its agony, about four feet above the ground. Lancer saw the distressed woman cover her face with both hands as the dog hit the side of a barn, from where it fell to the ground and ran off yelping, its thin, injured leg held up awkwardly as it went.

'Blasted animal!' Owens muttered, adding, 'Get that food going, woman. Me'n Ted have got an early start the morrow.'

When the meal was ready, all three of them sat around a table constructed from a rough but reasonably flat piece of wood to which four rough posts had been nailed. The woman sat opposite to Lancer, head down, as silent as her ugly husband was garrulous.

'I'll do the meal hauling down from Newton in the morning, Ted, while ye can plant the top field with tatties,' Owens said, breaking bread with hands that were as large as shovels, muscles standing out in bunches on bare arms that were as thick as tree trunks. 'That'll let me have the rest of the week to clear Arthur Browne's meadow.'

Nodding agreement, not really taking in anything the farmer said, Lancer ate his meal with nothing in his mind other than the two months' money he would eventually collect. That wasn't strictly true, for he wondered a little about how the woman across the table from him had become involved with a cretin such as Euart Owens. Although now dragged down to her husband's level so that she blended with the decaying surroundings of the farm, Nancy Owens would seem to Lancer to have known better days.

Later, when Owens had taken one of two blackened-glass oil lamps to go out and bed down the horses for the night, she revealed that she had similar difficulty in fitting Lancer into the situation at the farm. She spoke for the first time since his arrival, her voice low-pitched and seductively husky – totally out of keeping with her unkempt appearance.

'What are you doing here?' she asked urgently.

'Earning some money,' Lancer gave the obvious answer.

'That's not what I mean.' She shook her head of wild hair. 'Men like you don't work for the likes of Mr Owens.'

There was more sadness than amusement in the way she had given a title to her oaf of a husband. Calling him 'Mister' came from fear not respect, and Lancer made a comment that contained an in-built question.

'Women like you don't marry the likes of Mr Owens.'

Using a forearm to push her hair clear of her face, she looked into his eyes, unspeaking, her black eyes strangely compelling. He guessed that she was trying to read something with which to measure him, to gauge his sincerity before she was prepared to commit herself to even a short exchange of words. She had all the restless insecurity of a caged but untamed animal. Then she asked, her eyes still holding his, an arm remaining raised to keep her hair back from her face, 'Why are you pretending an interest in me?'

Patched and repaired very neatly, the thin material of the dress she wore was ripped under the arm. As profuse as that on her head, her underarm hair bushed out, alive with a fundamental sensuality.

'I am not pretending,' Lancer told her, and his honesty reached her.

'It's a long story,' she said wearily, letting her hair fall back over her face and turning away.

'I'd like to hear it,' he assured her.

'I'm not sure that I could bring myself to tell it—' she was saying, a tangible sorrow having settled on her, but she broke off as Owens walked back in.

Replacing the lamp he carried on the table, he picked up a hardboiled egg and put it whole, sideways, into his mouth. Chewing the egg, he spat fragments of white and yellow out as he jerked a thumb at the door and spoke to Lancer.

'You'll find straw to lay on in the first barn, Ted.'

Nodding, Lancer walked out into the cool night air. Standing still, head raised to the quarter moon that glowed orange in an unsettled sky, he filled his lungs and ran his hands through his long hair as he tried to expel an image of the harassed and abused Nancy Owens from his mind. Not a man to ever wear his heart on his sleeve, it perplexed him that in the short time that had passed since he had been pulled from the sea he had met three women, and was unable to free himself of any of them.

Sometime in the depth of that night he was awakened by the sound of raised voices coming from the house. Euart Owens' voice was shouting, and Lancer believed he heard Nancy make some kind of verbal protest before there came the unmistakably meaty sound of a fist hitting flesh, which was followed by a muffled scream.

It took Lancer a long time to get back to sleep after that, and he was weighted down with tiredness at dawn when Owens kicked the side of the barn to rouse him. He was shown the field in which he was to spend the day digging, and then Owens mounted the cart to head for Newton Arris. There was no sign of Nancy, a fact that Lancer wasn't pleased to discover, disappointed him.

At noon on that day of bright sunshine he saw her coming up the sloping field towards him. Her hip-swinging gait was more pronounced on rough ground, and she carried a small parcel in one hand and a jug of modest size in the other. She had used a strip of sackcloth to tie her unruly mop of hair back from her face. Really seeing her for the first time, Lancer noticed that the walk had painted a touch of colour into her thin cheeks, and that the narrow paths of grey swathed through her hair enhanced her appearance rather than detracting from it.

'I've brought you some food,' she said diffidently, gesturing with the hand that held a clumsy lump of bread and irregularly cut cheese.

She was wearing a different dress from the previous day. It was blue, and in slightly better condition than the one Lancer had seen her wearing on her slender, small-breasted body. As he studied her now, causing her cheeks to flush a darker, deeper pink, the leaves of the elm tree behind him were stirred by a weak movement of air to play shades of light and dark over the dress that he was fairly sure she had purposefully put on.

'Sit down,' she suggested rather than ordered, indicating a grassy bank at the foot of the tree.

Sitting, Lancer realized for the first time that day how painfully stiff his body was. He had undertaken no physical exertion since the shipwreck and it was telling now.

Taking the hunk of orange-hued cheese and the grey bread, he was breaking it in preparation for eating when she held out the jug, asking.

'Drink?'

'What is it?'

'Cider.'

'No thank you.' Lancer gave an emphatic shake of his head. Since coming to Devon he had seen how cider had first robbed men of the use of their legs, and then their brains. Where some of the older men were concerned the latter effect had been permanent.

'I think I could get you to like it,' she said, and there was a mixture of trepidation and daring in her husky voice.

'I think not,' a determined Lancer told her.

Looking at him levelly for a few moments, standing just feet from him, she then closed her eyes, tilted back her head and parted her lips. Raising the jug she put it to her mouth and drank. Then she stooped to place the jug on the grass, coming very near to him as she did so. He caught the scent of her hair, a natural perfume that was her very essence.

She bent over him then, so close that he was erotically awash in the body aroma that the long walk on a hot day had generated in her. Her eyes, just inches away from his, had clouded so that he couldn't fathom what was going on behind them. Held in her spell, a powerful entrapment that no witch could cast, he waited what seemed an eternity to him as her face came closer and closer. Then her mouth was on his.

It wasn't a kiss, but merely a fairly meaningless contact. Initially mystified and disappointed, Lancer then found his senses reeling as he realized what was taking place. She was transferring cider, warmed and sweetened, from her mouth to his. He drank from her lips as eagerly and hungrily as an infant at its mother's teat.

He was reaching out to hold her when, all too soon, the magically arousing exchange of liquid ended and she jerked back upright, away from him.

Coming up from his sitting position, arms outstretched, Lancer found himself clutching nothing but air as she stepped back, let out a strangled 'No!' in what was almost a shout, and turned to hurry away. He watched her making her way back down to the house, body held stiffly, shoulders hunched, not once looking back at him.

The flea-bitten wreck of a family dog did its best to bound towards its mistress as she walked across the yard. Nancy stooped to pat the animal while still on the move. The cur circled her in an exercise that involved the offering and seeking of affection. Observing this, Lancer was aware just how much both the woman and the animal were in need of tender consideration. He willed her to turn her head his way, mentally pushing the message through the clear spring atmosphere. But he failed to reach the woman. She went straight into the house, with neither herself nor the dog looking to left nor right.

Picking up his spade, Lancer recommenced digging, the sun hot on his back, the woman and her unexpected, blood-racing action on his mind. He toiled on for half an hour at a task that in normal circumstances was too mundane to occupy him.

These were far from normal circumstances, and he swung the spade down with one hand to cut a deep, symbolic entry into the earth. Leaving it there, he threw his head back, eyes closed, letting the sun burn his face with all the power of high noon.

It was a brief but meaningful communication with nature. When it was over he used both hands to smooth back his hair before walking off down the hill in the invisible track left by Nancy Owens.

When he silently entered the house she was standing at some task, her back to him. Her stance was so obviously saying that she didn't know that he was there and that she wasn't expecting him, that he knew it was false. The opposite was the case, and she turned as he took one step towards her.

For just a moment apprehension had command of her face. But then her needs chased all fear away as she waited for him to come to her.

Sarai Adams rarely went riding so late in the day. When she did so it was in the hope that the rushing wind might whisper a solution to her worry as she rode along the cliffs. The chance meeting with Joby Lancer that morning was at the root of her problem. In the short time she had been with the erudite, intelligent man, his presence had caused her to take stock of her personal situation. Finding that Gray Sawtell was waiting for her had cancelled out or, hopefully, postponed the resolutions she had made while with Lancer. It had suddenly come to Sarai that she was heading fast towards trouble. The cellars of Adamslee House were now packed to the ceilings with contraband. John Nichol had abandoned his vigil, but he was so astute that this was no consolation for Sarai. One day, sooner or later, the Revenue officers would pounce.

For the first time since she had been engaged in the heady business of smuggling, Sarai was more aware of the dire consequences of being caught than she was the thrill of carrying out the illicit work. Drifting along, in the control of her physical urgings rather than her well-educated mind, she had become caught up in all the lower-class trappings of the people she had been mixing with. The greatest tragedy of all was that she had accepted without thinking the standards of the likes of Gray Sawtell and those of his ilk.

Although Joby Lancer had made neither a comment nor an observation, just meeting him had caused Sarai to question everything about the sump of iniquity into which she had so willingly descended. Boredom, she was aware, was at the root of her difficulties. They were self-imposed difficulties at that. For the past ten months she had dallied in answering a proposal of marriage from Emil Edelcantz, a Swedish nobleman whom she had met during one of her sojourns on the Continent. Should she accept, then in the way of the majority of aristocratic marriages, every angle but love would be taken into consideration. Yet being the wife of Emil Edelcantz would be the kind of achievement that destiny had planned for Sarai since her birth into the distinguished family of the Devonshire Adamses.

Easing Caesar down into the lowland of the village, Sarai walked the horse along the edge of a beach where Ruth Heelan was struggling with a massive bundle of seaweed. With a rope tied around the bundle, the crippled girl was pulling on the end of it, her defective foot increasing the strain for her. With the district's soil being of poor quality, Ruth conversely earned a pittance in providing a valuable commodity.

Watching the girl, who, drooping from exhaustion, had to pause frequently in her task of hauling the seaweed inland, Sarai found herself envying Ruth. The crippled girl didn't have a large house and unlimited wealth, but she had what was close to being a calling. Unlike Sarai, Ruth had a definite purpose in life.

Riding on, Sarai sent the stallion at a canter up a gradient that would take them up to the cliff at the other side of Adamslee.

There was a little breeze and a cloudless sky created an evening sea that was a beautiful indigo blue. As she rode through this uncommonly pleasant spring weather, Sarai hoped that it would hold for May Day. On this social event of the year for the villagers she turned her grounds over to the Adamslee folk for their revels. Sarai quite enjoyed the occasion for she always had guests, and they, like her, found entertainment in watching ordinary folk at play.

Last year had been the best ever May Day at Adamslee House. Sarai had been honoured then to have the Duke of York and his party as guests. Recall of that occasion impressed on her even more how ludicrous was her present position, and made her all the more determined to bring about a huge change for the better in her life. There would be no royalty numbered among her guests this year, who would all be local dignitaries, although a letter she had recently received from her Swedish suitor had stated his intention of spending May Day at Adamslee House. No doubt he would take the opportunity to reiterate and reinforce his proposal of marriage. In the meantime she had to come to a decision as to what her response would be.

Dusk had now begun to blur far horizons. It was a time when Gray Sawtell would be putting out to sea. Very soon she would have to ensure that he was no longer in her present but firmly back in a past that she was determined to reject. It wasn't going to be easy, for even then a mental picture of the muscular Sawtell moving lithely around his ketch stirred her.

Turning for home, she rode into a twilight that was rapidly surrendering to night. Off to her right she could hear dog-foxes giving the double-bark with which they hoped to influence a female on heat. Despite her strong and fearless character, Sarai found herself trembling a little as she awaited the inevitable reply that would come from the vixen and was the most frighteningly eerie sound to be heard at night.

She had heard the men of the outdoors, of all callings including smuggling, cite the mournful wailing of the curlew as the one thing that would strike fear into their hearts in darkness. But in Sarai's opinion that bird could not compete in horror with the grim howl of a vixen, particularly when she had cubs to protect.

It came then, piercing through the night, causing her the terror that she knew it would. She continued to shiver until the foxes tired and went silent. When the gentle hooting of owls resumed command of the night, Sarai rode homeward. Recognizing that the sounds of the night had taken her back to a far away childhood, she knew that now she must make an effort to reach a maturity that was long overdue.

They had believed that the night would go without a hitch. Young Willie Brickell was wearing a huge, pleased grin, Abe Wilson, a powerfully built, middle-aged petty thief who was the fourth crew member, gave Lionel a satisfied smile and a wink, and even Gray Sawtell had visibly relaxed. Having been prepared to wait out at sea for the Frenchman to sail up, they had found her to be already in position when they'd arrived. The contraband had been taken on board swiftly, secretly and silently. Both the French crew and they had taken great care not to have a crate or keg collide with each other to create sounds that would carry for miles on that still night. But now as the Revenue boat came out of the darkness to bear down on them they realized that they had been under surveillance throughout. The Revenue officers had waited, biding their time. Not wishing to spark off an international incident they had ignored the French ship so that Gray Sawtell's ketch was their sole target.

'This is John Nichol's doing,' Sawtell yelled to Lionel, as he steered his ketch at speed on a course parallel to the shore.

Lionel knew this to be the truth. They had become more and

more aware of the Customs man's increased activities. Abe Wilson, who used a heavy stick to bludgeon his robbery victims and, if necessary, beat any witness into silence, had been all for them paying Nichol a visit at his lodgings in the Ship Inn and using violence to deter him from any further investigation.

Gray Sawtell quashed this idea. Although he was angry by the dire effect Nichol was having on the smuggling, he said that the Customs man was too tough a nut to be cracked by intimidation. Sawtell, in fact, seemed to hold Nichol in some esteem. Lionel noticed this, and it wasn't the first time it had struck him how fair minded the taciturn smuggler was when judging those around him.

Sawtell's interest in Arabella and himself was as strong as ever. Lionel knew, although he made no protest, that he was being paid far in excess of the share the others got. But now Lionel's luck, which had improved a thousandfold since he had joined up with Sawtell, was clearly about to suffer a reversal from which he would never recover. Instead of ensuring the comfort of his mother and sisters before marrying Arabella, he looked set to spend long years in prison.

A massive depression settled on him as Sawtell suddenly sent the ketch on a zigzag course. They had to cling on tightly as the boat pitched this way and that, the bow rising high over waves of its own making.

With a superior speed and manoeuvrability, the Revenue boat was staying with them, coming dangerously close in the sharp turns that were being made. Sawtell took skilful avoiding action as one of the officers yelled orders at them through a megaphone. The rushing of the water as the boats ploughed through it drowned out the Revenue man's words. Yet it didn't take a clever mind to deduce that they were being ordered to heave-to, and told that they didn't have a chance of escape. This was true, for the ketch could never outrun the Revenue boat.

Sawtell signalled to his three crewmen. Getting the message, Lionel's spirits dropped even lower. They were being told to jettison the smuggled goods. All three of them were in despair about throwing into the sea everything they had toiled for that night. But they knew better than to disobey an order from Sawtell. A bit at a time, they dragged the valuable but illicit cargo to the side of the ketch, then tipped it over into the sea where it quickly sank. Working beside Wilson, Lionel thought that the man was uttering a prayer, but then he caught the string of foul words and realized that the older man was cursing.

'Heave-to!' a Revenue officer issued the order through the bullhorn.

Checking that everything incriminating had gone over the side, Sawtell gave Lionel the nod. At this, Lionel picked up the sea anchor, a canvas bag that was held open at one end by a wooden hoop and was attached to a line. Throwing this out in the direction from which a moderate wind was blowing, Lionel saw it float on the surface for a moment, then go to the stern where it filled with wind and held the line taut. Slowing down, the ketch was then held fast and steady by the anchor.

Bumping against the ketch, the Revenue boat was then secured as armed officers left it to climb into Sawtell's boat. Catching sight of the guns, held in a threatening way, Lionel shrank back. But Sawtell faced the Revenue men with his usual arrogance. The officers were aware of what had taken place, and their anger showed. Making a pointless search of the ketch, the Revenue men clambered back onto their craft, with just a senior officer, a big, black-bearded fellow, staying to give Sawtell a mirthless smile with teeth made to look blazingly white in contrast to the dark surround of hair.

'You won't always be this lucky, Sawtell,' the Revenue officer said, adding by turning his head as he climbed back onto his own boat, 'At least I have the satisfaction of knowing that I have cost you a small fortune this night.'

Making no reply, Sawtell stood glaring at John Nichol, who looked back steadily from the Revenue boat.

'One of these days, Nichol, one of these days ...' Sawtell gritted through clenched teeth.

The bearded officer spun round to shout a question. 'Are you threatening one of my officers, Sawtell?'

Giving no answer, Sawtell moved his ketch off, his hard face set against the spray and the world as he headed the boat for the shore.

Five

MAY DAY DAWNED in Adamslee with a wraith-like rising of ground mist that predicted a brilliantly sunny day. When the sun had set the previous evening, bonfires had been set ablaze in the village streets. Every household had contributed logs and helped to tend the fires. Relatively prosperous villagers set tables before their doors, inviting neighbours and passers-by to help themselves to wine and cake. Those people set apart by disputes during the year, put aside their differences and gathered at each other's tables to shake hands. The victims of the *Paloma* disaster were not forgotten, but their tragedy had been put into perspective because life had to go on. Every house was decorated with birch boughs and branches of trees. In keeping with tradition, flora was brought to the heart of each home. Men, women, and children, the old and the young, joined together in a community spirit that must have had love of some kind as a catalyst. It was the end of months of winter confinement with little money for fuel and light, of retiring to bed early and arising in darkness to shiver through another day.

This special day started for Arabella Willard more joyfully than any other day in her life. As she stood among villagers who were coming into some raggedy semblance of a formation in the awkwardly-shaped triangle that was known in Adamslee as 'the square', Arabella was pleased that her mother's friend of long years, Josephine Heelan, was spending the day with her.

The two women would enjoy themselves talking about old times. Arabella had promised her mother that she would bring her back a present. She couldn't afford much, but she knew that her mother would treasure some next-to-worthless trinket.

The procession that would make its way to the grounds of Adamslee House was forming up. The maypole was of enormous length. It was decorated with flowers, bound round with ribbons from the bottom to the top, and painted in variable colours. Standing ready to carry it was Farmer Blaketon's ox, with sweet nosegays of flowers tied to the tips of its horn.

With everyone anxious to move off, to start the festivities for real, the Reverend Worther climbed awkwardly up onto a cart, where he precariously balanced his swollen-stomached body on short, bent legs, to address the assembly.

'As you know, brothers and sisters,' the clergyman began, 'I am no kill-joy.'

A few of the village boys gave shouted, unflattering opinions of what the Reverend Worther was. Their elders who turned on them with cries of 'Shame' silenced them.

When order was restored, the cleric carried on with what was partly a speech and partly a sermon. 'There are those among you, people who have carried wise heads through long years, who have expressed to me their fears that on this day we are to celebrate a day when once heathens indulged in gluttony as well as leaping about in dance and fornication to dedicate the celebration of their idols. These sages have pointed out, quite rightly, that this' – he pointed to the maypole – 'was once regarded as a stinking idol.

'I was able to reassure these good-thinking folk, just as I this very minute assure all of you, my brothers and sisters, that I have called upon the Lord to bless our festivities this day as a Christian welcoming of summer.'

'And so shall it be,' several of the crowd shouted in a disjointed chorus.

'Are ye telling us that no young maiden will have her cherry taken in the orchard this year, your worshipness?' an old woman called.

The crone was shouted down by some, laughed at by others, but what she had said momentarily spoiled the day for Arabella. With disgust she recalled the drunkenness and lewdness of other years. The goings-on, with couples lying shamelessly in the bushes, or standing pressed together behind trees. She prayed that there would not be anything at all like that during her day as queen.

An amateur trumpeter, his homemade silver suit as offensive to the eye as his discordant music was to the ear, blew a fanfare. Helped down from his impromptu pulpit, the Reverend Worther took his place beside Dr Rupert Mawby at the head of the procession. Bracing itself for the weight of the maypole, the ox broke wind in a rattlingly loud way that brought forth roars of laughter. Unofficial stewards, self-appointed and with eyes already washed out of focus by cider, cajoled and bullied the procession back into order, and Arabella, who was to be crowned at the grounds, was put into her place of prominence. Ruth was at her side, her plain face already showing the effects of pain from her foot and leg, but bravely ready to march alongside the rest. A contingent of village maidens fell in behind Arabella, when with a strident clashing of cymbals the parade moved off, flanked by Morris-men jerkily waving handkerchiefs as they did their strangely hopping half run. Somewhere in the line someone with a passable voice falteringly started up a song. Others gradually joined in until everyone, including a deliriously happy Arabella, was lustily singing as the procession proceeded along the track out of the village:

> Worship ye who have been lovers this May,
> For your bliss the Kalendis are begone;
> And sing with us, away, winter, away!

Come, summer, come, the sweet season and song.
The fields' breath sweet, the daisies kiss our feet,
Young lovers meet, old wives a-sunning sit,
In every street these tunes our ears do greet.

Just inside of the grounds, where a radiantly smiling Lionel was waving to Arabella, a farm cart decorated as a platform waited. It had been done so cleverly that Arabella didn't realize there was a cart underneath as she was helped up and seated upon a waiting chair. The lame Ruth was lifted up onto the makeshift stage then, to stand at Arabella's right side, a hand resting upon her shoulder. Four little girls with long hair and wearing angelic dresses stood one at each of the corners of the decorated cart. Another fanfare was sounded, and the girls then blew showers of golden leaves from cups of gold.

Tears stung Arabella's eyes as the wives of Worther and Mawby, both elderly ladies, draped garlands over her head. Not passing the lids, the tears just misted up her eyes so that she couldn't see for a moment; these were tears of happiness mingled with tears of regret that her mother couldn't be there to share this with her.

Morris dancers, themselves now garlanded, pranced around the periphery of the platform as Rupert Mawby advanced on Arabella, a purple cushion bearing a crown in his shaking hands.

Cheap and constructed from scraps, it was more of a tiara than a crown. But this meant nought to Arabella, nor to the crowd that let out a roar of approval and congratulations as the doctor's trembling hands placed the crown upon her head. It was all a charade, sheer make-believe, but no royal queen in history could have been as ecstatically happy as Arabella was right then. Feeling Ruth's fingers squeeze her shoulder, she looked out across a sea of bobbing, smiling, shouting, laughing, friendly faces.

From her side came Rupert Mawby's stentorian voice, addressing the crowd in the serious tone of someone pronouncing a prison sentence in court: 'Lenten is come! Good people of Adamslee we are going a-Maying. Behold our queen!'

A mighty cheer went up, and Arabella's tears welled over the dam of her lower lids and rolled down her cheeks. Beside her she could hear Ruth sniffling and snuffling, and felt a great surge of love for her crippled friend.

Later, when Arabella was walking through the crowd on Lionel's proud arm, exchanging pleasantries with well wishers, Ruth proved to be a dedicated attendant. Once the ceremony was over, Arabella had felt foolish wearing the crown, but each time she tried to remove it, Ruth made sure that it stayed firmly on her head.

As they toured the ground with interest, taking in the sporting events which had village boys competing against each other, and the games of chance from which the proceeds would go to the upkeep of Reverend Worther's church, Lionel spotted Gray Sawtell and Willie Brickell up ahead. He guided Arabella closer to them.

When they drew nearer they could see that Sawtell, although he was as sure-footed as ever, was belligerently drunk. There was an air of aggression about the man that deterred even Lionel, who steered Arabella off at a tangent away from his friend and employer.

Behind a table with a huge hamper on it, packed with a variety of food, most of which was too expensive ever to have entered the Willard or Heelan houses, were the two ladies who had put the garlands around Arabella's neck.

Mrs Mawby spoke to Arabella, putting bottom teeth excessively on show in the manner of most elderly people. 'Just a penny a time, Bella, my dear. Write your name on one of these pieces of paper, then screw it up and put it in that glass jar with all the others. The winning names will be drawn down at the rostrum at seven o'clock this evening.'

'I must have a try,' Arabella told Lionel enthusiastically. 'I have a penny, and I would love to win all that food for Mamma.'

Unable to contain herself, having a good feeling, a kind of certainty that on this day of all wonderful days she would win the hamper, Arabella wrote down her name, squashed the paper into a ball in her hand, tossed it into the jar, closing her eyes and made a wish that could probably be best described as a prayer.

She was passing over her penny to Mrs Mawby when Lionel gave her three more coins, telling Arabella, 'Make sure of it. Have three more tries.'

'You write your name down,' she protested, a little surprised that he was prepared to gamble so much money. Of late he had been morose, constantly complaining because he wasn't earning as much as he had been.

'No, I want you to win it for your mamma, Bella,' he insisted with a kindly smile.

'Then when we win we'll share it between both our families,' she told him and Ruth firmly as she wrote down her name three more times.

'No,' Ruth objected, her bland face registering something like resolve. 'Your mamma has been very sick, Bella, and this will help her a lot now that she's getting better.'

'That is what I was thinking,' Lionel backed his sister.

Putting a loving arm round the waist of each of them, Arabella went on up through the grounds. They came to the extensive, raised lawn outside of the house, where Sarai Adams and her sophisticated guests sat on white chairs beside white tables, sipping drinks as they disdainfully watched the peasants at play.

Arabella had often seen Sarai Adams ride by, as proud, beautiful and unapproachable as one of the queens of Ancient Egypt she had seen depicted in a book when once she had been invited into Rupert Mawby's library. It astonished Arabella to discover that today, for the first time, she didn't envy the lady of the manor. Riches couldn't buy friends such as Lionel and Ruth Heelan. Neither could they purchase the new harmony that had been developing fast between herself and her mother as the latter's health recovered.

She could see Sarai Adams walking among seated guests on the arm of a slim, distinguished-looking man. Arabella was watching the woman, wanting to study her graceful style, intending to attempt copying it later, when a disturbance to her left made her spin round.

There was so much shouting and action that the scene was confusing. But Arabella was able to deduce that John Nichol had been sitting at a table in conversation with an elderly lady, when the drunken Gray Sawtell had crossed the frontier between *us* and *them* by dashing up the grass bank and grasping Nichol's clothing to lift him up out of the chair. The table had been knocked over, the elderly lady had left her chair in fear, and was staggering around in danger of collapse, and there was much screaming and shouting.

Leaving Arabella and Ruth, Lionel ran to the angrily violent little scene, where Abe Wilson and Willie Brickell joined him. The three of them eventually got Sawtell's arms pinned to his side and dragged him back into the society in which he belonged, but not without Wilson receiving a bloody nose, while the upper lip of young Willie was split and bleeding. Calmly standing back from it all, John Nichol was using a cloth to dab at the drink that had been spilled down his clothing.

Hurrying up to them as fast as his too-short legs would allow, the Reverend Worther immediately took in what was happening, speaking sharply to the held but still struggling Sawtell.

'You will behave yourself, Sawtell,' the clergyman said commandingly, 'or you will be expelled from these grounds. Now, my good man, what is it to be?'

After some time, Gray Sawtell ceased to fight those holding him, and gave an almost imperceptible nod to Worther. Lionel and the other two released him, and Sawtell walked surlily away. Watching him go, Arabella couldn't understand the effect the incident had had upon her. She felt a deep cold as if her skeleton was made of ice and not bone.

She pulled the dress up slowly over the small breasts that seemed inadequate for the oversized nipples they supported. These days having Lancer see her thin body naked no longer embarrassed her. Nancy had changed a lot since they had become lovers, now being much more outgoing. She liked to fool a little now once the act that was all consuming for her was over. Of late, she had been jokingly calling him 'Ted', a ridiculing of her husband that she would once never have even dreamt of engaging in. Lancer had still to hear anything of her past, but he wasn't in a position to pressure her for her story, as he had told her nothing about himself.

It was noon on Sunday, May Day, and his urge to go to Adamslee was dampened by his worry over Nancy. He was certain that Euart Owens was aware of what was going on between them. Nancy wouldn't accept this, reasoning that her husband's temper was so volatile that he would have done something about their relationship immediately. But Lancer was convinced that when they had lain together on the straw in the barn one day he had seen a shadow flit past the partially open door. Once again Nancy had argued that her husband was a creature of habit. On the day in question he was due to deliver meal in Footehill, which meant, on her reckoning, that he would have been delivering meal in Footehill.

The next time he had gone to town, Jamie, the boy who always helped them unload, saved Lancer, who had intended to ask a discreet question or two, the trouble.

Called 'Ted' by Owens, as was every other male of the

farmer's acquaintance, Jamie commented to Lancer, 'Was Master Owens ill or summat on Wednesday, Joby?'

'Not that I know of,' Lancer has answered. 'Why do you ask?'

'Cos he didn't come here with no meal. First time in years that he'd missed, far as I know,' the puzzled lad said. 'Mr Shrewton said it was the first time he'd ever known Euart Owens miss a delivery.'

That had been evidence enough for Lancer, but he couldn't understand why Owens had not reacted to his wife's infidelity. The brutal farmer had total confidence in himself as a fighting man so it wasn't fear of Lancer that was holding him back. Owens had taken delight in recounting how he had stamped on the guts of an employee who had peeped at Nancy. Lancer had done much more than peep, but without repercussions of any kind.

With Owens due back from Newton Arris that afternoon, Lancer was reluctant to leave Nancy. This would be the first time he had really been away from the farm, and it could be the opportunity that the farmer was waiting for to punish his erring wife.

'I don't think that I should leave you alone,' he said, meaning it.

Walking over to him, doing up the top button of her frock, she stood close to him, looking adoringly up into his face. At a time like this, her natural body scent was too earthy for a description of fragrant, but it was a compulsive aroma that he was ready to believe dated back to the Biblical Fall.

'You must go, Joby,' she told him in her soft, husky tones. 'I will not keep you from what you wish to do, but I trust that you have no women at this village you are to visit.'

'No,' he assured her with a smile, but he had an underlying feeling that he was not only lying to her, but to himself as well. Of late he had been thinking about Arabella a lot. She was wholesome, so sweet, and so totally honest.

In accepting that his desire for Nancy had, if anything, increased since their relationship had begun, she had nothing like the emotional hold on him that he recognized, in all modesty, that he had on her. In less than a week his two months at the farm would end. He would collect what was owing to him and walk away. There would be poignancy in leaving her, but he was honest enough to know that this would wane once he was over the first hill, and flee completely when he met the next attractive woman. But what of Nancy? She had told him many times how much he had altered her life. Could she go back to nothing but being afforded the same treatment as her half-famished dog?

Lancer hadn't told the woman that his days at the farm were numbered, and he guessed, as she and her husband didn't seem to carry on normal conversations like other couples, that Owens had said nothing to her about the terms that dictated the duration of Lancer working there. When the time came, later that week, Lancer was planning just to walk away without a goodbye. It was perhaps the coward's way, but he felt that it would be emotionally easier for them both.

'I'm worried that he may harm you when he gets home,' Lancer said, aware that Owens would be returning mid-afternoon.

'There's no need,' she assured him. 'I've been here for fourteen years, and he's caused me no real hurt in all that time.'

This snatch of her history was the most she had ever said about herself. The news that she had lived for fourteen long years isolated on this farm with only the brutal Euart Owens as company was too depressing for Lancer to contemplate. Adamslee was calling, and he started towards the door.

Crossing the room to stand in his path, she stretched up to give him a slack-lipped, lingering, deeply arousing kiss before whispering huskily, 'Hurry back to me, Joby.'

Outside, physically free of the woman but tethered by an

invisible cord to her compelling femininity, he walked away from the building. Increasing his rate of walking as he put distance between them he strode along the track to Adamslee with the unhappy confusion of his feelings for Nancy retreating from his mind as anticipation of meeting the folk from the fishing village again, Arabella in particular, took over.

The day had immeasurably exceeded Arabella's expectation. She had been much in demand: judging fancy-dress competitions, starting races and other games, and leading the dancing round the maypole. After some five minutes of the latter she had been exhausted and a little dizzy after so many strenuous hours taking part in everything, and she had laughingly given up, leaving it to the younger girls who continued to skip around the pole, weaving a colourful pattern with the ribbons they held.

Lionel had been there, waiting for her, and she had clung to his arm thankfully. Ruth was at hand, too, as she had been throughout the day, smiling and ready to support Arabella in any way. The stalwart brother and sister, both of them filled with love and kindness for Arabella, were the cause of her acute guilt at the way she had reacted to spotting the long, yellow hair of Joby Lancer in the crowd. Trying to control herself, she had failed, and was certain that Lionel had noticed how keenly she had made her way to where Lancer was standing talking to Rupert Mawby.

Delight on his handsome face as he saw her coming towards him, Lancer excused himself to the magistrate and stepped forwards to greet her. He held both of her hands, asking how she was and enquiring after her mother's health.

Giving him the good news about her mother, Arabella blushed a little at noticing that neither on them were in a hurry to break the contact between their hands. To her right she saw Lionel making pretence of watching boys wrestle. He was hurting, she was all too aware of it, and Arabella was ashamed of herself because she was unable to prevent it from happening.

'And you, Joby?' she enquired with great interest. 'What have you been doing?'

'I've had short-term work on a farm. I finish next week.'

'What will you do then?' Arabella had hoped this question would sound casual, but it didn't.

Lancer shrugged. 'First I will pay back what I owe your mother and yourself.'

'You will not. Neither Mama nor I would dream of—' She broke off her protest as a boy came through the crowd calling out her name.

'Bella Willard! Bella Willard!'

'That's me,' she called to the lad. 'What is it?'

'You're wanted at the rostrum, mistress,' the boy told her.

Coming towards her, a huge smile on his face, Lionel called, 'It's seven o'clock, Bella!'

Squealing happily, clapping her hands as she jumped up and down in glee, Arabella, uninhibited by joy, cried out. 'I've won! Oh, I've won!'

The three of them, Arabella, Ruth and Lionel, hugged each other, dancing around in a little circle. Ruth broke up the cuddling group to catch hold of Arabella's hand and pull her along. 'Come on, Bella, let's go and have you claim your prize.'

Being pulled away by her friends, Arabella remembered Lancer and turned to him. He smiled at her, not understanding, but waving a hand in a short gesture that said he accepted that she had important business with her friends.

Desperate to take possession of the hamper, already imagining the impact she would have when struggling into the house carrying it, Arabella hurried through the crowd, Ruth holding one of her hands, Lionel the other.

Consoling herself with the thought that Lancer would be

staying at the event and she would see him later, she called above the general noise to her friends.

'I'm going to share it with you, I promise.'

'You've won it, Bella, it is yours.' Ruth smiled happily at her and Lionel was nodding agreement.

The rostrum was in sight now. The decorations had sagged as the hours had passed, but it still had an imposing appearance. Arabella could see the Reverend Worther and Rupert Mawby up on the platform with several others, all awaiting her arrival. Then a daunting thought struck her, stopping her in her tracks, and pulled Ruth and Lionel to a halt.

'Whatever's the matter, Bella?' the crippled girl asked, worried by the look on Arabella's face.

'I'm the May Queen,' Arabella gasped.

'We know that,' Lionel said, gallantly adding, 'and the prettiest one ever!'

'But …' Arabella stammered, 'won't people think there's been some cheating because I've won the basket of food?'

Both the brother and the sister scoffed at what they saw as a preposterous suggestion, and Lionel said, 'You played the game the same as everyone else, Bella. No one would ever think that you would cheat, and there's no reason for anyone even to think so.'

'I hope that's right,' Arabella murmured, only partly reassured. But the excitement of winning, the thought of the magnificent prize she would be taking home, came back to her and she let her two friends impel her towards the rostrum. Like most people who have reason to expect little are suspicious of good fortune should it happen to come their way, she was uneasy.

As Arabella was covering the final few yards to the rostrum where Worther and Mawby stood watching her approach, she was suddenly numbed by the ridiculous thought that this day was so wonderful that she would never know another to match it. Slowing her steps, she wanted to achieve the impossible of having her time as May Queen stand still so that her happiness would stay with her forever.

But then she had another, more substantial, worry. The clergyman and the doctor both wore frowns. Seeing this, Arabella's heart sank. She had been right to be wary, because someone must have lodged a protest over the May Queen winning the major prize of the day.

Ruth and Lionel pulled her along, still smiling, and Arabella told herself that she was being unnecessarily anxious. Everything had gone so well that her prize must be secure.

Even so, she knew that something had to be wrong when she reached the platform and neither an unhappy-looking Worther nor an equally dismal Mawby made any move towards her. In fact, they kept their faces turned a little from her. Arabella was pondering on this strange behaviour when something odd happened. Josephine Heelan detached herself from the little group around the two men. She ran forward, head back and mouth wide open in grief as tears streamed copiously down her face. The distressed woman dropped to her knees at the edge of the platform, arms spread wide in a posture of supplication.

'Oh! Arabella, my love. It's your mama. She's just died!' Josephine Heelan cried.

It wasn't a coincidence, Sarai Adams knew that. Not long ago she had shown Joby Lancer where she lived, and now he had strayed from the village celebrations and was standing in the shadows cast by a hedge. A mysterious semi-stranger. An exciting semi-stranger, with his unusual colour of hair given a sheen by the lights coming through the windows of her house. A chill had come late in the evening to send her guests inside. Sarai looked over her shoulder to be certain that she was alone. Count Edelcantz had been constantly at her side since his arrival from Europe. In his eagerness, the poor fellow, every inch an aristocrat, handsome and disdainful, was oblivious to the fact that the monotonous reiteration of his marriage proposal was destroying any possibility of Sarai's acceptance.

Walking over to share the shadow with Lancer, she enquired seductively, 'Do you seek me?'

'No,' he told her, a deliberate rebuff that first annoyed but then intrigued her. Nothing worth having came easily, and Sarai included men in that self-composed adage. 'I've come about the job as estate manager.'

'Three months too early, and you know it.' She gave a little chuckle.

'I've always had an eye for the future,' he said, and she noticed how the shadow flattered him so that he was even more startlingly good-looking than when she had met him on the trail.

'Methinks that you have an eye for more than the future, Joby Lancer,' she said softly, hoping that he wouldn't notice that she had taken half a step towards him. That was a vain hope. He was too astute to miss such a planned move.

'I heard you singing,' he told her.

This thrilled Sarai. About an hour ago, after much pleading from her guests, she had sung for them on the lawn. Hardly had she reached the end of the first line of her song when a hush had descended on the villagers who were gathered not far away. It had pleased her to know that they were listening, but she would have been ecstatic had she known that Joby Lancer was among her audience.

'I was singing just for you,' she informed him in a half whisper.

'How did you know I was here?'

'I could sense your presence within ten miles,' she replied, poking a forefinger lightly into his chest.

This wasn't true, but it was harmless, as both she and he knew that it was a lie. But it added a mystique to their being together that Sarai was sure he appreciated as much as she did.

Doing a quarter turn, she said invitingly. 'Come, let us take a walk. The gardens at the rear of the house are beautifully scented at night.'

'What of your guests?' he asked, not moving.

'They still eat; they still drink, so they will not miss me for a short while.'

'What about Gray Sawtell?' was his second question, and he made no attempt at taking a step.

For a brief second Sarai was rocked slightly off balance. This handsome fellow was even more perceptive than she had thought. Turning back to face him, moving in close, she put her hand flat on his chest this time as she whispered, 'Why should we concern ourselves with others? In my experience there is always one more song to be sung.'

A shiver of erotic anticipation hit her as he placed his big, powerful hand over the one she had left against his chest. They were already close, but Lancer applied a gentle pressure that brought her nearer to him: ever closer. Aware that he had rested his mouth and nose lightly on top of her head to breathe in the aroma of her hair, Sarai was tipping her head back, slightly parting her lips, when her name was shouted across the lawn.

'Sarai?' Emil Edelcantz's slim figure was standing in the doorway of the house, backlit by the orange glow from the oil lamps inside. It made him into a silhouette, the shape of which she found she didn't like.

'Sarai? Are you out there?'

'Who is that?' Lancer asked in a terse whisper.

'The man I am probably to marry.'

'When?'

'Most likely when he stops asking me,' Sarai replied, aware that it was no real answer for Lancer, but it was the only honest one she could give. She turned her head on his chest to entwine her slim fingers with his long, sensitive but very masculine ones as she gave him first instructions and then a warning. 'You will have to leave here now. But you hear me, Joby Lancer; I shall expect you to return.'

'I will be back,' he told her, and then he was gone, moving along close to the hedge so that the night quickly hid him.

Disconsolate, trying not to let her anger show her annoyance at Emil Edelcantz for intruding on her precious moments with Lancer, Sarai walked slowly over to the Swedish man, commenting idly, 'I just felt like some fresh air and a little peace and quiet after so hectic a day.'

'I agree,' he smiled, cupping her elbow to lead her into the house, looking over his shoulder to observe, 'The peasants have gone home to their hovels, I see.'

Sarai found that she detested the arrogance of his remark, while at the same time recognizing that it was the sort of thing that she would say, the kind of thoughts that she had, about the villagers. So she reasoned that it wasn't what Edelcantz had said that she didn't like, but it was Edelcantz himself, the smooth, suave, elegant nobleman that she detested.

When back inside with guests she cared little for, her circle of hatred widened swiftly and gained venom as it did so. Stuck with Edelcantz and the others, while every fibre of her being longed to be with the enchanting Joby Lancer, it was a terrific strain on Sarai to remain polite and engage in small talk for what was left of the evening. That she made it was something she regarded as a minor miracle. She even managed to shake off the more persistent than ever Swede.

The festivities dragged on until two o'clock in the morning, and Sarai had been in bed for only half an hour, and asleep for something like ten minutes, when she was awakened by a light tapping on the bedroom door. Edelcantz had been drinking all through the previous day, and alcohol in a man often makes him either a danger or a nuisance to a woman.

Getting out of bed, donning a robe, she gave thanks to any god that might be listening at that time of the morning that she'd taken the trouble to bolt the bedroom door. How was she to handle Edelcantz? The only course open to her was to leave him outside on the landing where he would only embarrass himself if other guests heard him. To open the door and allow him make an advance towards her would result in Sarai revealing that he repulsed her physically.

Why this should be, she didn't know. Edelcantz was good-looking enough, and his body, though a little over slender for a man, was in good shape. If modesty should permit, then there would be a long queue of spinsters from England as well as on the Continent, desiring to marry the eligible nobleman. Yet there was some clash of chemistry, or whatever, between Edelcantz and herself that caused Sarai's flesh to creep. When she married him, as it seemed she inevitably would, then she would not deny him his rights. But Sarai knew that she would need to close her mind as well as her eyes when she had to submit to him.

'Who is it?' she called softly, the short spell of sleep having put a croak into her voice.

It was her maid's trembling tones that replied. 'It's me, Mistress Adams. Forgive me for calling you at this hour, Mistress Adams, but something …'

Unbolting the door, Sarai opened it sufficiently to see a shaking Elsa standing there, wearing a cloak over her night-dress and a white nightcap on her head. The expression on the maid's round, crimson face warned Sarai that something really serious had taken place.

'What is the matter, Else?'

'Please, Mistress … please … something really bad has …' Elsa stuttered and stammered.

Grasping the maid by the shoulders, Sarai pulled her into the bedroom. Still holding her firmly, she ordered Elsa, 'Get a hold of yourself, girl, for goodness' sake. Now, first take a deep breath and then tell me whatever it is you have to say.'

Doing as she was told, the maid breathed in so deeply that it caused her to explode in a fit of coughing. Doing her best to recover, clearing her throat, eyes watering, the girl sat on the edge of Sarai's bed, a liberty she would never normally take. From there she looked up fearfully at her mistress as if the message she was about to impart would spell her doom.

'Something really bad has happened, Mistress Adams,' she at last managed to utter words that were strung together. 'It is Master Nichol, the Customs man. Oh dear, oh dear. Mistress Adams, he is lying out on the grounds at the side of the house. He's dead, Mistress Adams. Somebody has beated him to death!'

Six

'I TOLD YE when I took ye on that things weren't too rosy, but I didn't know then just how bad they were, Ted.'

Euart Owens was evasive and shifty-eyed, as he spoke. He had lost much of the super self-confidence that comes easily to the ignorantly unintelligent. It was noon on the day of Lancer's departure from the farm, and he stood with Owens at the far end of the second barn. Still not having mentioned to Nancy that he was leaving, Lancer sensed that she had learned it through the mysterious communication that exists between a man and woman who have been intimate. A few moments before he had caught a glimpse of her inside of the window of the house. Nancy was wearing her best frock, such as it was, and it worried him that she could be contemplating joining him when he moved off.

Having anticipated trouble from Owens, he had considered that the farmer would physically attack him for having had Nancy, or perhaps would have picked a fight in which he would hope to pound Lancer to a pulp without giving a reason. But Owens was trying to explain, as reasonably as possible, that he couldn't afford to pay him for his two months of hard work.

The thought of having spent two whole months of toil for no reward angered Lancer. Becoming aware of this, Owens held up both hands, palms facing Lancer, in a gesture that said he should calm down because there was an answer to the difficulty.

'Now, now, there's no need to get your dander up, Ted,' the farmer said pleading for common sense to prevail. 'I told ye before, and I'll not back away from it, that ye'll get a good deal from Euart Owens. We've got a way of settling things in these parts, I think ye'll find more'n fair.'

Hearing this made Lancer suspicious. His guess was that the farmer was about to challenge him to a fight. If Owens won then his debt to Lancer would be erased, while if Lancer became the victor he would be paid double. The odds against him winning were stacked pretty high, Lancer estimated. Leaning against the sloping, semi-collapsed wall of the barn close to Owens' right hand was a hoe with a thick, heavy handle. It had been positioned there for the farmer to grab if, or as soon as, hostilities began.

But Owens was speaking again, and Lancer found his supposition proved false as the farmer told him, 'Ye've worked hard for me, I'll grant ye that, Ted. What we do 'ereabouts at a time like this is let the hired hand take a calf away instead of money.'

This sounded like a reasonable answer to Lancer, until he remembered the sickly calf that had surprisingly survived through all the time he had been at the farm.

'You offering me the sick calf, Owens?' he asked, an edge to his voice.

Giving a spit-spraying laugh, Owens said, 'Ye are the most cussed, mistrusting creature I ever did meet, Ted. I've said that ye did good work, and I told ye what a fair man I am. Ye go into that barn there and ye take your pick, Ted.'

Astonished, Lancer's mind went to the sturdy black and white calf, the best of the bunch. The animal would fetch a good price at Footehill, much more money than he would have got from Owens if that farmer had been able to pay him in cash. It didn't seem possible that the offer to have him take his pick would extend to the fine calf.

'I'd take the black and white one,' he said tentatively, bracing himself for a refusal. With what he could sell the calf for he could reimburse Arabella and her mother. Even then there would be enough money left over to start the new life he had promised himself.

'If that's yer choice, Ted, then go ahead and take the beast,' Owens said affably.

Going into the barn, Lancer tied a short rope around the neck of the calf to lead it, and picked up a stick to drive it along when necessary.

At all times in the semi-dark he was on the alert, expecting Owens to launch a sudden attack. But nothing happened, and when he came out of the barn with his prize calf, Owens was standing there displaying the nearest thing to a friendly smile that his ugly face could manage.

'You've got yourself a fine animal there, Ted, but, like I says, you worked hard for 'im,' Owens said, taking a step closer, tentatively holding out his right hand. 'This is where we parts, Ted. We've worked well together, and I'd like to shake you by the hand.'

Tempted, Lancer hesitated. There had been nothing about Owens that he liked, but the farmer was showing a sense of fairness now that Lancer hadn't believed him capable of. With the calf now his, a handshake wouldn't be much to give. But he found that he couldn't take the hand of a man whose wife he had coveted.

Without a word, Lancer turned and walked off with the calf. He expected Owens to be angrily offended, but the farmer didn't seem in the least hurt as he called. 'Good luck to ye, Ted.'

Not turning, Lancer gave a backwards wave of his hand and walked on. He could feel that not only Owens was watching him depart. Nancy's eyes were boring into his back, making him feel terribly guilty. She had come to him in the barn last night, the first time she had taken a risk like that with her husband in the house. It was obvious to Lancer then that she either knew, or strongly suspected, that he was about to leave. He had rejected her, telling her that it would be disastrous for her if her husband discovered them.

He hoped that he had successfully convinced Nancy that this was his reason for turning her down. It had been impossible for him to tell the same lie to himself. His meeting with Arabella in Adamslee had an effect on him that still had influence. The subsequent short time he had spent with the blatantly seductive Sarai Adams had diluted the feeling, but not to any serious degree. Arabella had looked so radiant as May Queen that he still had a clear mental image of her lovely, smiling face, her happily sparkling eyes, and her glorious mass of copper-coloured hair.

He was unable to shake from his head a notion that Arabella Willard figured large in his future. With Lionel Heelan on the scene it was difficult to envisage how this could come about. But the idea was fixed there in his mind, and no amount of thinking could move it. Sarai Adams refused to be dismissed from his deliberations, yet Lancer saw working for her as nothing but a way to remain in Adamslee so as to eventually get to Arabella. Sarai was both a means to an end and a diversion. Admittedly, she was an excitingly vibrant diversion.

As they walked the deserted track that would eventually take them to Footehill, the calf was faring better than the man who was leading it. The day was oppressively hot, and a tongue-swelling thirst gripped Lancer. When he joined a dusty road, using the stick to drive the calf ahead of him, and a public house came into view he bitterly rued the fact that he had no money.

The inn stood at the side of the road, the only building to be seen for miles, but it somehow avoided appearing to be a lonely place. Close enough now to read a sign that said The Lamb Inn, Lancer could sense the comfort the place had afforded travellers throughout the years. Although standing alone and miles from

civilization, The Lamb Inn gave the impression of being a destination. He supposed that in an ephemeral kind of way it had
been a destination for countless thirsty, hungry and weary travellers.

Pausing outside of the inn, Lancer took a rest by sitting on a
low wall. Standing placidly beside him, the calf leaked opaque
saliva from its wide mouth. Why, Lancer wondered, was the
young cow so moist in the mouth while he was so dry? He
considered entering the inn and requesting a drink of water, but
pride, an original sin that he had ever been guilty of, prevented
him from doing so.

'Ah ha!' exclaimed a voice behind him, and Lancer turned his
head to see a young man coming out of the inn, looking from
him to the calf as he advanced. 'What have we here, eh? I see
before me an animal that will fetch a fine price in the market,
and a man badly in need of a drink.'

He smiled at Lancer in a friendly way. Of average height and
of good build, he had brown hair, carefully parted and combed,
above an oval, good-looking face. The young fellow was expensively clad in a blue frock-coat with yellow buttons, a black
waistcoat, and light-coloured cashmere trousers. The over-all
impression was that of a country gentleman, one of the idle rich.
But Lancer judged that the wealth of this young man was
neither inherited nor legal. He was certain that it was a highwayman who was speaking to him.

'You're right about the calf,' Lancer replied, 'but wrong about
the man. I was resting awhile, but now I must be on my way.'

Shaking his handsome head, the young man argued mildly,
and it grieved Lancer to accept that the obviously affluent
fellow had him down as destitute. 'I still believe that I am right.
A long, cool drink will soon slake that thirst that I see raging
inside of you, my good sir. You see, I am not out to offend your
sense of self-respect, but to buy your company for a short while.
You will be doing a lonely man a great service by accepting my

offer, sir. Now, tie your animal to that stake, and you can treat it to a bowl of water when you leave the inn.'

Needing a drink more than ever now that it had been spoken of, Lancer secured the calf and walked towards the door with the elegant young man, who asked, 'May I ask what name you go under, sir?'

'Joby Lancer.'

'It has a pleasantly unusual ring to it, Joby. I detest the formities of this world, such as uniformity, conformity.' He gave a smile with good teeth, and offered a smooth, white hand that had never known manual labour.

'Thomas Oliver, Joseph Infield; take your pick. I'm known mostly on the road as Buckingham Joe.'

Lancer shook the proffered hand, taking an instant liking to Buckingham Joe, who now paused before they entered the inn, to say in his fascinating style of speaking, 'You may have noticed, Joby, as I most certainly have, that life does not follow a straight line, but moves in cycles. Less than two years hence I was standing outside of this very inn, penniless due to an idiotic lack of foresight. A fine gentleman in a coach pulled up and insisted on purchasing a drink for me. That was the most satisfying drink I ever had. I often taste it over and over again in my memory.'

'No doubt you were in a position to repay the man,' an unhappy Lancer said, as he thought of the increasing number of people to whom he was becoming indebted.

'Oh yes, I repaid the gentleman, of course,' the elegant young man said, turning to point in the direction of Footehill, asking, 'Do you see that bend in the road up ahead there, Joby?'

'I do,' Lancer nodded, looking to less than a quarter of a mile away to where the road took a lazy, meandering route between two small hills. 'And that pair of trees standing together as stiffly as lovers having an argument?' Buckingham Joe waited for a nod from Lancer before continuing, 'I stepped out from behind those trees as the fine gentleman's coach approached. I repaid him by relieving him of the remainder of the money he had with him.'

The self-confessed highwayman was chuckling, pleased with his story that Lancer wasn't sure could be believed, but felt that it could well be the truth. But he had no time for further contemplation of the subject, for they were inside and Buckingham Joe was ordering drinks for them from a surly, unshaven landlord.

The only other patrons were a group of three women and two men when Lancer took to be itinerants, and who were engaged in a noisy argument that seemed guaranteed to shortly erupt in physical violence. But Lancer ignored them and everything else about his surroundings as he drank a long, beautifully cool, golden-tasting mug of ale.

'You'll have another,' the highwayman said in a way that let it be known he would brook no argument, going on to shake Lancer with a perception that had to be some kind of unerring instinct. 'Something about you tells me that you have served with the military, Joby?'

'Some time ago,' Lancer conceded. There wasn't any likelihood of a man known on the road as Buckingham Joe, turning him in to the forces of law and order.

The answer proving him to be right pleased Lancer's new friend. 'That's a good thing, for a man who has never known discipline can never really enjoy freedom. We would make a great partnership, Joby. I like the cut of you. We could reach the heights together, but I fear that you have personal things you wish to do, a definite destination towards which you are heading.'

'I do and I have,' Lancer confirmed, 'and I must be going now so as to reach Footehill before sunset.'

A disappointed Joe said resignedly. 'So be it. There is no meeting without consequence, so perchance we shall meet again, Joby, maybe even in a life to come. If there is a Lamb Inn in the hereafter, then I pray that Joby Lancer and Buckingham Joe will meet outside of it.'

'And the calf,' Lancer joked as he drained the mug and made ready to go to the door. 'I don't know how I'll do it, Joseph, but one day I will repay you for these drinks.'

'Then I had best be wary when I reach that bend by the trees ...' the highwayman said laughingly, but was interrupted by the dispute between the itinerants exploding into fisticuffs.

One of the men, a hulking brute of a fellow, punched a lightly built woman full in the face. She went flying backwards, passing between the standing Buckingham Joe and Lancer, blood spurting from her mouth and nose.

The fellow came after her, preparing himself to jump on her with both feet when she hit the floor, but Buckingham Joe put out a foot to trip him neatly. As the itinerant was pitching forwards, the highwayman swung his arm to hit him hard on the back of the neck so that his face smashed into a table to the cracking, creaking sounds of bones breaking and gristle giving way.

Raging like an angry bull, the second man launched himself at the highwayman. But Lancer was standing between them. Turning his back on the charging man, Lancer timed it just right to drive his right elbow hard into the itinerant's midriff. The body blow knocked the man back a few steps, and he made a noise that was a blending of a grunt of pain, a belch, and the beginning of a bout of vomiting. Without turning, working through some kind of sixth sense that had served him well on the battlegrounds of the world, Lancer flung his right arm out behind him to smash the man in the face with a mighty, back-handed blow.

With the two itinerant men lying on the floor of the inn, senseless, both of them bleeding heavily from the face, Buckingham Joe coolly finished his drink, straightened his frock-coat daintily, and commented to Lancer, 'I told you we could do well together.'

They went towards the door, with Buckingham Joe putting a hand on Lancer's shoulder to say, 'I will walk with you to Footehill, Joby. We could go further together were it not for this woman who is so important in your life. Am I right yet again?'

'You are,' Lancer answered simply, glad that not even this apparently all-knowing highwayman could see that there were three women playing major roles in his life. Yet the situation had righted itself for Lancer in the past few hours, with everything settling into its proper place. He would never see Nancy Owens again, although his guilt where she was concerned would follow him down through the years. The promiscuous Sarai Adams was there to be used, to provide well-paid work, possibly even allowing him to share her bed, but Sarai was and always would be a stranger to the kind of fidelity that Lancer wanted when he settled down. That just left Arabella Willard, his ideal woman.

They stepped out of the door into a sunlight that was initially blinding. When Lancer's eyes adjusted he saw two men standing beside his calf. At first thinking he was about to be robbed, he started forwards, expecting his new friend to be there offering support. But Buckingham Joe had gone, either back into the inn or running off round the building.

Lancer was alone, and now realized that the two men were not brigands of some kind, for they were both well dressed. Not speaking to either of them, he reached to the rope, intending to untie the calf and continue on his way. But one of the men grabbed his wrist and held it, preventing his fingers from reaching the tether.

'Where are you taking this animal?' one of the men asked. He was tall, broad-shouldered, and had a face that he hadn't been born with, but had been remodelled by fists at some later date.

'To Footehill, where I will sell it,' Lancer replied.

'It's not yours to sell,' the second man barked, of short stature, as broad as he was high, but even the fat he carried was stacked in a way that said he could use it to his advantage in a rough-house.

'It belongs to Euart Owens,' the tall man informed Lancer, adding, 'I am Constable Githam, and this is Constable Price.'

'You are mistaken, gentlemen,' Lancer explained calmly, understanding now why Buckingham Joe had deserted him. 'I worked for Owens and he gave me the calf because he didn't have the money to pay me.'

'Are you named Joby Lancer?' Price asked.

'That's right.'

Githam gave a satisfied nod. 'Mr Owens gave your name when he reported that you had stolen his best calf.'

This staggered Lancer. Not only did he know he was in serious trouble, but also that Owens had got the better of him for being cuckolded. The burly farmer obviously hadn't fancied his chances using brawn against Lancer, so he had used brain. Lancer had to grudgingly admit that, for a man so intellectually limited as Owens, the farmer's plan had been a clever one.

'I am telling you the truth, but I don't suppose it will end here,' Lancer said to the constables. 'What happens now?'

'We will take you back to the farm,' Githam replied. 'If Mr Owens can identify both you and the calf, then the animal will be returned to him and you will be arrested for theft.'

There was no point in arguing, so Lancer went along with the constables. The long trek back was a dismal experience for him. He was retracing as a prisoner the steps he had taken as an entrepreneur leading on a rope a source of capital that would launch him into an ambitious new life.

The constables spoke little to each other, and not at all to Lancer as they walked. When they came over the rise where Owens had halted the cart on that first day to proudly show Lancer his farm, a massive depression descended on Lancer as he looked at the ramshackle buildings. Neither Owens nor Nancy were to be seen anywhere about the place. Only the skinny cur was there, sitting on its haunches, mouth opened and drooling as it howled over and over like some demented wolf that had mistaken the sun for the moon.

The dog's howling struck Lancer as ominous, disturbing him greatly for a reason that he was unable to fathom.

Not seeming to notice them as they walked up, the cur kept the unearthly wailing going. Githam shouted, 'Mr Owens?' thrice without getting a reply, before instructing Price to put the calf in the barn.

Holding Lancer by the arm, Githam took him in through the door of the house. A familiar smell brought everything back to Lancer. As he blinked to get his eyes used to being without the bright sun, he thought of Buckingham Joe's theory that life moved in circles. This was a tight circle indeed, for it had brought him back to his miserable starting point within just a few hours. His dread was that he would find himself face-to-face with Nancy. That would be a shameful experience that he hated to think about.

But only Euart Owens was there. Half slumped where he sat at the table; his bulging eyes were red-rimmed as he looked up at Githam and Lancer. He moved his heavy jaw and his slit of a mouth opened but no words were uttered. Even before he caught the stench of cider, Lancer was aware that the ugly farmer was drunk to the extent that he was close to being insensible.

'There's the man who calls me a thief,' Lancer said contemptuously to Githam, who nodded an uncomfortable head uncertain what his next move should be in this situation.

Both Githam and Lancer turned as they heard Price coming in the door behind them. His face was white and he wiped a trembling hand over it before he tried to speak. Even then his lips wouldn't obey him, and all that came out was a mumble.

At last he managed to blurt out a shocking statement. 'There's a young woman hanged herself in the barn. I cut her down, but it seems to me she's been dead for some time.'

Since I walked out of here this morning, Lancer estimated bitterly, feeling sick and sad. His mind couldn't cope with imagining Nancy lying cold and dead where she had lain with him when she had been full of life and passion. In the grip of a deeply depressing feeling, it was as if his own life had just come to an end.

The small group of mourners had returned to the Willard home after the funeral. As well as being filled with sorrow, Arabella couldn't free herself of the astonishment that had been caused her by the single cloud that had come across the sky to rain on them just as her mother's coffin was being lowered into the ground. It had seemed to her like heavenly acknowledgement of the sadness in the life that had just ended. Arabella had never seen her mother truly happy, although she had bravely tried to appear to be so for her daughter's sake. For most of her life it had been plain to Arabella that her mother had undergone some traumatic experience from which she had never fully recovered. It was either before Arabella had been born, or when she was too young to understand what was going on around her. Often having tried to summon up the courage to ask, Arabella had found the whole issue held in some kind of black void. Now it was too late to put the question.

Uncomfortable at what now seemed a somehow strangely empty house, Arabella felt Lionel touch her arm and signal with a sideways inclination of his head towards the other room. Glad to escape from a group of mourners eager to convey their sympathy but unable to speak one word, Arabella followed her man. On that day that needed nothing to increase its misery, Lionel gave her more bad news when they were alone, standing in their dark clothes, sipping Josephine Heelan's weak tea.

'They've arrested Gray Sawtell and Willie Brickell for the murder of John Nichol,' Lionel solemnly informed her.

Added to Lionel's upset over the arrest of his friends, it was obvious to Arabella, was the desolation he felt at the grim, soul-destroying truth that he would no longer be earning good money.

'When one door closes another one always opens, Lionel dear.' She offered words of consolation that sounded patheti-cally ridiculous the instant they passed her lips.

Dejected, Lionel countered fantasy with stark reality. 'With the arrest of Gray Sawtell the only door of opportunity to open for me closed forever, Bella.'

'Let us wait until this sad day is over, then we can think straight,' Arabella advised. 'We can make a new start because this house will be ours to rent.'

Although he gave a half-nod of agreement, the expression on Lionel's face as he took a sweeping glance around the hovel showed that he was far from impressed by the prospect.

At Owens Farm, Githam and Price had commandeered a cart and a pony that they harnessed to it. They had cut down Nancy's body and laid it in the bed of the cart. Her lovely face had been contorted into a ghastly grimace by strangulation, and her eyes stared sightlessly at a horrified Lancer. Covering the woman's body with sacks, they had ordered Lancer to get up on the cart. Then what was a nightmare ride for him began, with every jolt of the cart causing the Nancy's corpse to move around under the sacking. The worst of the journey ended when the constables stopped in a town that Lancer didn't know to carry Nancy's corpse into a small building.

The constables returned to the cart and the journey continued until Dorchester was reached. There he was taken to the Police Office to be examined by a magistrate. He had an hour-long wait until a hard-worked magistrate named Merrifield came, red-faced and sweating, into the building.

'Stand up,' shouted Sergeant Foster, who had now taken over as Lancer's captor.

With the image of Nancy's dead face filling his mind, Lancer was not really aware of what was happening around him. He heard the magistrate complain that he 'Didn't have time to waste', and then Foster pulled him roughly up on to his feet.

The magistrate solemnly but hurriedly read out the charge that Lancer had stolen a calf the property of one Euart Owens from Owens Farm, Symingham, Devon.

'Have you any observations to offer on the charge, Lancer?' Merrifield enquired.

Forcing himself to take an interest, Lancer replied, 'I did not steal the calf. Owens gave it to me as payment for two months' labour on his farm.'

'Mr Owens says differently,' Merrifield sneered. 'Mr Owens is a respected member of the community, whereas you apparently are some kind of itinerant. I understand that when you were arrested outside of an establishment known as the Lamb Inn you were wandering without visible means of sustenance. Is that correct?'

Accepting that he was in a no-win situation, Lance made no reply.

'I will take the absence of a response from you as confirmation,' Merrifield said smugly. 'Constables Githam and Price have noted that you left the Lamb Inn in the company of one Joseph Infield *alias* Thomas Oliver, better known as Buckingham Joe, a highwayman who has previously languished for many days at the prison in which you will reside anon when you leave here.'

'Someone left the inn soon after me,' Lancer's habitual need to oppose authority temporarily defeated his despair over Nancy's death.

'It is noted that you were drinking with Buckingham Joe while inside the inn.'

Lancer shrugged. 'There were several people there. I didn't ask the name of any of them.'

'This attitude of yours is doing you no favours,' the magistrate cautioned.

Lancer responded with another shrug.

'Get a grip of yourslf, lad, and show respect. Mr Merrifield is a Justice of the Peace,' Sergeant Foster ordered angrily.

'Leave it, Sergeant, thank you,' Merrifield said quietly, then raised his voice to address Lancer. 'If you have anything to say, now is the time to speak up.'

'Owens Farm is in Devon, so why have I been brought to Dorchester?'

'That's because The Lamb Inn, where you were arrested lies just inside the Dorset border. That presented the arresting officers with a choice – Devon or Dorset, and it was convenient for them to bring you here,' Sergeant Foster replied.

'I would imagine that when you are tried in court you will be taken to Exeter Prison,' Merrifield explained, revealing that he had already found Lancer to be guilty. 'Take him away, Sergeant.'

Snapping a pair of handcuffs on Lancer's wrists, Foster grunted. 'Come on, lad. The sooner I get you out of my sight the happier I will be.'

Resigned to believing that Joby Lancer would never return to Adamslee, Arabella had said yes when Lionel had proposed marriage. It hadn't been the joyous acceptance of someone madly in love, or in love at all, she had realized. Rather, it had been one of the big compromises that those facing just two options are forced to make in the knowledge that she could either face a bleak life of soul-destroying poverty alone, or face a bleak life of soul destroying destitution with a partner. Her sole asset was the tenancy of the house she had taken over on the death of her mother. Admitting to herself that she was acting out of cowardice, unable to face a dismal future alone, she had agreed to marry Lionel Heelan, who was then in poorly paid work as a fisherman.

No wedding day in an impoverished community is a spectacular event but Arabella's big day went largely unnoticed. Not one solitary soul stood in the doorway of any of the cottages to see her pass by on her way to the church in the badly fitting white dress Lionel's mother had made for her. Waiting inside for her at the door of the church was Dr Mawby who had willingly agreed to give her away, and Ruth Heelan, her bridesmaid.

The doctor gave her an encouraging smile as she took his arm and they started slowly down the aisle together. The only people in the church were Josephine Heelan and her two youngest children. The Reverend Worther stood in front of an altar had been sparsely decorated with a few small bunches of wild flowers. Lionel Heelan stood in the front row of pews with his older brother Malcolm at his side, having travelled down from London to act as supporter. Lionel turned to watch Arabella's approach, the expression of utter desolation on his face too much for her to endure.

Footsteps slowing, Arabella would have turned and run out of church had not Rupert Mawby applied pressure on his arm that linked with hers, and gently kept her moving in the direction of the altar. Once she was there, and his brother had nudged Lionel out into the aisle to stand beside her, the kind Reverend Worther rescued the ceremony from total gloom by conducting it in a vigorous style that made it seem that the church was packed with well-wishers there to ensure that the *happy* couple are properly launched into a life of wedded bliss.

Finding it easy to join in the illusion created by the clergyman helped Arabella to get through to the finish of what had seemed an interminable wedding ceremony. But when they stepped out of the church into the gloom of the village's deserted streets, and Lionel abruptly shook his arm free of her hand, the memory of Reverend Worther's well-meant pretend enthusiasm disappeared. Arabella realized that a happy marriage needs more than a church blessing. Much more.

Neither Arabella nor Lionel spoke as they walked back to the house that now held no promise of security. She broke down and wept once inside what was once a home but was now just a crude building in which her sobbing echoed hollowly.

The one saving grace for the prisoners confined within the damp, depressing walls of Dorchester Gaol, was the knowledge that life could get no worse. Joby Lancer was the exception, although his fellow convicts were unaware of this. There was a rule against prisoners talking to each other. As enforcing this rule caused trouble for the warders it was largely ignored. That displeased Lancer, who had no wish to either mix with or speak to the other inmates. The prison wasn't the cause of his depression: he was haunted by the knowledge that he was the reason for Nancy Owens having taken her own life. His sadness would be just as upsetting had he been free and living in luxury with Sarai Adams in Adamslee House.

Having just finished a frugal meal in the refectory he was about to stand up when he sensed another prisoner standing close, and heard him exclaim, 'At last, a true gentleman among the riff raff! Joby Lancer, I presume?'

Astonished that someone should know his name, Lancer looked up to see a handsome young man who was wearing a smart smock coat, smiling down at him. Obviously new to Dorchester Gaol, the fellow's charming persona didn't fool Lancer. It failed to disguise the ruffian that lay just beneath the surface.

'Did you learn my name from someone in here?' Lancer enquired as he stood up.

'No, no, no. It may help if I introduce myself,' the prisoner suggested, proffering his right hand to Lancer. 'I am John Longley.'

Ignoring the invitation to shake hands, Lancer said, 'That name means nothing to me.'

'Mmm.' Longley pursed his lips before trying another name. 'John French?'

Lancer shook his head.

'One more try.' Longley smiled. 'The Kentish Youth or the Kentish Hero?'

'I have heard both those names,' Lancer confirmed, as he became aware of an under-warden, a sly man by the name of Moses Heron, covertly eyeing them.

Heron was mistrusted by the convicts and gaolers alike. It was well known he had betrayed many by going to the governor of the gaol and repeating what he had been told in confidence or half overheard.

'I am certain that you have, Joby, as we have a mutual friend.'

'Buckingham Joe.' Memory fragments clicked together in Lancer's mind as he recalled the highwayman having once mentioned the Kentish Hero. 'How could you have recognized me?'

'It wasn't difficult. Buckingham Joe emphasized that when describing you,' Longley replied, pointing to Lancer's yellow hair. 'He spoke highly of you.'

That is more than he did of you, Lancer thought, as he recalled that Buckingham Joe hadn't a good word to say about this disreputable fellow. He noticed that the under-warden had inconspicuously moved closer to them.

'We got on pretty well,' Lancer said.

'Everyone likes Thomas. That's his real name – Thomas Oliver,' Longley informed Lancer. 'Me and him were good together. I made more gilt along the road when I was with Thomas than I ever did. We would be wealthy men today had we stayed together. I'd like to catch up with him when I get out of here. When did you see him last?'

Now confident that Longley, probably under the directions of Moses Heron, was pumping him for information about

Buckingham Joe, Lancer gave a vague answer. 'It must have been several months ago, I don't really remember.'

'Where would that have been?' Longley enquired, the mask of friendliness he had worn until then noticeably slipping.

'If I remember rightly it was at Haldon Races,' Lancer lied deliberately. Speaking from the side of his mouth, he added a warning, 'Moses Heron is circling us.'

With an almost imperceptible nod, pretending to appreciate the caution, Longley replied *sotto voce*. 'We will talk later.'

I will make sure that we won't, Lancer made a silent promise to himself.

Seven

LANCER FACED THREE magistrates when he arrived in court, none of the three being the Justice of the Peace named Merrifield before whom he had appeared on arrival at Dorchester. He was placed in the dock standing between two uniformed constables as the clerk of the court read out the charge in a monotone. Perhaps because he wasn't really paying attention, the words droning around the courtroom seemed nothing to do with Lancer.

'Is Mr Euart Owens in court?' the chief magistrate asked officiously but unnecessarily, as it was obvious that only the policemen, the court officials and Lancer were present.

The police sergeant got to his feet to reply to the magistrate. 'No, sir. Constables Githam and Price obtained a statement from Mr Owens that together with the overwhelming evidence produced by the said two officers, establishes a clear-cut case against the accused.'

'Is there anything you wish to say?' the magistrate asked Lancer.

'There is nothing for me to say other than I did not steal the calf.'

'Yers,' the magistrate murmured the word in a drawn-out manner that signalled his utter disbelief.

Following this, the three magistrates took time to study the papers in front of them. While they were engrossed in that examination, Sergeant Foster cautiously did an animated display for Lancer by pretending to have a noose put over his own head and pulling it tight. When he had finished the charade he pointed at Lancer to indicate that hanging would be his fate. Aware that the police sergeant was nought but a cowardly bully, Lancer stared hard at his would-be tormentor until the imbecilic grin faded from the sergeant's face and embarrassment made him eventually turn away.

The three magistrates began discussing the case among themselves. Lancer waited, totally unconcerned as to what the verdict might be. Whatever it was it would never amount to the punishment that guilt over Nancy Owens' death was inflicting on him.

'We have thoroughly considered every aspect of your case,' the chief magistrate finally announced gravely. 'We are appalled by the callous act of theft that you committed against a poor farmer in these difficult times when so many are struggling so hard to make ends meet. There is no facet of your behaviour that would in any way allow us to consider leniency—'

The magistrate broke off as the colleague on his right leaned close to him to say something *sotto voce*. A lengthy inaudible conversation ensued in which the third magistrate joined.

Lancer was jolted out of his reverie by the very real possibility that he would be sentenced to transportation to Australia. After many years in the army, he saw a convict colony as something similar: the kind of life he didn't want to return to. For the first time since he had been taken back to Owens' farm by the police, Nancy was not on his mind. He prepared himself for the worst as the conversation between the magistrates came to an end.

A belch, that was made more noticeable by his attempt at stifling it, rumbled out of the fat-lipped mouth of the chief magistrate as he went to speak. He waited for a second, less explosive escape of stomach gas, and then addressed Lancer. 'I have been reminded that we have recently considered quite a number of cases very similar to yours. That similarity suggests, no, more than suggests mark you, that farmers giving employees an animal in lieu of wages may be a ploy of some kind. Therefore, we have decided to be compassionate in imposing a sentence on you. You will be taken from here back to Dorchester Gaol to await transportation....'

This hit Lancer like a hard punch to his stomach. He tried but failed to convince himself that whatever the magistrates' decision he could accept it with an uncaring shrug. Strong in the face of enemy guns, heroic in hand-to-hand combat, he discovered that his nerves were getting the better of him in a fetid smelling rural court. He managed to concentrate on what the magistrate was saying.

'... to Devon County Gaol, Exeter, where you will be imprisoned for three months.'

Relief flooded through Lancer, who had suspected that the magistrate had used phraseology and a deliberate pause to cause him anxiety. For the first time in weeks he felt good but this feeling collapsed as his escort snapped handcuffs back on him. Nancy Owens had swiftly returned to continue her haunting of him.

'At the risk of being rejected, I think that we have reached the point where a decision has to be made, Sarai,' a petulant Emil Edelcantz said, as he leaned forward to pat the neck of his horse.

Of all the grand scenery in the area this was Sarai's favourite spot. She made no reply, not wanting yet another of his persistent proposals to spoil what was for her ever a divine experience.

They had left the seashore where they had enjoyed an exhilarating gallop along the edge of waves breaking gently on the sand. They had climbed a hill that was of different soil, into a new and pleasantly refreshing air, riding up into a different world. The atmosphere had continued to lighten and the soil grew pale with chalk, trees were few and huddled together. Reining up, they now sat side by side, physically close but widely separated by their incompatible inner selves.

The curve of downs below them was a drunken, absurd confusion of small red and yellow flowers and the fluttering white and golden wings of butterflies. There were a few fluffy-white clouds in the sky, and an unnatural clearness that betokened a summer shower.

An unearthly stillness raised Sarai into a higher conscious-ness. She felt as if she were passing through time as she looked with reverence down a wooded slope to where the river rushed and foamed. A late afternoon sun pictured roaring flames on the water far below. She knew that wherever she may go, whatever may happen in life, this scene would forever be a part of her. There was soil here on which no man had ever set foot. The downs held no water so no one had ever constructed a building or even pitched a tent. The Roman legions may have marched through here, a soldier or two leaving the column to relieve themselves behind a bush or tree, but no one stayed to love, or hate, or set up house, or gossip with the neighbours. These downs were free of the leftover human emotion that taints so many places, often to an ominous degree.

Her reverie was ended abruptly by the sound of Emil Edelcantz moving his horse away. Surmising that he was peeved by her lack of response to his proposal, she watched him ride slowly down the hill on the palomino horse that was his favourite while staying at Adamslee House. Not yet free from the effects of her communion with the mysterious, he seemed to be a legendary figure of her imagination. Sad to abandon her fantasyland to re-enter her increasingly unhappy world, she reined her horse about and followed him.

When she reached the stables he had already dismounted and stood waiting for her, a sulky expression on his face, unspeaking. Little Ben Morley, her groom was there to take the reins of her horse. Coming lithely down from the saddle, she strode towards Emil with a confidence that she didn't feel.

On the way down the hill, she had appraised her present situation. Without Gray Sawtell as a distraction, life had become boring. In truth, referring to him as a distraction was inaccurate. Since his arrest she had analysed her feelings for the tough smuggler, and realized that she loved him. But the present day savage machinery of law and order meant that soon Gray Sawtell would be no more. Emil Edelcantz would make a poor substitute for a real man like Sawtell, but she had no other option. Living alone for most of the year on an isolated cliff top had lost the attraction it had once held for her. To continue in that way of life would probably see her finish up as mad as Oliver Adams, her arsonist ancestor.

'Please forgive me, Emil,' she pleaded. 'I must have appeared to be most rude when we were on the hill. My only excuse is the effect that the view from up there always has on me.'

'There is nothing for you to apologize for, Sarai, I understand perfectly what that delightful view means to you,' he replied reassuringly, although she sensed an underlying tone of resentment in his voice.

Feigning a deep interest in him, she moved closer. Looking puzzled, he took a half-step backwards. Sarai could understand why. Perhaps more than anyone he knew her well enough to doubt anything she might say. But she could put on a good act when it was in her interest to do so.

'You left before I could respond to what you said to me on the hill, Emil,' she told him, placing a hand lightly on his arm.

Though there was an expression of excitement on his delicate aristocratic face there was also fear that she could be about to mock him, not for the first time. Struggling to control himself, he remarked, 'Long practice permitted me to predict your answer, Sarai.'

'You knew that I was going to agree to marry you?' she enquired in fake amazement.

'You mean...?' he began, before his voice let him down.

'I am serious, my dear Emil,' she assured him convincingly.

'I give you my word that you will never regret this moment, Sarai,' he promised, as he took her into his arms.

Face pressed against his jacket, fighting back tears because it wasn't Gray Sawtell holding her, she was already filled with the regret he promised she would never know.

In late evening outside Dorchester Gaol, Constables Githam and Price kept Lancer close between them as the three of them climbed up on the box of the Traveller coach that would take him to Exeter.

As they travelled through a night that was chilly for the time of year, Lancer realized how much imprisonment had weakened him. Having spent countless nights on battlefields in arctic weather, he now found himself shivering violently while riding on top of a coach during a summer night in England.

Noticing his discomfort, the coachman remarked, 'It looks to me as if you are suffering, my friend.'

Githam merely glanced at Lancer uninterestedly but Price expressed genuine concern. 'I am sorry that we haven't a greatcoat to lend you, Lancer.'

'Don't worry, Constable, I'll survive,' Lancer replied with difficulty, through chattering teeth.

'You should get the doctor to take a look at you when we get to the gaol,' Price advised.

After that brief exchange there was no further conversation between the four people up on the box. It seemed an eternity to Lancer before they reached the outskirts of Exeter. Then they were passing the imposing entrance to Exeter Castle that in the moonlight framed a section of the Assize Courthouse. This was a fitting introduction to the Devon County Gaol that loomed up as a dark silhouette that intensified the grimness of the huge building.

As they pulled into the yard a side door opened and two warders came out ready to relieve the constables of their prisoner. Price reached out a hand to assist Lancer down from the box. But he managed it alone. Having reached the end of the journey he had recovered significantly, even though he found the prospect of another three months in prison daunting.

'Lionel and me are close to starvation now, so I absolutely dread the thought of having a third mouth to feed,' Arabella lamented, her unhappiness exacerbated by shame on discovering three weeks after her marriage that she was pregnant.

Chin dropping to his chest, Dr Rupert Mawby knew the probable consequences of agreeing with a distraught Arabella Heelan. But the alternative was to lie, to offer hope where there was no hope. Procreation in all animals other than man was a beautifully balanced system. When circumstances were adverse in the jungle, or on the prairie, all the wild creatures, the elephant, the lion, the buffalo or the coyote instinctively limited breeding until nature righted the deficiency. Not so man, the intelligent being. When bogged down in poverty and not knowing which way to turn, men and women went against all logic by speeding up their rate of reproduction. Other than London's slums, there was no more depressing an example of this defect in nature than Adamslee.

Forced into cowardice by the situation, Mawby passed the buck by saying, 'I will ensure that you get the best medical care throughout your term, Arabella. But you also need the kind of support that a physician is incapable of providing. With your permission I will ask the Reverend Worther to call on you.'

'But I have sinned, Doctor. My child was conceived out of wedlock.'

'You have been through a traumatic time of late, Arabella. I am certain that Reverend Worther will grant you forgiveness, just as Jesus was ready to forgive. You must not bear this alone. You must make sure that Lionel is here with you when the Reverend Worther calls,' Mawby advised. 'You must have his support.'

Tears welled up fast in Arabella's eyes and spilled out to run down her cheeks. She attempted to excuse her husband as she said. 'Lionel doesn't say much these days. He is working all hours but brings home very little money. I try to talk to him about our financial difficulties, but he refuses to listen.'

'He must face up to his responsibilities, Arabella.'

'I know that, Doctor, but he just refuses to do so.'

'What about the baby?' Mawby probed. 'How did he respond when you informed him that you were pregnant?'

'He didn't say anything ...' Arabella began, but a sudden onset of sobbing stopped her. Mawby slipped a comforting arm around her thin shoulders, and she managed to continue halt-ingly. 'He has refused to discuss it ever since. Every time I mention the baby he walks away from me.'

'I'll ask Reverend Worther to speak to you both,' a defeated Dr Mawby lamely murmured.

Still dispirited by the Nancy Owens tragedy, even after eight weeks had gone by, Lancer barely noticed that he had been moved from Dorchester Gaol to the Devon County Gaol. Yet he did show a spark of interest when on a landing one night just prior to lock-up time, he met the burly Abe Wilson, a former member of Sawtell's smuggling crew.

Pleased to see Lancer and keen to bring him up to date on the Adamslee criminals, Wilson began with his own misfortune. 'I could handle the smuggling lark right enough, but when Gray Sawtell got tooked and things were real hard, I tried highway robbery. I weren't much good at it though. I seed this crusty-looking bloke coming along in a one-horse carriage and chanced my luck. It was dead easy. I bashed him over the head and tooked his fat wallet. I'd just got to the nearest pub and ordered a drink but didn't have time to take a bloody sip before this police sergeant and constable walked in and lifted me.'

'Now you're awaiting trial,' Lancer guessed, only slightly interested.

'Naw, that's all over, Joby. All I'm waiting for now is trans-portation to Australia.'

'I am sorry to learn that, Abe.'

Wilson shrugged. 'It could be worse. There's twenty-eight poor souls in here waiting to meet the hangman. Gray Sawtell and Willie Brickell will be joining them afore long. Their trial is due to happen any day now.'

'That boy had nothing to do with the death of John Nichol, I am sure of that,' Lancer declared, saddened by the thought of another young life being snatched away.

'You are right there, Joby. Neither did Gray Sawtell.'

'I wouldn't go so far as to say that,' Lancer said, shaking his head. 'If not Sawtell, who else could have done it?'

'You don't know what really happened, Joby.'

'Then you tell me,' Lancer ordered urgently as he saw a warder heading in their direction.

Also noticing the warder, Wilson spoke rapidly. 'It was that Heelan kid, Lionel. He's got a wicked temper. For the first time in his life he had been earning good money, and Nichol had put an end to that by breaking up the smuggling.'

'Why doesn't Sawtell speak up?'

'He intends to make sure Willie Brickell is cleared when he gets to court,' Wilson said.

'But Sawtell should be freed as well if he's innocent.'

Shaking his head sadly, Wilson presumed, 'That would mean young Heelan being arrested.'

'That's what should happen,' Lancer stressed. 'Otherwise Sawtell could be hanged.'

'It is certain that he will be, Joby, but he's determined not to point a finger at Lionel Heelan.'

To protect Arabella, Lancer realized gloomily as Wilson and he were moved apart by the warder. As he was marched to his cell Lancer was tormented by the memory of recent events. He had walked away from Adamslee so that his relationship with Arabella would not cause problems between her and Lionel Heelan. It now seemed that he should have stayed there to protect her from a boy who had proved himself capable of the worst crime of all. This latest incident convinced him that fate was making him pay dear for having miraculously survived the sinking of the *Paloma*.

Even the lift that knowing that he had served two-thirds of his prison sentence had given him in the past few days had deserted Lancer the following morning. His spirits fell even lower when a warder arrived to announce that a police officer wanted to see him. As he was escorted to the under-warden's office, he speculated on what the policeman could want of him. His biggest fear was that something bad had happened to Arabella.

It was Constable Price who was standing waiting for him in the office. Delaying speaking until the under-warden had left, Price then began hesitantly. 'I have taken a risk in coming here, Lancer. Having spent a considerable amount of time in your company I feel it insulting to ask you this, but I must have your assurance that what passes between us here will forever remain secret.'

'You have my word. You have always treated me fairly and with respect, Constable Price.'

'It was easy for me to do so, Lancer.' Price managed a brief smile. 'You are the type of person I don't normally come across in my line of work. Why I was so cautious a little while since is because I broke the rules when we attended Owen's Farm. Githam was not involved, neither does he know about it.'

'Neither do I,' Lancer informed him, guessing that Price was worried that he may have noticed something while there.

'That never occurred to me,' Price assured him. Reaching into his pocket he pulled out a folded sheet of paper and held it out to Lancer, saying. 'For my first time as a policeman, at the scene of a death not due to natural causes, I withheld evidence from the coroner. It seemed to me that you are the rightful person for this to go to.'

Taking the paper not knowing what to expect, Lancer opened it to read a penned note:

My darling Joby,
I have prayed that it will not affect you badly to read this when I am no longer in the world, but I feel it necessary to let you know the truth. I have been for many years planning what I am about to do. Long before I met you, dear Joby. Please do not regard what follows as self-pity. I realized that I was destined to have an unhappy life even before an awful union with Euart Owens was forced upon me. By coming to the farm you extended my life for several wonderful weeks, Joby. It was seems to me that our being together, even for so desperately short a time, may have been God's way of compensating me for the misery of the remainder of my life.

Thank you for coming my way and for making it possible for me to die happy from having known and loved you. Please believe that my last wish is for you to live your life to the full.

With my eternal love, goodnight and God Bless You.
Nancy.

Folding the note, Lancer attempted to hide how deeply he was moved by commenting, 'How could an obviously well-educated woman such as this be married to a monstrous creature like Owens and living in such terrible conditions?'

'Those were exactly my thoughts, so I did a bit of asking

around. I gather that Nancy was the daughter of a travelling woman who went by the name of Black Nance. The girl travelled round West Country fairs until she was aged four. That was when her mother, a drunken slut from all accounts, died. Little Nancy was looked after by various travelling people until Mrs Thomasine Westerhall, the widow of an army general, learned of her plight and fostered her. Nancy was highly intelligent and a fast learner who was so well tutored by Mrs Westerhall that she was destined to become a schoolteacher at the age of ten, when Mrs Westerhall passed away.

'That was when the good life ended for poor Nancy. A travelling woman claiming to be a close relative of Black Nance took the girl back on the road. I understand that Nancy's life was horrendous at that time. The story goes that she was rescued from that terrible travelling life by farmer Euart Owens.'

'That is an abuse of the word *rescued*,' Lancer remarked.

'I couldn't agree more,' Price said, as he shook Lancer by the hand. 'Take care of yourself. I do hope that we shall meet again.'

'That is also my wish, and I am most grateful to you for coming here today,' Lancer replied, at last freed of guilt by Nancy's letter.

'This has truly been a day to remember, Sarai,' Mildred, the wife of one of the Members of Parliament for the City of Exeter, trilled.

Managing a smile that she had to reach for, Sarai who was already trying to forget her five-hour-old marriage, agreed. Her high-society marriage ceremony at the Cathedral Church of St Peter at Exeter had been conducted in grand style by Henry Phillpotts, the Lord Bishop of Exeter. In the way that the frivolous antics of the highly privileged inexplicably attract the under privileged living on the breadline, the streets around the cathedral were thronged with as many spectators as to a royal wedding. Leaving in a four-wheeled Jenny Lind buggy, she and

Emil had pulled the curtain of the carriage back to smile and wave at cheering crowd who didn't know them, and whom they wouldn't want to know.

Farcical, Sarai whispered to herself now, as she saw Elspeth, the count's sister coming towards her out of a mass of guests, most of whom were inebriated.

'It is a unanimous decision, Sarai,' Elspeth shouted at the top of her voice. 'We want the bride to sing for us.'

There was a concerted roar of support. 'We do, we do.'

'Sing *Amazing Grace*,' a male voice called.

'It's a beautiful new hymn,' a woman agreed.

'For my beautiful new bride to sing,' the count, swaying drunkenly shouted as he raised his glass to Sarai.

Not in the mood to sing, Sarai protested. '*Amazing Grace* is not a new hymn. It was written in 1789 but has only just been published.'

'It was worth waiting for,' a man shouted.

He was immediately supported and then a chorus of many voices chanted her name. 'Sarai, Sarai, Sarai, Sarai, Sarai, Sarai, Sarai, Sarai....'

Defeated, Sarai signalled to the pianist, an elderly man who nodded assent and put out his hands to the keyboard.

As the introduction ended, a hush instantly fell on the assembly as Sarai's voice filled the hall. Needing to fight an urge to flee had the surprising result of her singing being at its best. But getting through the song was tough for her, because the lyrics were about the sea, about boats, and about danger. It brought an image of Gray Sawtell to her. Memories of the magical times she had spent with him did a replay through her mind. Nearing the end of the song she realized that she and the handsome smuggler had been, still were, soulmates. That was something that her husband could never be.

As if to prove that point, when she reached the close of the song rapturous applause started up, only to die away fast as

Emil Edelcantz shouted, 'Well done, my darling,' before losing his balance and falling sideways, crashing to the floor.

There were cries of concern and people rushed to kneel beside him. Taking advantage of the confusion caused by her husband's heavy fall, Sarai slipped from the ballroom unnoticed and hurried up to her room.

When early on a Thursday morning Gray Sawtell and Willie Brickell were brought to stand trial for murder they had to pass through a crowd of sightseers assembled outside the entrance to the Crown Bar Court in Exeter Castle. There was little chance of any of these spectators gaining admission to the court. Most of the seats had been reserved for Devon's VIPs, the aristocrats and gentry and their ladies.

The Judge, Baron Cecil Lawes, was already infamous for both his bias and harshness. The prosecutor was Barnaby Ryall, an Exeter solicitor who had retained barrister Abraham Weyland. No witnesses were called for the prosecution as all the evidence was circumstantial. Sawtell could not or would not account for his movements on the night John Nichol had died, and neither could Willie Brickell. Sawtell had paid a solicitor, and could have afforded a barrister, but he saw no point in paying for one as counsel were not allowed to address the court on behalf of those accused of a felony.

In the dock Sawtell was well groomed and smartly dressed but Willie Brickell, an undersized, painfully thin lad with a mop of tangled curly hair, was, in contrast, scruffily clad. The indictment of wilful murder was read out. Sawtell was charged with beating Nichol to death, and Brickell of aiding and abetting.

Weyland, the barrister, cleverly presented what had to be an unarguable case for the prosecution, and even the heart-rending episode when Willie Brickell's ailing mother was carried into the court to testify that he had spent the whole evening and night of the May Day celebrations with her, didn't seem to register with the jury.

Seemingly bored by the long-winded summing-up by Judge Ryall, they fidgeted and appeared to be wishing they were somewhere away from the stifling, fusty smelling courtroom. They were at last permitted to retire at ten o'clock in the evening, to return within minutes, and the foreman gave a unanimous verdict of 'Guilty' against both the accused.

On hearing the verdict, Willie Brickell bowed his head, tears running down his cheeks and his skeletal body convulsed by sobbing. The clerk of the court asked both the prisoners why the sentence of death should not be passed on them. The boy showed no sign of having heard, but the tough-looking Sawtell faced the judge confidently.

'My lord,' he began. 'I do not intend to plead for mercy for myself, but I am not going to permit you to send this innocent boy to his death. Neither you, my lord, nor any other man or woman in this courtroom can consider for one moment that if I had set out to batter a man to his death I would take this poor little wretch to assist me. That is too ridiculous even to contemplate. Willie Brickell is innocent.'

The judge was already lifting the black cap but hesitated, and there was a concerted gasp in the courtroom, as a voice cried out in praise of Sawtell. 'By gad, sir, you are a noble fellow!'

The general astonishment in court was increased by the shout having seemingly come from the clerk, who was then staring down at something on his desk.

Recovering, the judge donned the black cap and addressed Sawtell and Brickell. 'Prisoners at the bar, you have been convicted following a painstaking and impartial trial. Upon the facts that have been diligently and meticulously presented to the jury, the jury then came to this conclusion. That leads me to presume that they hold the opinion that the weight of evidence against you is compelling. In my address to the jury, you will have noticed that I placed the evidence and the facts of the case before them in every sympathetic point of view for you.'

There was a stirring in the court as Sawtell interrupted him. 'I have a statement to make, my lord. Please hear me. I ask you not to send an innocent man to the trap. This lad by my side is innocent of murder. I know him well as he has worked for me for some time, and proved himself to be a hard worker. Every penny he earned he spent on his mother, that poor lady who, despite being very sick, insisted on being brought into this court to swear the innocence of her son. This boy, my lord, is as incapable of committing murder as you are.'

'We must be regulated by the evidence given, on which the jury have found you both guilty—'

'I am trying to stop you hanging an innocent boy, not contesting the verdict pronounced on me, my lord,' Sawtell emphasized.

'I recognize that, and admire you for it,' the judge acknowledged. 'Nevertheless, I can add nothing to what I have said before. You cannot find mercy here. All that is open to me is to strongly suggest that you immediately focus your minds on appealing for forgiveness and mercy to the only quarter now open to you.

'It is now necessary for me to perform my unwelcome duty to direct that you Gray Sawtell, and you, William Brickell, be taken to the place from whence you came, and thence to the place of execution, and there to be hanged by the neck until your bodies be dead. That you be then interred within the precincts of the prison – and may the Lord have mercy upon your souls!'

As the words of the judge faded away, Willie Brickell made a strange barking sound that changed to an eerie noise like the howl of a wolf. Echoing alarmingly through the courtroom, the relief of everyone there could be sensed as it died away. A motionless Sawtell seemed not to be aware of the howl as he glared stoically at the judge. Then, as the screech started up again, he reached out to hold the boy tightly and, to the relief of all present, silence him.

After a shaky start, Sarai's relationship with Count Edelcantz settled into what could best be described as a parody of marriage. This compromise was largely due to her decision to tolerate her husband's lack of consideration for others, which was the infuriatingly childish egotism of those privileged by birth. She could never love him, but due to his self-interest he didn't seem to notice. It was a married state of mutual benefit; with him enjoying the esteem of having a dazzlingly attractive wife, and she the prestige of belonging to Swedish nobility.

Yet it was a fragile arrangement that she realized must one day fracture beyond repair. This was never more evident than the afternoon when Kendall Harrison, who owned a newspaper in Dorchester and was an old lover of hers, rode up to Adamslee House. Emil was away from home at a meeting with the local aristocracy, but Sarai panicked because she expected him back at any moment.

Hurrying from the house she confronted Harrison before he had the chance to dismount. She brusquely enquired, 'Why have you come here, Kendall?'

'I am delighted to see you again, too, Sarai,' he responded sarcastically. 'I have just come from the courthouse at Exeter Castle and have news.'

He was in the act of dismounting when Sarai stopped him. She spoke sharply. 'I question why you have come here today, Kendall. Our liaison, such as it was, ended long ago. Please leave, now. My husband is an extremely jealous man.'

'With good reason I don't doubt,' he remarked, settling back in the saddle. 'Then he will welcome the news that he need no longer fret over your lover whom I understand was a major threat to your marriage. You can read about it in my newspaper, Sarai.'

Pulling on the reins, he was wheeling his horse about and she frantically ran a few steps after him, raising her voice to ask, 'Who are you speaking of, Kendall?'

'Now you want to learn my news,' he chuckled, as he reined his horse to halt.

Sarai realized that he was enjoying the moment immensely. It was she who had ended their clandestine relationship, and he had reacted angrily. When they had met socially afterwards he never concealed the bitterness he felt toward her. Whatever news that had brought today it had to be something that would cause her distress.

He leaned over in the saddle to bring his face close to hers as he said, 'In the court today, Judge Baron Cecil Lawes sentenced Gray Sawtell and William Brickell to death.'

Shocked at hearing this, feeling faint, she reached out to steady herself against the horse. But Kendall Harrison quickly moved the animal forward. As he rode away she lost her balance and fell weeping to her knees on the hard ground.

Eight

'THE RT HON Montague James has invited us to dinner this evening, darling,' Emil Edelcantz proudly and excitedly announced, the moment that he arrived back at Adamslee House. 'It will be a grand time, I assure you. The Home Secretary and his lady will be attending, and it has been said, although Montague wouldn't confirm it to me, wanting it to be a surprise I presume, that a member of the Royal Family will be present. Everyone will, of course, be longing to hear you sing. I shall be the proudest man there when that sweet voice of yours rings clearly through Cavendish Hall.'

She and Emil differed in many ways, the principal one being his penchant for needing to impress the aristocracy. Despite her breeding, if push ever came to shove she would desert the patricians and join the ranks of the plebeians.

The way she felt right then, Sarai had grave doubts that she would be able to sing that evening. Yet her husband, who took advantage of her looks and singing voice to boost his own ego, which didn't need help anyway, would be angry if she let him down. Being subjected to a furious Emil Edelcantz was a far from pleasant experience. Frantic with worry over the probable fate of Gray Sawtell, she was worried that he might notice her eyes were red and swollen from her having ceased crying only minutes before he had come home.

Conversely, when the evening arrived, Sarai, having dreaded

it throughout the afternoon, was surprised to discover that being part of a crowd dulled but didn't significantly alleviate her mourning for Gray Sawtell. Mingling with others was enough to enable her to sing, but she conceded to herself that her performance was below par, even though her enthusiastic audience plainly didn't notice.

Late in the evening, worry over Sawtell had her covertly contrive a conversation with Trevor Bolland, the Governor of Dorchester Prison, a dour but kindly man who seemed to her to be in awe of the power he held. She turned the subject to capital punishment. Saying that she had heard of two local men being sentenced to death at Exeter, she disguised her worry by asking, with a distinct tremor in her voice, 'I understand that the laws of England provide that murderers, unless respited, have to be executed within forty-eight hours of pronouncement of sentence.'

'That is no longer so, I thank the Lord, my dear Sarai,' Bolland replied uncomfortably. 'That harsh law was of constant concern to me in my position. It must undoubtedly mean that I, as a prison governor, have been an accomplice in sending many an innocent man to the gallows.'

'That law doesn't apply now, Trevor?' Sarai double-checked, afraid to believe that Sawtell would have another opportunity to prove what to her was his undoubted innocence.

'A Bill was passed changing the law some six weeks ago, my dear Sarai.'

Relief flooding through her, Sarai asked hopefully, 'Then it is possible that both of those local men may yet be respited?'

'I understand that Judge Lawes was about to set off from Exeter to open the Cornish Assizes when he was delayed upon receiving an impressive memorandum from the defence solicitor, together with other deputations. The judge has made a concession: he is to return to Exeter within days to study both cases prior to fixing an execution date.'

'Could I ask you a favour, Trevor?' Sarai enquired nervously, being encouraged to continue by a smile and a nod from the governor. 'Could you possibly keep me informed as to any developments at Exeter Gaol?'

'Of course I can. We have been friends for a very long time, Sarai. Please be assured that you can rely on my discretion,' he said, from which she gathered he had perceived her need for secrecy.

Heartened by this, but shamed by the perceptive Bolland having detected her extra-marital reason for enquiring, Sarai saw her husband hurrying towards them. He was sober, having curbed his drinking of late.

Smiling at the prison governor and her, he said politely, 'Forgive me for interrupting. When you are ready, Sarai, folk are clamouring for you to sing again.'

'I'll be happy to do so, Emil,' Sarai heard herself say.

Arabella Heelan could understand her child's reluctance to enter the dark and desolate world that she inhabited. If the souls waiting to enter the world had a choice, which she disbelieved, no child would opt to be born in Adamslee, the forbidding place where its penniless ancestors had suffered and starved. Neither was it just a past generation's heartbreak. A similar destiny awaited her unborn son or daughter and its eventual descendants. Arabella wanted more for her child than a struggle to survive against overwhelming odds. She no longer wanted to be where poverty caused people to live together in fury and bitterness, suspecting, misinterpreting, over-dramatizing, denouncing, resenting and conspiring.

The dream she had long had of a better life had breathed its last in the first few weeks of her marriage to Lionel Heelan. Fantasy could not survive in a relationship with a husband who became increasingly remote and distant every day. She mourned the dream's passing now as she huddled under a torn and inadequate blanket in her squalid bedroom. She was terrified that devoid of her mental equilibrium she wouldn't be able to endure the sheer agony of childbirth.

She lay trying to concentrate on the sound of the gentle waves of August lapping against the shore. This helped to block out midwife Granny Galpin's demented muttering to herself while fumbling with barely adequate items that were needed. In the flickering light from two candles the witch-like crone's wrinkles became ancient furrows.

Light-headed with the pain that began in her grotesquely swollen belly and went down through her legs and reversed from there up into her mind, Arabella regretted refusing Ruth's kind offer to sit with her. Having someone for whom she cared and who cared for her present at this time would be wonderful. But she couldn't have subjected her sensitive best friend to such a harrowing experience.

Suddenly she became aware of the beat and the clamour of the child quickening in her womb. Her whole body trembled and fought. She turned her head to one side, and her teeth were bared, her face glistening. It was her time, and Arabella Willard was afraid. Why was she thinking of herself in terms of her maiden name? What was happening to her was the unknown. It was something large and frightening and uncanny, human, yet past human comprehension. It was a complete mystery even to medical science and theology. Both the physician and the clergyman came into the world the same way as everyone else, and were therefore just as ignorant as the masses.

She had a sudden sharp and demoralizing memory of once having overheard the Reverend Worther commenting that, 'The easiest childbirth is more traumatic than the worst death.'

'That young man of yours should be here at this particular time,' Granny Galpin pointed out, managing to force a coherent sentence through her gabbling.

'He's out at the fishing,' Arabella lied, not knowing where

Lionel was, but in no doubt that he wasn't at work as a fisherman.

The change in Lionel had been both upsetting and inexplicable. He seemed to have retreated to a place deep inside himself. Of late he had spent little time in the house, mostly coming home just to sleep. As he had no money, Arabella supposed that he was wandering alone somewhere in the hills. There was no longer any intellectual level ground for conversation between them. Unlike Arabella, who was always able to look with new eyes at the parade of sensations, thoughts and feelings that made up her inner world, Lionel was now never tempted to think for long about things that were clearly beyond understanding, or to ask questions that are unanswerable.

As if summoned by her thinking of him, Lionel entered the house at that moment. Closing the door behind him, he didn't look in the direction of either her or Granny Galpin, but walked off into the other room as if they were not there. Then she was gripped by awesome pain, shaking her head, her eyes unseeing, and turning suddenly to bite at her arm like a snared animal. When she cried out the old woman came to bend over her.

'It's all right, lass. Think of the little one you will soon hold in your arms, not of that heathen who has just passed by as if you and the child he has fathered don't exist. Do you want me to scold him?

Arabella stared at the bulging ceiling, and when she spoke it was in a startlingly calm tone, as though the agony of a moment ago had been entirely forgotten. She knew that it wasn't wise to anger Lionel, who had been violent to her recently when losing his temper.

She pleaded, 'No, please don't. I wouldn't want you to upset him.'

'Humph!' Granny Galpin snorted. 'I'd do more than upset that ignorant lout if you allowed me to.'

The old midwife tried to cover Arabella's feet that she had

thrust out from under the bedclothes, but realized that she was struggling to press them against the bars at the bottom of the bed. There was an expression of concern on Granny Galpin's craggy face. In prevailing conditions that had child-bed fever mean death for many women, and in which babies were frequently born blind and terribly crippled, she seemed to dread what the fast approaching night would bring to add to the difficulties that already beset them.

Able to sense the witch-like woman's worry, Arabella asked. 'Will it be long now?'

Granny Galpin murmured an unintelligible reply. Feeling all alone and suffering terribly, Arabella noticed the old woman's body jerked each time a cry of pain escaped involuntarily through her clenched teeth. It increased her anxiety to see this sign of the veteran midwife's fear for her and the baby.

It was a long night. As dawn neared, a cock crowed and the clip clop of a horse being led past the house could be heard, Arabella's twisting and writhing on the bed became convulsive.

The Heelan baby arrived at six o'clock on that morning of 5th February. Its crying filled the cabin as Granny Galpin came into her own. Washing the child in warm water that had been previously boiled, binding its belly with gentleness and patience, and bundling it in a blanket, she spoke clearly. 'It's a girl, Bella, a beautiful little girl.'

Tears mingling with the sheen of sweat on her face, Arabella closed her eyes for a moment. Then she opened them to look around the room for her husband. He was not there.

The Governor of Dorchester Gaol had kept his word. In one way, Sarai wished that he had failed to do so. A horseman had ridden up to Adamslee House, a young lad who had obviously been instructed by Trevor Bolland to first check that Emil Edelcantz was not at home, and then asked to see her. Since that moment she had been so stunned on hearing the message she had been given that it seemed she was only partly in the world.

Doubt about Willie Brickell's guilt had led to his execution being put off until 26 August, but Friday 12 August was the day that Gray Sawtell was to be executed. Though aware that it would be a terrible ordeal, Sarai's conscience permitted her no choice other than to attend the ghastly event.

Arriving in the City of Exeter at seven o'clock in the morning of the execution, a bewildered Sarai spent the next two hours watching the continuous arrival of sightseers assembling at the prison gates to see the hanging that was due to take place at ten o'clock. They came in carriages, on horseback, and on foot, chatting and laughing as if attending some festive event.

Sarai's heart skipped several beats and she had difficulty with her breathing as she saw Sawtell led out of the condemned cell into the courtyard. Shielding his eyes from the brilliant morning sun, he could have been strolling out to go to his boat on a normal morning. Governor Bolland stayed at his side as far as the door of his own house, where John Smith, the Under-Sheriff of Devon who was in charge of the execution, took over. A procession was formed to lead Sawtell down the long walk to the prison gates through rows of javelin men carrying white batons drawn up on each side. John Smith led the procession, with two prison chaplains close behind reading the burial service aloud as they walked, with Sawtell, who was flanked by an escort of two more javelin men, coming next.

Smartly dressed in a light-green coat, dark-green waistcoat, cashmere breeches, green worsted stockings and calf-length boots, Sawtell held his head high. His face was noticeably pale, and Sarai found herself wondering pointlessly whether this was due to his confinement, or because he was the principal player in a real-life tragedy. It was heart-breaking for her to realize that it made no difference as he would be dead in a very short time regardless.

Possibly to deter them from future law-breaking, other prisoners had been brought under guard from the prison to witness the execution. Sarai noticed the young Willie Brickell was among them, looking in every direction but at the gallows that had been erected just outside of the gates.

The procession reached the gallows and Sawtell nonchalantly climbed a short flight of stairs to a platform. At one end was the press room that was packed with newspaper reporters and prison officials. Conspicuous at the other end of the platform was the coffin that awaited Sawtell's body.

He stood for a moment calmly looking out over the crowd. A force beyond her control pushed a reluctant Sarai through to the front of the crowd. Once she was there she felt compelled to look up at Sawtell but feared the thought of making eye contact. She looked up, and it happened. He stared down at her. Face expressionless, he held her gaze for what seemed an eternity. Something mysterious passed between them that had an endearing touch to it that was spoiled by Sarai's realization that it was an exchange between her and a dead man.

She could see the effort it took Sawtell to break off the contact. Looking away, he spotted Calcraft, the hangman, and walked over to him. Sarai could see a short conversation take place between the two men, and then she forced herself not to look away as the executioner pinioned Sawtell's arms. Then, kneeling, Calcraft fastened heavy weights to the condemned man's right leg. His task finished, the executioner stood and used both hands to explain something to Sawtell about his head and neck, to which Sawtell must have responded with a witty remark, as Calcraft smiled and patted him on the shoulder.

Always having been in awe of Sawtell's courage, Sarai's admiration of him soared to fresh heights as she observed his coolness in such an appalling situation. The whole drama was being played out on a balmy summer day before a mass of spectators occupying an area that stretched out to Longbrook Street, Northernhay, and St David's Hill.

The crowd had been quiet throughout to show respect for the fearless man about to die, but now a ghostly hush settled on the gathering as the condemned man's last words were eagerly anticipated. The two clergymen had stepped out on the platform beside Sawtell to resume the burial service. They paused while one of them asked Sawtell if there was anything he wished to say.

Despite the warmth of the day, Sarai's body suddenly turned so cold that she was shivering as she heard Sawtell's deep voice firmly reply, 'I have just one thing to say, and that is to tell each and every one of you here that I make no protest about being found guilty. But William Brickell, the boy who was on trial with me, is totally innocent. That is all.'

In the silence that followed, Calcraft pulled the cap down over Sawtell's face while the voice of one of the clergymen continued the service. When he reached the words 'any pains of death to fall from thee', the executioner drew the bolt of the gallows and Gray Sawtell was plunged into eternity.

The impact that the gruesome sight had on Sarai convinced her that something of herself died at the same time as her love.

It had been a long climb up to Adamslee House on an oppressively hot day. It had been much more exhausting for Ruth Heelan, and Arabella was shamefaced at having asked her crippled sister-in-law to accompany her. But there was no way she could have faced the haughty Sarai Edelcantz alone. Ruth lacked the nerve to speak in the situation ahead but her support just by being there was essential to Arabella.

A maid answered the door to them, and they followed her into a study where Sarai Adams sat behind a desk leafing through a stack of documents.

'Mrs Heelan is here for an interview, ma'am,' the maid announced shyly.

'Thank you, Elsa,' Sarai said, without raising her head.

Arabella, who had become aware of the imposing presence of her prospective employer immediately on entering the room, became increasingly nervous as Sarai Edelcantz continued to inspect the documents, neither looking up nor speaking. It was just as if she was alone in the room.

A grandfather clock standing at the side of the room ticked away the passing minutes agonizingly slowly for Arabella. Then she was startled as Sarai picked up the documents, holding them with both hands as she tapped the pile into shape on the desktop, then placed them to one side.

Raising her head to flash a smile at the girls, she said, 'Living up here on the cliff top I lose touch with Adamslee folk. Please remind me, which one of you two ladies is Arabella Heelan.'

'That's me, ma'am.' Arabella said, as she silently thanked the maid for revealing the correct term of address. 'This is Ruth, my husband's sister.'

'Forgive me; I should have recognized you as our May Queen. What sort of employment are you seeking, Arabella?'

'Anything, ma'am. I am a hard worker.'

'I am sure that you are,' Sarai agreed, then went on to reveal that she wasn't as out of touch with Adamslee as she had professed. 'I believe that you recently gave birth to a child.'

'That's right, ma'am.'

'That makes it difficult for me to consider employing you, Arabella. There are no facilities here to care for your baby while you work.'

Fearing that the opportunity to earn money was slipping away, Arabella hastened to give an explanation. 'That won't be necessary, ma'am. Ruth and her mother will take turns in looking after Thelma, that's my daughter.'

'I see,' Sarai said doubtfully. 'But surely a child so young needs its mother full time?'

'If my situation was different, ma'am, I would want nothing more than to be with my baby day and night,' Arabella replied.

'But we are very poor, and Thelma needs things that I can only give her if I earn money.'

To Arabella's surprise Sarai responded sympathetically to this. 'I should have realized that, Arabella. Please excuse my ignorance. I am prepared to offer you work in the kitchen. It will be on a trial basis, more in your interests than mine. If your arrangements for your baby prove to be impractical for either of us, then your employment here will end. If that should occur, then as I admire your pluck in attempting to improve your lot in such difficult circumstances, I will ensure that you leave here with a financial reward for your courage in trying.'

'That is very kind of you. I am most grateful. ma'am.'

'I hope that everything works out for you,' Sarai said with a smile. 'I'll call Elsa and have her take you down to the kitchen and introduce you to Mrs Winchell. You'll find she is a very nice person.'

Walking in an easterly direction from Exeter following his release from prison, Joby Lancer reached a point that presented him with two options: he could continue straight ahead to arrive at Adamslee, or follow a north-east trail that would take him to Adamslee House. The first possibility beckoned strongly to him by offering to reunite him with Arabella, the second would mean renewing his brief relationship with Sarai Adams, a prospect that appealed to him far less than being with Arabella again.

Yet Adamslee could not proffer any paid work, whereas Adamslee House held the promise of the position of estate manager. Considering this to be the deciding factor, Lancer took the left fork.

Half-an-hour later his trail merged with a well-worn track that was somehow familiar to him. Hot and thirsty from the long trek, he rejoiced when coming to a clear stream flowing from a rocky area. Deliberately delaying the need to satisfy a raging thirst, he sat on his heels to scoop up handfuls of cold water and spatter it over his face. Only then did he slowly kneel to drink water that was unbelievably refreshing.

Straightening up, relaxed and stretching his arms above his head while enjoying the luxuriant grassed, treeless countryside around him, a memory clicked in. Then he knew that he had stopped here on the day that he had walked away from Adamslee.

Dwelling on this memory, he became instantly alert at the dull sound of the hoofbeats of a horse at a walking pace on a grassy surface. Pulling himself tight against a stone ridge in preparedness, he offered up a prayer that the approaching horseman would not mean trouble just a few hours after he had left prison.

He was puzzled on vaguely recognizing the front of a horse as it emerged round a slight curve in the track, and was then astonished to see the rider was Sarai. She wore a red merino shirt with black buttons, a belt, and a pale-green skirt. Her hair cascaded down, long and full, from under a wide-brimmed hat that had a domed crown, which she pushed up off her forehead as she looked down at him. A mysterious creature, the bloodline of the unknown ancients she had descended from was reflected in her dark eyes and flowing, blue/black hair.

As if this was an arranged meeting, she calmly remarked, 'The miracle man who walked alone out of the sea of the dead to join the living. What brings you here, Lancer?'

'I have come to take up the position of estate manager that you promised me.'

'Hold on there,' she advised, dismounting and wagging a finger at him. 'As I recall I *offered* the position not *promised* it. There have been changes here since we last met.'

'The position is no longer open?'

Shaking her head she replied, 'That is not correct. The principal change is that I am married. I am now Sarai Edelcantz. My husband is Emil.'

'I take it that he is now managing the estate.' Lancer stated rather than questioned.

'You take it wrong. Emil Edelcantz is capable of drinking two or three bottles of brandy of a night but would definitely be unable to manage as much as a chicken run. Having said that, I should warn that though I feel free to criticize my husband it is not open to others to do so.'

'Will he be giving me orders if I become your estate manager?'

'He will not. I am still my own woman.'

'Then I will have no reason to criticize him,' Lancer decided.

One foot in the stirrup, Sarai spoke as she swung up into the saddle. 'If you care to walk up to the house we can discuss the possibility of your employment.'

'I'll be there,' a pleased Lancer promised.

'And I will be waiting for you,' she said, giving a little tug on the reins to hold back the stallion who was about to move off. 'There is one other item: something that can't be mentioned in the company of my husband. I understand you were in Exeter Gaol at the same time Gray Sawtell was there.'

'I was.'

'Did you have the opportunity to speak to him?'

'No. Why do you ask?'

'Because ...' She replied hesitantly, her usual arrogance replaced by coyness. 'Well ... I suppose I would like to know how he was during his last days.'

'That suggests that he meant a lot to you.'

'What grounds have you for making such a supposition?'

'The first time we met he was waiting for you a little further along the trail. From your reaction to him being there I judged that the two of you weren't just going to exchange polite "Good afternoons" as you passed by.

'For a potential employee you are grossly impertinent, Lancer,' she protested.

Glaring angrily at him, she rode off fast without uttering another word. He was left wondering if he had blown his chances of becoming estate manager prior to even reaching Adamslee House.

'Willie Brickell has been released, he's back home.'

Delighted by this news, Arabella was also thrilled by the fact that this was the first sentence Lionel had spoken to her in many weeks. He had completely changed, having almost gone back to being the old Lionel. He had arrived home that evening earlier than usual, which was doubly surprising as his brother Malcolm had come back to the village for a few days. When she made it clear that she was making tea for them both, Lionel had meekly sat at the table. She decided to choose the right time, supposing that there was one, to tell him that she had found employment at Adamslee House. Lionel's temper had become so bad that it had recently manifested as frightening tantrums. Even so, his pride was intact. Considering himself to be the man of the house, she feared that he might well go berserk when she told him that she would be contributing to the household finances.

Staying with the subject he had introduced, she commented, 'I didn't think Willie was capable of killing anyone.'

'Maybe not doing the killing,' Lionel said. 'But they hanged Sawtell for that, and Willie always did as Sawtell told him, so he was probably guilty of helping.'

Though wanting to argue on Willie's behalf, Arabella was keen to avoid saying anything to upset Lionel now that he was talking to her again. So she agreed. 'You are no doubt right, Lionel.'

'I was pleased with the money Sawtell paid me,' Lionel reminisced, 'but maybe I did wrong by working for him. He rightly paid the penalty for murder, and perhaps I have been punished for getting involved in smuggling. I have a feeling that now my luck is about to change.'

This provided Arabella with the lead-in she desperately needed to break her news to him. 'I believe that you are right, Lionel. Our luck is changing for the better. I have got myself work in the kitchen at Adamslee House.'

Hearing her own words echoing around the barely furnished room, Arabella waited in dread. Expecting him to explode in a terrible rage at any moment, she was staggered to hear him speak in a calm voice and call her by name for the first time in weeks.

'That is good news, Bella, really good news.'

'You don't mind me going out to work?' an incredulous Arabella managed to enquire.

'Of course not,' Lionel assured her. 'It eases my mind to hear that you will have money coming in. You see, I was about to tell you that Malcolm is going back to London tomorrow, and I am going with him. He says that he can get me well-paid work either on the docks or at sea.'

The limited but brighter world Arabella had been building since her return from the successful visit to Adamslee House, collapsed. She wept uncontrollably. That he ignored her distress confirmed one devastating: Lionel Heelan would never return to her, or to Adamslee.

Sarai Edelcantz remained standing when she invited Lancer into her study, and she didn't ask him to sit. Not speaking, she turned her back on him to gaze unseeingly out of the window. There were times when she didn't like herself, and this was one of them. Though the horrific image of Gray Sawtell's face and eyes minutes before his death would be with her forever, she was mortified by how rapidly her feelings for him had faded. Now the presence of Joby Lancer in the confines of her office was awakening Aphrodite, the Greek Goddess of love who had dwelt within her since puberty.

Turning to face him she asked for forgiveness, 'Please excuse my rudeness.'

'No apology necessary,' he declared with a smile. 'I was aware that you had things on your mind.'

If you deduced that, she thought, I am glad that you are not a mind-reader. Maybe that isn't so! If you knew what I was thinking at this moment we could both take a short cut to what I know we both want, and then discuss the estate manager business afterwards. Control yourself, Sarai, she silently commanded, with a reminder that she was the lady of the manor about to interview a prospective employee, not some painted up strumpet looking to turn a trick.

'Your prompt arrival tells me that the job interests you,' she ventured. 'Am I right?'

'I need work, Sarai.'

'The position is yours, but there are one or two stipulations. Alfred Gribble, your predecessor, was a perfectionist, a really dedicated worker who ran this estate as if it were his own. I have no doubt that you will be equally as efficient, most probably more so, but I want to be involved. Gribble took decisions, brought about changes, without consulting or even considering me. It was as if I did not exist.'

'That won't happen with me, Sarai,' Lancer guaranteed. 'You have existed for me, often frustratingly, since we first met at the place where we were reunited a short while ago.'

Obviously pleased by this, she told him, 'You have a way with words, Lancer, and a manner that proves you have had your way with many women. I would be impressed if you had not walked away from me the day we first met, only to come back to me months later after spending time in prison.'

'That's easily explained. But I have already incurred your wrath by mentioning Gray Sawtell.'

'I was angry with myself rather than you,' she declared. 'Maybe I'll tell you why at some time, maybe I won't.'

'It's your prerogative, Sarai.'

'It will be difficult for me to get used to having someone

around who uses big words,' she said with a short laugh. 'Most of the people I encounter each day find it difficult to grunt intelligently.'

'When there are other people around I will grunt if you wish,' he offered humorously.

'If there should be an occasion for you to grunt, it will be when we are alone,' she couldn't stop herself from advising suggestively. Though pleased to see his reaction, she recovered from this lapse to adopt a business-like manner. 'You will not be expected to share the servants' quarters downstairs, but will have a room on this floor. However, there are some house rules. When we are alone I will be Sarai to you, and you will be Joby to me. When there is anyone else present, be it a servant or a guest, you must call me Mrs Edelcantz and I will use your surname when I address you.'

'I'll obey the rules, Sarai,' he promised.

'Good. Now we must discuss your salary.'

Nine

ON HER FIRST morning at Adamslee House, Arabella entered the large, spotlessly clean kitchen with trepidation. Aware as she stepped over the threshold into the kitchen that she was a simple village lass invading the intimidating world of the upper-classes, Arabella had the daunting impression that she was treading on hallowed ground. A middle-aged woman and a young girl, neither of whom Arabella knew, were standing at a table kneading dough. They glanced at her briefly in what she thought was an unfriendly manner. Mrs Winchell, who had been pleasant when Arabella had come to Adamslee House to apply for the job, appeared to be forbidding as she stood with arms folded waiting for her to approach.

Taking a few tentative steps forward, it was an immense relief for Arabella when Mrs Winchell gave her a welcoming smile and introduced the two kitchen workers, first indicating the woman. 'This is Ida Sutton, who has worked here for so many years that she is a part of the furniture now. Ida is both a hard worker and an incessant talker. This pretty little wench is Nelly Wellman, who I'm sure will be delighted to have a work-mate of around her own age. Ida, Nelly, meet Arabella who has joined our little band.'

'It is nice to meet you, love,' Ida Sutton said, adding jokingly, 'and I know that I speak for Nelly, too. She don't say much but her heart is in the right place even if her brain ain't.'

'That ain't a nice thing to say, Ida,' the girl admonished the older woman, wearing a smile that enhanced her prettiness as she advanced to hug Arabella. 'I do hope we can be good friends, Arabella.'

'I am sure that we will be, Nelly. Everyone calls me Bella.'

'Then that's what we shall call you,' Mrs Winchell announced. 'Now, we know who each other is, and there is work to be done. You can start over here by greasing these pans, Bella.'

Relieved by the welcome she had received, Arabella hurried over to eagerly start the chore she had been assigned.

'That should not have happened,' Sarai declared both lazily and unconvincingly.

Eyes closed she lay at Lancer's side, absently chewing on a blade of glass. They had started out on a dark and dismal afternoon on a ride to acquaint him with the perimeter of the estate. Along the way the sun had been anxious to be seen, parting heavy curtains of cloud so that it was pleasant enough to stop and take a rest on a low hill.

'Is that your way of telling me that you regret it?' Lancer enquired.

'Certainly not,' she declared, raising herself up on to one elbow to look down at him. 'It was really very special, if that term can be used to describe a civilized couple making wild love in the long grass like a pair of gypsies.'

Lancer sat up. Still not accustomed to being free, even the scenery seemed out of perspective. The downs gave the impression that they were unnaturally close. It was as though he could have stretched out a hand and touched them. His prison-conditioned body had reacted gratefully to the sunlight with a feeling as if he was bathing in warm golden water. The soft skin and fragrance of a woman always had a therapeutic effect on him.

'I always fancied the gypsy way of life, and now I know why,' he remarked.

'I don't know whether to believe that or not.' Sarai sighed. 'I always found an air of mystery in a man to be attractive, but you are a total enigma, Joby Lancer. You give nothing of yourself.'

'I have never had any complaints.'

Exasperated, she complained, 'You are deliberately misunderstanding me. I am not referring to what happened here. All I know about you is that you walked out of the sea like some mythical figure, an ancient legend. You had to come from somewhere. I am aware that the *Paloma* was a troopship. Were you a soldier?'

Lancer hesitated, undecided. Sarai had given him much-needed employment at a high rate of pay, more money than he had ever been paid. She had a right to know more about him, but it would be disastrous if his past should be generally known. The hills and dales of the countryside were as evil as the dark and dangerous alleyways of the cities, perhaps more so in some different way. Records would show that he hadn't been among the dead, so there would now be a bounty on his head. There was doubtless many a poverty-stricken Judas around who would sell him out to the political dictators in London.

'This has to be just between you and me, Sarai,' he stipulated, before venturing further.

'As a married woman, Joby, I trust that everything between you and me is strictly between you and me.'

Still hesitant, Lancer pointed out, 'Your good name is safe with me, Sarai, but I have much more to lose.'

'That sounds very serious.'

'Believe me, it is.'

'Even so, you are in no danger from me, but you must obey your own counsel, Joby.'

'I find that difficult where you are concerned.'

157

'I am sorry that I pressed you,' she replied, in a tone that conveyed she was miffed.

'I wasn't complaining, but was trying to pay you a compliment in a twisted kind of way,' he attempted to explain. 'I was a captain serving with the 38th Regiment of Foot. But on the *Paloma* I was a prisoner being brought back to England to face a court martial on a charge of cowardice in the face of the enemy.'

Impulsively embracing him, clinging to him tightly for some time before speaking, Sarai then said, 'I wouldn't believe for one second that a man like you could be accused of cowardice, Joby.'

'Thank you for your support, Sarai, but the army believes it and the court martial will believe it, so whether or not it is true is academic. '

'If they are unable to find you there won't be a court martial,' she rationalized. 'No one here, other than me, knows anything of your history. I certainly won't be revealing it to anyone.'

'I know that,' he confirmed. The sap from the blade of grass had moistened and put a gloss on her full lips, and he couldn't resist kissing her. 'I am pretty sure that I can spend the rest of my time here in Devon without being discovered by the army. I think I might try the Romany way of life.'

Aware that he was trying to lift their spirits, she chuckled. 'Don't expect me to join you; I have to keep up appearances. It wouldn't be possible for me to mingle with royalty one moment and squat on my haunches making clothes pegs the next. Which reminds me, not the clothes peg part the aristocracy, Emil will probably be back at the house now. We had better be on our way.'

Gaining something from having shared his secret with her, Lancer's good feeling increased as they rode through the beautiful countryside. This lasted only until they neared the house and he saw a tall man walking along the terrace, putting garden furniture back into place now that the threat of rain had passed. This was his first sighting of Count Edelcantz.

A light breeze that smelled of the river and pine woods and forest flowers plucked gently at the leaves on the trees that they passed through as they rode in. Edelcantz stood waiting for them. Slender and urbane, his fair hair clustered in natural curls on his long, aristocratic head, he greeted Sarai but afforded Lancer nothing more than a superior glance. It was enough to free Lancer of any guilt he might have felt, but didn't, about cuckolding the haughty Swedish nobleman.

'This is Joby Lancer, Emil,' Sarai said in an attempt at creating a normal situation.

Edelcantz's right hand moved as if about to offer a handshake. Sunlight sparkled off the big black stone set in a ring on his middle finger as he thought better of the potential handshake by pulling his hand back and walking away.

'Emil has a tendency towards snobbishness,' Sarai offered apologetically.

'I would say that's only one of his problems,' Lancer observed with an indifferent shrug.

Becoming quietly insightful, Sarai murmured, 'Our marriage is a sham, Joby. I don't love him, in fact I don't even like him, but by agreeing to be his wife I do owe him respect.'

'You weren't being very respectful just a half-hour ago,' Lancer reminded her as they walked their horses to the stables.

'That was a cruel thing to say,' a saddened Sarai complained. 'I have regretted my actions countless times in the past, absolutely detesting my weakness, but my nature is a family legacy that I have no control over. Perhaps my behaviour borders on insanity, but at least I can satisfy my primitive urges in the natural way. Oliver Adams, one of my ancestors of just a few generations back, was completely mad. He burned this place to the ground and himself with it. His portrait hangs at the top of the stairs, and I shiver every time that I pass it.'

'You should stop and have a word with him' Lancer advised drily. 'Perhaps you could persuade his ghost to set Emil alight.'

'You are wicked, Joby Lancer,' she chided him smilingly. 'I would probably take you up on that idea if I could trust Oliver not to burn me to ashes as well.'

'I think you could trust him not to set fire to one of the family, Sarai.'

'The fact Oliver set fire to himself would not seem to guarantee that. Anyway, Emil wouldn't be here now if you had come back to me sooner,' she affirmed.

'I would have done so had I not unavoidably been delayed, Sarai.'

Aware that Emil Edelcantz was approaching, a nervous Arabella kept her head down, eyes on the washboard on which she was scrubbing aprons and kitchen linen. Ida Sutton had explained to her that Sarai Adams had recently married Edelcantz who, until that moment, Arabella had only glimpsed from a distance.

His shadow fell on the ground beside her as he came to a halt, and her prayer that he would move on went unanswered. He spoke in a friendly manner with a foreign accent. 'Are you the new girl, Arabella?'

'Yes, sir.'

'I have been watching you from a little way off, and find that Mrs Winchell was correct when she reported that you are a hard worker. We are lucky to have you.'

'Thank you kindly, sir,' Arabella responded, worried as to whether a curtsy was expected or would be in order.

'You are from the village I understand.'

'I am, sir.'

'That pleases me, as I have a need to get to know the local folk,' he explained. 'I would like Adamslee House to become a part of the community, and I wonder if you would be kind enough to assist me. A personable girl such as yourself must know just about everyone in Adamslee.'

'I would be happy to help you if I can, sir.'

'We have already made a start. Mrs Edelcantz has taken on Mr Lancer as our estate manager.'

Heart missing a beat, Arabella's voice deserted her. Even if it hadn't she had no idea what to say. She had heard that morning that Joby Lancer was now working at Adamslee House, and had thrilled at the thought of meeting him again. Yet she couldn't trust herself to speak of a man who, in his absence, had come to mean more and more to her.

'I would imagine that Mr Lancer is a born and bred Adamslee man,' Edelcantz speculated.

Able to speak, although humiliated to hear herself stammering, she said, 'No, sir, Mr Lancer came here a short while ago when the *Paloma* was wrecked in a tempest.'

'I wasn't here in Adamslee at that time, Arabella and know nothing of that night. Am I to take it from what you say that Mr Lancer was one of the survivors?'

'Oh no, sir. He was the *only* survivor.'

'Dear me, what a tragedy,' Edelcantz murmured. 'I have always held an interest in shipping. If I am not mistaken the *Paloma* is, or rather was, a troopship, so many men must have perished on the night you refer to?'

'Many hundreds, men, women and children, sir.'

'Good Lord. The fortunate Mr Lancer was a member of the crew?'

'I do not believe so, sir,' Arabella replied, finding it difficult to admit, not so much to the questioner but to herself, that she knew little or nothing about Joby Lancer.

'Then he must have been a trooper,' Edelcantz said, more to himself than to Arabella.

'I really don't know, sir.'

Really stressed now, Arabella relaxed a little as Edelcantz

showed signs that he was departing. He said. 'You have been most helpful, Arabella. I enjoyed our little talk immensely. Goodbye.'

'Goodbye, sir.'

'You would have been wise to hide your horses.'

Lying together in a little grassy hollow miles from any buildings, believing they were alone, Sarai Edelcantz and Joby Lancer were startled by a voice addressing them. Partly freeing each other from a close embrace they both looked up to see Emil Edelcantz standing just feet away on a hillock looking down on them. Face reddened by rage, he was holding a shotgun.

'No, Emil!' Sarai cried out in fear.

'Do either of you believe that you deserve better?' he snarled.

'Stay here, don't move,' Lancer quietly instructed Sarai as he stood up and started to climb up the slope towards where Edelcantz stood.

'Please, Joby!' She called his name beseechingly.

Unheeding, Lancer continued steadily up the grassy gradient.

'Stop!' Edelcantz shouted at him hysterically, tersely adding, 'One more step and I will blow you to pieces, you scoundrel.'

By that time, with only a yard distancing him from the muzzle of the shotgun, Lancer looked to Edelcantz's right and cried out a warning, 'Go back. He is armed!'

Unnerved, Edelcantz did a quarter turn to glance behind him. Moving at a tremendous speed, Lancer closed the distance between them to grab the barrel of the shotgun with both hands to wrench it out of the other man's grasp. Pulling the weapon towards him, Lancer then thrust the butt hard into the midriff of Edelcantz, who instantly doubled over in pain. Swinging the shotgun, Lancing whacked Edelcantz across the head.

Leaving the unconscious man lying at the top of the bank, Lancer hurried down into the hollow to help the sobbing Sarai to her feet and hold her close.

'This is the end for me,' she murmured through her sobbing. 'What on earth can we do now, Joby?'

'First we have to get your husband back to the house and tend his injuries, Sarai.'

'What?' she gasped in disbelief. 'He was going to shoot us, Joby!'

'If I was him I would have pulled the trigger,' Lancer admitted, filled with remorse. 'He was the wronged one in this situation. Come, we must find his horse and get him back to the house. He isn't a fighting man. I could well have injured him seriously.'

'But you can't be there when he regains consciousness, Joby.'

'*If* he regains consciousness,' Lancer corrected her grimly. 'You are my responsibility so I must be there to protect you.'

Bad news awaited Arabella when she reached the Heelan cottage to collect Thelma that evening. Ruth was standing in the open doorway with the baby in her arms.

'Oh Bella,' she sobbed. 'Mum's been taken real ill.'

Rushing into the house behind the crippled girl, Arabella found an obviously seriously ill Josephine Heelan lying in bed, and asked Ruth, 'Have you sent for Dr Mawby?'

'I don't need a doctor, Bella,' Josephine protested weekly. 'I will be right as rain tomorrow morning.'

Taking Ruth to one side, Arabella expressed her anxiety. 'As you said, she is extremely sick, Ruth. It is vital that Dr Mawby sees her. Do you agree?'

'I do agree, of course. I am terribly worried about her.'

'If I run to the doctor's place can you look after Thelma for a little while longer, Ruth?'

'She will be fine with me. Please hurry, Ruth.'

Ruth did hurry, rushing through the always near-deserted streets of Adamslee to hammer on the door of Dr Mawby's small cottage. The old doctor, ever one to turn a call-out into a crisis, became flustered as he donned his coat, picked up his case, and closed the door behind him to hurry up the road at Arabella's side.

'Of late I have been concerned about Mrs Heelan,' the old doctor puffed, out of breath through trying to keep pace with Arabella. 'She hasn't looked well for some time.'

'I hope it isn't serious.'

'Chin up,' Mawby advised in a half whisper as they went in through the Heelans' door.

Sitting beside the sofa on which her husband lay, Sarai was nervous even though she knew that Lancer was in the next room. Unconscious for half-an-hour, the Emil had just started struggling to open his eyes. A folded cloth that had been soaked in cold water and rung out lay across his bruised and swollen forehead.

Fearful about what to expect, she saw his eyes open. At first unfocused, they then returned to normal to look at her. She waited, holding her breath. Not speaking, he reached up to explore his forehead gently, fingers lifting one end of the cloth.

'That is to reduce the swelling and the pain,' she told him. 'Would you like me to rinse it in cold water again?'

'How long have I been lying here, Sarai?'

'It is well over half-an-hour since we brought you back.'

'We?' he questioned her sharply.

Sarai hesitated, apprehensive as to what his reaction would be. Make-or-break time had arrived. Within the next few minutes she would learn whether or not she was still married. More worrying still was the fact that she didn't know whether or not she wanted to be.

'How did you manage to get me back to the house?' he enquired in a surprisingly conversational way.

'I didn't,' she began, having decided it would be best to provoke the inevitable showdown, 'Joby Lancer did.'

Amazing her by taking this calmly, he asked, 'Where is he now?'

'In the next room.'

'I must thank him for doing so. He could well have abandoned me. I probably deserved to be left there for letting a moment of jealousy turn me into a madman.'

'You were justified,' Sarai conceded. 'My behaviour was unforgivable.'

'If Lancer hadn't stopped me I would have shot you, Sarai.'

'That is probably what I deserved.'

'No,' he corrected her. 'What you deserve is a considerate, sensible husband, which is something I have never been since our betrothal. What I have been is the term that I have heard the Adamslee *hoi polloi* use. I have been a bloody fool, Sarai.'

'I can't say that I understand what you are telling me, Emil.'

'That is because I don't know exactly what it is that I want to say,' he confessed. 'I feel that we have both learned a lesson today: a lesson that we can utilize to save our marriage and remain together here in Adamslee House.'

'And what of Joby Lancer?'

Obviously in pain, Edelcantz kept his head still while waving a hand vaguely in the direction of the door. 'Close that door, Sarai.'

Obeying, glad that Lancer wouldn't overhear whatever decision her husband had made about him, Sarai came back to sit by the bed.

'Lancer can remain as estate manager.'

'You mean,' a stunned Sarai exclaimed, 'that you forgive him?'

'Forgiveness is not one of my traits, Sarai, but revenge is.'

'But you must not tackle Joby Lancer, Emil,' she blurted out in a dilemma, unaware that she was criticizing her husband's manliness. 'Lancer is a fighting man. He was a soldier.'

'Ah, that is what I had surmised,' he muttered smugly. 'Now, my sweet Sarai, I want you to tell me everything that you know about your lover. I have a plan that permits him to stay here in the short term providing that I have your promise that there will be no further intimacy between the pair of you.'

'My nature, which I find difficult if not impossible to control, prevents me from making you such a promise. Emil.'

'If my head didn't hurt so much I would be shaking it now,' he said. 'Drink does not help your problem, Sarai. It is a sexual stimulant, and you imbibe it too freely. Limit your intake and help me with my scheme to make Lancer pay dearly for the liberties he has taken with my wife. We must begin with you telling me everything, every detail that you know about him.'

Having known that she had never liked him, at this very moment Sarai become conscious that she loathed Emil Edelcantz. It maddened her that she had no option but to go along with what would certainly be his fiendish plot to harm Joby Lancer, who was a thousand times more of a man than her husband would ever be.

It had added to Arabella's unhappiness to find Sarai Edelcantz so distant that it was difficult to talk to her. Leaving Thelma yet again with an understanding Ruth, she had started out on the climb to Adamslee House soon after Dr Mawby had left. Before going he had taken Arabella to one side and told her the bleak news. Josephine Heelan did not have long to live.

'I feel it best that you tell Ruth,' the old doctor had whispered.

Aware that it wasn't cowardice on the part of Dr Mawby, but compassion for the crippled daughter of the ailing mother, Arabella had agreed. It was on her conscience that up to now that she had not mustered enough courage to pass the sad tidings on to Ruth. Unable to force herself to do so before she had left, she was deeply troubled by the awesome task that she faced on returning to the village.

'I am sorry to hear the sad news about your friend's mother, Bella,' Sarai sympathized, every bit as distracted as she had been since Arabella had arrived at the house.

'I am afraid that with Ruth having to take care of her mother I will have no one to look after my baby.'

'So you will have to leave us?' Sarai assumed, without showing any real interest.

'I'm very sorry to let you down, Mrs Edelcantz.'

'We will be sorry to lose you, Bella,' a plainly inattentive Sarai said, adding in an attempt at covering her abstract disposition, 'Mrs Winchell can't praise you highly enough.'

'I was happy working here,' Arabella said, surprised to grasp how sad she was to be leaving.

'Maybe when your circumstances alter you can come back to us. Goodbye, Bella.'

'Goodbye, Mrs Edelcantz.'

Going out of the house, Arabella felt hurt at being dismissed so coldly. During the short time that she had worked at Adamslee House she had met Sarai on a few occasions. Each time the older woman had stopped for a short but friendly chat, whereas today she had been unapproachable. Coming to the conclusion that her former employer had some pressing worry, Arabella's mind now turned to her own predicament. Never having been avaricious or selfish, but out of concern for the future of her child and herself without an income, she had been disappointed when Sarai had not honoured her earlier promise to make Arabella a financial gift should circumstances prevent her from continuing her employment.

When she got back to the village and paid Ruth and her mother for minding Thelma, she would have just enough money, if eked out, to live a fraction above a survival level for one week. What then?

On reaching the top of the slope down to Adamslee, it hit her hard to discover how much her brief spell of employment had been a much-needed escape from the village. It increased her melancholy to look down at the jumble of decrepit buildings that housed neighbours who were overly curious, overly critical, or overly obsequious, all drowning in a world that they had never completely entered. Long ago recognizing this, she knew that she had to be different, must make something of herself. But her ambition had come to nought.

Unable to force herself to walk on down to the village, she sat on a flat rock. Elbows on her knees, face held in her cupped hands, her dismal contemplation of a desolate future drifted into memories of an equally hopeless past. There had been a few good times, such as when her mother and she had enjoyed an occasional happy event, and the early months of her relationship with Lionel.

One highlight had been her short-lived delight as Adamslee's May Queen, now a sad memory that glowed dimly under the shadow of her mother's death. The sudden emergence of Joby Lancer had lightened her life, but that, too, had been cut short when he had walked away. Though he had returned once, when she had been pleased that he had seen her as the May Queen, he had not come back since, and she doubted that he ever would.

The shadows were lengthening around her, and she was ashamed at having burdened Ruth with Thelma for so long. Pushing herself up from the rock, she wiped away tears caused by her poignant reminiscences, and started on the way down to the village.

It was late afternoon when Lancer rode back towards Adamslee House. After a visit to a tenant farmer who was behind with his rent, he rued the fact that he had applied pressure that had resulted in an agreement of regular payments that would include fixed amount off the arrears.

Aware of the hardship the arrangement would cause the farmer and his family, Lancer was far from proud of himself.

Yet this didn't interfere with his intuition. On the battlefield he had learned never to ignore an inner voice whose whispered warnings could he could hear above the roar of guns. It was telling him now that he was being followed.

Although still summer there had been an autumn dampness in that dawn. Dismounting, Lancer concealed his horse in a small copse and swiftly climbed a cliff, moving behind a projecting rock to look down on the trail that he had just left. Disturbed by Lancer's arrival, a bird probing for worms at the water's edge of a nearby stream took flight.

Lancer waited for some fifteen minutes without any sign of whoever he was sure had been following him. Throughout that time he blamed the startled bird for warning off the man, or men, trailing him but so much time had passed now that he was ready to accept that he had been mistaken. However, he waited a further ten minutes before moving on.

On a slow ride back he was once again certain that he was being tailed. Slowing his horse to a walking pace a couple of times didn't produce any results, and he was ostensibly alone when he rode into the grounds of Adamslee House.

When the old groom, always sycophantic but at that time strangely secretive, had taken his horse, he entered the house and went to Sarai's office to report the arrangement he had made with the tenant farmer. The office was empty. About to leave, he was prevented from doing so by Emil Edelcatz standing in the doorway. The recent history that they had shared created an invisible, acutely embarrassing barrier between them.

'Ah, Lancer, you are back,' Edelcantz began self-consciously.

'I was expecting Sarai to be here,' Lancer said, making a motion with his hand for Edelcantz to stand aside.

Ignoring this, the Swedish man cleared his throat before saying with authority, 'Mrs Edelcantz is indisposed at the moment, but there is a matter that you are needed to take care of in the stables.'

'I don't take orders from you, Edelcantz,' Lancer pointedly but calmly advised.

'I am not giving you an order, Lancer, but merely repeating a message that Mrs Edelcantz implored me to convey to you. It is a matter that I would willingly attend to myself were my equine knowledge practically non-existent. Caesar, Mrs Edelcantz's stallion is ailing and she is extremely worried.'

This demolished Lancer's reluctance, and his gesture to have Edelcantz move aside was obeyed. Striding out of the house, Lancer hurried in the direction of the stables. Seeing Morley at the corner of the building, he was about to call to him to learn something of what the problem with Caesar was. But the under-sized groom had spotted him, and hurried off behind the stables.

Both the half doors on Caesar's stall were closed. Filled with apprehension as to what he might find, Lancer pulled the top door open. He had to jump to one side as the head of the huge stallion, pleased that his stall had been opened, came out fast. Caesar showed his appreciation by swinging his head in a circular motion while blowing and spluttering through extended lips.

There was nothing wrong with the stallion: it was in excellent condition. For a moment bewildered by this, Lancer then grasped the situation. Edelcantz had tricked him into coming to the stables. But for what reason?

Head down, pondering on this, Lancer turned on his heel. Determined to return to the house and demand an explanation, he raised his head and his whole body was electrified by shock.

Some ten yards from him stood five soldiers spread out in an arc, each of them holding a Brown Bess musket at hip level, all of the weapons aimed at him.

Ten

'YOU MUST COME and stay with me now, Ruth,' Arabella said firmly, as they left the cemetery after the burial of Josephine Heelan.

Ruth's mother had died on the stroke of midnight three nights earlier. The time of her death struck Arabella as being significant, though she could not comprehend why. Often in the past strange happenings had importance for her but she had never been able to fathom out what message they held. She had been tempted to ask the Reverend Worther for advice, but something had warned her against such a move.

At that moment she had to concentrate on the known, not the unknown. What she was certain of was that she wasn't going to leave the grief-stricken Ruth alone in the empty house. Though the crippled girl could make no contribution, being as destitute as she was, Arabella kept telling herself that they would somehow manage.

'Are you sure that I won't be a nuisance to you, Arabella?' Ruth questioned falteringly.

'Don't be silly,' Arabella protested. 'You are more than welcome. I will be glad of the company; you can stay as long as you like. The longer the better as far as I am concerned.'

'You are a good friend, Bella,' Ruth stammered gratefully, struggling to hold back tears as they walked through empty streets. 'Would you like me to carry Thelma for a while?'

'Thanks, but I can manage,' Arabella answered with a white

lie as she moved her baby from one arm to the other to ease the strain.

When they entered the house Ruth collapsed into a chair and sobbed incessantly. Unable to think of any way to comfort her, Arabella settled the baby in her cot and listlessly searched bare shelves for something that might possibly be conjured up to make at least a semblance of a meal. It was a hopeless task that depressed her so that she was reduced to tears that streamed down her cheeks as she cried for Josephine Heelan, her own mother, the sorrowful past and the doomed to failure future.

One solitary, hollow echoing sob burst from her. An immense effort enabled her to stifle further sobbing but only momentarily. Then the wretchedness of it all returned in full force and she collapsed across the table, her body convulsing with each gulping wail.

Though his surroundings were limited to the three walls of a guardhouse cell and a door with a small barred window, Lancer knew where he was. Three days ago he had recognized the town of Aldershot as the army carriage in which he sat between his escort had passed through. A short while later when crossing heathland he had looked out with interest at the almost completed construction of an army base on his right. While still serving in the army he had heard of a planned garrison for this area. His escort didn't share his keen interest. The two burly, surly soldiers took no notice of the scenery. Neither of them had uttered one word to him on the long journey.

Lancer was plagued by memories of the circumstances of his arrest at Adamslee House. There was no possibility that the army had traced him to Adamslee. Somebody had informed the military that he was in Devon. Sarai was the only person he had told about his past. It was significant that neither Sarai nor Emil Edelcantz were to be seen when the armed soldiers who had been waiting outside of the stables had moved in on him.

Skirting the house, weapons held at the ready, the soldiers had taken him to where several military carriages were concealed among trees at the rear of the building. When he had been roughly shoved into a carriage and was moving out, the clip clop of the horses' hoofs had brought Sarai to an upstairs window from where she had peered down at him while clutching a curtain in the hope it had hidden her.

Annoying his escort by moving to ensure that she was aware that he had seen her, Lancer hoped that he had shamed her. The fact that she had betrayed him had caused his past three nights in the cell to be sleepless. Sarai's reason for doing so had doubtless been to save her marriage. It appalled him that she had been willing to sacrifice his life to rescue her unsatisfactory and unholy state of matrimony to Edelcantz. That knowledge had caused him much pain from the moment he been taken from Adamslee under armed guard. Nonetheless, it was impossible to share the earth-shattering passion that they had known and ever again be completely separated. Consequently, he still held deep feelings for her, although with a future that would last only until the court martial sentence was pronounced, yearning for Sarai was meaningless.

He had decided that on the eve of his death he would pen a letter to her. Common sense made it evident that her betrayal meant that she was a worthless person who did not deserve one kind thought; he was willing to concede that while in a state of despondency she had been influenced by Emil Edelcantz.

He was lying on his cot composing the letter to Sarai in his mind when the cell door was unlocked and a young second lieutenant stepped in. The door was closed behind him and locked from the outside. Handsome in an aristocratic way, the officer's diffident manner had him stand uncomfortable and speechless.

Moving in the hope of breaking the silence, Lancer got to his feet. His ploy worked. The officer extended his right hand saying, 'I am Second Lt Hugh Driscoll, your defence counsel, sir.'

'Pleased to meet you, Lieutenant,' Lancer said as they shook hands. 'But the sir is unnecessary as I no longer hold a rank.'

'Having been passed your record, I use your rank out of respect for an experienced and courageous officer. I am a lowly second lieutenant who has yet to fire a shot in anger or for any other reason.'

'You are young and have plenty of time to gain experience,' Lancer consoled him. 'I don't doubt that you will gain promotion quickly.'

A rueful Driscoll nodded agreement as he spoke ashamedly. 'I will. That is beyond a doubt, sir. You see, I am the only son of Brigadier Arbuckle, sir. You can imagine how I feel in the presence of someone such as you who has come up through the ranks.'

'I have to admit that I would have preferred to have done it your way, given half a chance, Lieutenant.'

'It is impossible to see you as a privileged brat, sir.'

'Believe me, you show no sign of being that yourself … can I call you Hugh?'

'I would regard that as a compliment,' Driscoll said, smiling for the first time since his arrival. 'My second confession is that I have had no legal training whatsoever, sir.'

'The kind of court martial that I face is fairly new to the British Army, and I suspect that no one from the trial judge advocate will know what he is doing. None of this is of any consequence, Hugh. There will only be one verdict.'

'I don't like to think that way, sir. Though I fully realize my limitations, I intend to prepare the best defence that I can for you.'

Lancer shrugged. 'I really appreciate your kindness, but do yourself a favour by accepting that the outcome of my trial is a foregone conclusion.'

'I am determined to do everything possible to defend you, sir.'

'You do as you wish, Hugh, but I fear it will be wasted effort.'

Desperation forced Arabella to climb the hill to Adamslee House that afternoon. There were only a few scraps of food in the cupboard at home, and Mr Clinton, her landlord would be calling in the morning. She had no money to pay him that week's rent, and she already owed five weeks. Faced with the situation there was no alternative but to summon up enough courage to ask Sarai Edelcantz for financial help.

By the time Arabella reached the door of the big house her despair was rapidly increasing while her courage was waning equally as fast. She was about to turn and run away when the maid she had met on her first visit opened the door.

'Are you here to see the mistress?' the maid asked absently, seemingly preoccupied with some major problem.

'Yes.'

Making a listless one-handed signal for Arabella to enter, the maid led the way along the passageway towards Sarai's office.

'Is the master here?' Arabella enquired, prepared to flee if Emil Edelcantz was present.

Neither speaking nor turning to look at Arabella, the maid gave a negative shake of her head. On reaching the office door, she turned the handle to open it a little. Then she hurried away.

Lost for a moment as to what she should do, Arabella took a deep breath, pushed the door open, and walked into the office. There was a strong aroma that she couldn't identify. Sarai was standing looking out of the window with her back to Arabella. She didn't turn, which was nothing new for Sarai, who always displayed a lack of tact where greeting people was concerned.

Arabella coughed, but Sarai either didn't hear or didn't care. She cleared her throat again. This time Sarai turned, slowly. She pointed a wagging finger vaguely in Arabella's direction, her speech slurred as she said her name over and over again. 'Bella, Bella, Bella....'

Running her well-rehearsed plea through her head once more Arabella was about to speak when Sarai took one clumsy step. Faltering, she lurched back against a wall, from which she bounced to collide with a small bureau. The bureau toppled sideways and a stumbling Sarai caught her legs against it and fell heavily to the floor.

Panicking, Arabella moved hesitantly towards the fallen woman, wanting to help but not knowing how to. Coming close to Sarai she could hear her making tiny whimpering sounds. Then she retched loudly; and Arabella had to turn away as the prone woman vomited explosively, splattering the floor and Arabella's shoes.

The stench was awful, and Arabella quickly linked it with the odour she had noticed when first entering the room. It was alcohol. Sarai Edelcantz was hopelessly, helplessly drunk. Now she understood the maid's attitude. Disgusted by her first experience of such an inebriated person, Arabella fled from the room as another eruption of vomit splashed noisily on to the polished wood floor.

The court martial of Lancer was convened at 10 a.m. in a newly constructed wooden hut. Due to the unfinished state of the base, the whole set-up had a makeshift appearance that devalued the line of grim-faced officers of the court martial board sitting on each side of Captain Bluett, the trial judge advocate. That this court was an experimental one was evident by the civilian lawyer who sat in isolation from the uniformed figures, ready to advise should any legal difficulties arise.

Carrying a file of documents, Second Lieutenant Hugh Driscoll hurried into the hut to sit beside Lancer. Placing his file on the table in front of him, he leaned close to Lancer to inform him, 'I have made some substantive progress, sir.'

Grateful to the young officer for his diligence, Lancer tried to look pleased as he gave a neutral and unenthusiastic answer. 'Thank you, Hugh.'

'In all modesty I think, I pray, that I may well be able to prove you wrong as to your prospects, sir,' Driscoll responded, but then fell silent as counsel for the prosecution stood to relate the facts against the accused.

He was a lieutenant who spoke with a confidence and skill that strongly suggested that he was a either a lawyer or a blustering egotist. He gave an account of the night of Lancer's alleged offence in stark and vivid detail.

'Are you calling witnesses for the prosecution, Lieutenant?' the judge enquired, when the prosecutor had put his case.

'All who could have testified to this court to the events of that night are dead, sir,' the lieutenant replied. 'But their deaths bear silent witness to the fact that the accused deserted his post that night.'

'Witnesses for the defence, Lt Driscoll?' the judge invited.

Rising to his feet, Driscoll surprised Lancer by answering, 'I will be calling two witnesses, sir. The first is an *officier supérieur* of the Armée de Terre, Commandant Jacques-Pierre de Breteuil who was in command of the French unit involved on the night in question.'

Lancer's estimation of Lt Hugh Driscoll soared sky-high as the smart French Army officer took up his position as a witness. He stood to attention, the tunic bearing three rows of medal ribbons, the sleeves emblazoned with the mainly gold insignia of the artillery.

'I am conversant with Armée de Terre insignia, Commandant de Breteuil,' the judge began, 'but for the record I must ask if on this particular night you were in command of a *compagnie*, an *escadron*, or a *batterie*?'

'My command was a *batterie*,' de Breteuil replied with barely a trace of a French accent to confirm that he had been in command of an artillery unit.

This led to a series of questions skilfully posed by Hugh Driscoll during which the Frenchman revealed that, due to a breakdown in communications between the French and British Armies at midnight on that fateful New Year's Eve, his *batterie* had opened up on enemy positions without being aware that Captain Lancer and his men were occupying a forward post close to enemy lines.

'Did you make contact with Captain Lancer later that night?' Driscoll enquired.

'Personal contact, no, but it was brought to my attention that a patrol of our *compagnie,* that is infantry soldiers, had brought Captain Lancer back to our lines. He had been injured and was unconscious. The patrol explained that every one of Captain Lancer's men had been killed.'

'By a cannonade from your *batterie*?' Driscoll half-asked half-assumed.

'Very much to my regret, I have to say that is correct.'

The prosecutor came quickly to his feet to enquire, 'It is correct that quite a number of Captain Lancer's men died that night, Commandant?'

'I do not have the exact figures.'

'But Captain Lancer was the only survivor?'

'That is correct.'

'Something of miracle,' the prosecutor commented wryly to himself, yet loud enough for the court martial board to hear, as he looked down at the papers in front of him.

The civilian lawyer spoke quietly to the judge, who nodded in agreement before addressing the prosecutor. 'Confine yourself to evidence, Lieutenant.'

'I would call my second witness now, sir,' Driscoll said, when the hostile few moments came to an end. 'Sergent Henri Allègre of the Armée de Terre.'

The sergeant, who had the tough look of a battle-hardened veteran, answered through an interpreter.

Driscoll said, 'You led the platoon that found Captain Lancer in the wake of the cannonade, *sergent*. I understand that he was unconscious?'

'That is right.'

'Roughly what distance would you say separated Captain Lancer from his men at this time?'

When this question was translated for him, for some reason it bewildered the sergeant. Studying him worriedly for some minutes, Commandant de Breteuil then got to his feet to address the judge. 'Permission to answer for Sergent Allègre, sir?'

Before replying, Captain Bluett looked to the civilian adviser, who assented with a nod. Captain Bluett then signalled for Commandant de Breteuil to go ahead.

'I submitted Sergent Allègre's report with the file that I forwarded when the sergent and I were first summoned as witnesses,' the French *commandant* stated.

Captain Bluett turned to the lieutenant who was the assistant trial judge advocate, to ask, 'Do you hold a report by Sergent Allègre, Lt Marston?'

'I am not aware of ...' the lieutenant mused, as he reached for a file that he leafed through. 'No, sir, there is no such report in the file lodged by Commandant de Breteuil.'

With a frown creasing his brow, the judge apologized to the French officer. 'I am sorry about this, Commandant de Breteuil. As you no doubt realize, our legal system here at Aldershot is in its infancy and the administration section leaves much to be desired.'

'I understand, sir,' de Breteuil said.

Hugh Driscoll rose from his seat. 'In my opinion it would be unfair to the accused to proceed without this document.'

'I agree,' the judge said, although at the same time censuring the junior officer for his effrontery with a hard stare. 'How long would you estimate it will take to get a copy of the sergeant's statement to this court, Commandant de Breteuil?'

'No longer than two full days, sir.'

'Then we will now adjourn and, provisionally, reconvene on Thursday at ten o'clock,' he pronounced.

Speaking quickly as he saw Lancer's escort approaching, Driscoll commented on the missing witness statement. 'The outlook is brighter, sir.'

'That may be so,' Lancer conceded before adding a reservation. 'Everything depends on what Sergent Allègre has said in his statement, Hugh.'

'Is there any hope of getting you to look on the bright side, sir?'

'Don't be cheeky, Hugh,' Lancer warned with a grin. 'If I get off you might end up under my command.'

'If you don't get off I may ask Daddy to secure your command for me?' Driscoll quipped.

They were both still chuckling when Lancer's escort led him away to his cell.

Thunderclouds had been gathering from the west all that dark day, and there had been a constant deep grumbling beyond the horizon. The pain of Sarai's now ever-present headache had been exacerbated by pressure from the heavy, warm air. A blazing quarrel with Emil late that evening had turned the ache into agony. Tearfully escaping to her room, she had been unable to sleep and became agitated. Disagreements between them, teetering on the brink of violence, were far from rare now, but there was something different about the altercation tonight; something ominous.

At half-past one in the morning she lay, disturbed by the incessant beating of rain that was whipped against her bedroom windows by a gale-force wind booming in from the sea. Each attempt that she made to drive her recent shouting-match from her mind only served to increase her anxiety. The vicious wrangling had ended with the always self-assured, contemptuous

Emil Edelcantz collapsed in armchair, curled in a foetal position, his body violently convulsing as he wept.

That memory took on the awesome magnitude of a premonition that made it impossible for her to remain in bed. Donning a robe as she hurried along the landing, avoiding the insanely staring eyes of Oliver Adams as she passed his portrait, she went down the wide majestic staircase without knowing why she was doing so.

An oil lamp that had been lit in the hall was affected by a breeze that threw moving shadows around eerily. Standing on the bottom stair trying to calm herself by deep breathing, Sarai's heart thudded in her chest when she glimpsed the silhouette of a person inside of the front door. She had all-but convinced herself that she was mistaken when a flash of lightning came through the glass panes in the double-doors to light up the hallway ten time brighter than daylight ever could.

She gave an involuntary gasp as she saw her husband standing inside the door. As the flash of lightning was spent, the whole scene became even more surreal as it appeared she found she would be speaking to a silhouette.

Stepping off the bottom stair on to the floor, she enquired anxiously. 'What are you doing down here, Emil?'

'I am ...' he began, taking a few shuffling steps forward that brought him into the dull-orange glow of the oil lamp. 'I am taking the only course open to me, which is leaving.'

'Why? Emil, why?'

It took him a long while to answer. Sarai was shaken to see how haggard he looked. His face had become gaunt of late, and now the shadows cast by the lamp accentuated the lines and fissures. But guilt and shame compelled Sarai to face the undeniable truth. As she fully realized this, he spelled it out for her.

'You have to ask *why*, Sarai?' he asked in disbelief. 'I came to Adamslee a proud man, a man who commanded respect wherever he travelled in the world. Now I am looked upon as a buffoon, a foolish man with a drunken slut for a wife. A wife who treats him abominably, who talks down to him even in company belonging to the highest echelons of society. Nay, *especially* when among the top people. You lower me purposely in the hope that by doing so you can rescue yourself from the gutter in which you lie in filth with the other whores.'

Moved to tears by his censure, shattered to realize that she could deny nothing that he had said, she pleaded as an exceptionally strong gust of wind rattled rain against the window-panes. 'But you cannot leave on such a night as this, Emil. At least stay until the morning. That will give us the opportunity to rescue our marriage. I am sure that is something that we can achieve.'

'Rescue our marriage?' he questioned with a maniacal laugh that chilled her. 'That would take a miracle, you stupid woman, and I am convinced that the Lord God would not be interested in practising divine intervention at such a place of ill-repute as Adamslee House.'

Having hurled that final insult at her, he opened the door and the wild wind and rain exploded into the hall. He went out leaving the door open. Battling her way to the door that swung and juddered in the gale, Sarai had to use her shoulder and all her strength to ram it closed during a brief respite in the force of the wind.

Soaked to the skin, she staggered towards the stairs. Aware that she was the author of her own misfortune, she could find not one scrap of redemption in what had just occurred with which to console herself. Yet in the depth of her misery she could find a source of compassion for Emil in the fact that he had been weeping as he went.

Heading for bed and what she was certain would be a sleep-less night, she had climbed three stairs when she had a sudden change of mind. Hurrying back down, she made her way to the sitting-room. Returning, cuddling a bottle of brandy in her arms as if it were a baby, she went off up the stairs.

There was a faint smile of satisfaction on Lt Hugh Driscoll's face when the interpreter finished reading Sergent Allègre's affidavit to the court martial. The sergent had arrived on the scene before the dust from the cannonade had completely settled. He found the bodies of Lancer's men lying among the ruins of the enemy bunker. Allègre and his men had checked the bodies in the hope of finding survivors. They found only one man alive: that sole survivor had been an injured and unconscious Captain Lancer.

Driscoll was quick to ask the Frenchman through the interpreter. 'Captain Lancer was lying among the bodies of the men of his command?'

'That is so. At first his rank was not visible to me, just as initially there was nothing to suggest that Capitaine Lancer was still alive.'

'Captain Lancer had not left the enemy bunker from the time it had been demolished?' Driscoll double-checked.

'In his condition it would have been impossible for the *capitaine* to do so, sir,' was Allègre's reply.

Reseating himself, Driscoll commented to Lancer, 'That about wraps it up, sir. All that remains now is to get you reinstated in the army with adequate compensation.'

Unable to credit how swiftly his fortunes had reversed, words failed Joby.

Eleven

CAESAR, SARAI'S HORSE, was found the morning after the freak autumn storm that had devastated the local harvest. A shepherd on the way back from a dawn check on his flock had come across the animal standing dejected, dripping wet and saddleless close to the edge of the cliff just a few hundred yards west of Adamslee House. Though it was not unusual for the horse's owner to take an early-morning ride, the absence of a saddle was puzzling.

The alarm was raised and Sarai Edelcantz was found safe and well, although somewhat intoxicated, at her home. She could offer no explanation as to why her horse should not be in its stable, but her groom reported that he had found the stable doors open first thing that morning. A horse theft that had gone wrong seemed the likeliest explanation.

The mystery lasted only until 10.30 that morning when it was tragically solved by a longshoreman who discovered the extensively damaged body of Emil Edelcantz on rocks at the foot of the cliff almost directly below where Caesar had been found at the top of it.

Newly appointed Police Constable Coombes, a self-effacing young man unsuited for his chosen profession, went to interview Mrs Edelcantz at Adamslee House. He had got no further than, as tactfully as possible, giving her the sad news of her husband's demise, before returning *post haste* to nervously report that the lady of Adamslee House was in an exceedingly distressed condition. Reluctantly the constable had then done a quick about turn to head back up to the cliff top in the company of a concerned Dr Rupert Mawby.

Answering the door to the doctor and police constable, Sarai remained silent as she led them into her office. She deliberately walked slowly in the hope of being able to compose herself before having to face the two men. It was a vain hope.

Sad faced, Dr Mawby studied her both sympathetically and professionally, advising her. 'Be seated, Sarai, this is a terrible time for you.'

Welcoming the advice, Sarai, close to collapse, slumped into her chair, listlessly waving an arm as a signal for Mawby and Coombes to be seated. She waited, dreading what was to come. Hopefully, the opinion would already have been formed that Emil had unwisely decided on an adventurous horse ride on a stormy night. A foolish escapade that had cost him his life. She forced herself to pay attention as Dr Mawby hesitantly began speaking.

'In all my long years as a doctor I have encountered numerous tragedies, but each one has caused me as much pain as the one preceding it, Sarai. This is no exception. Most probably it is worse because I have known you since you were an infant, and have become quite fond of you.'

Liking the old doctor, but tormented by the circumstances that had brought him to Adamslee House, she conveyed with a nod that she understood his suffering.

'Have you any notion why your husband would set out on Caesar on such a horrendous night, especially without saddling up, Sarai?'

She spoke for the first time since the two men had arrived. The sound of her choked-up voice was alien even to her. 'I have tried to find an explanation since I heard the horrendous news of his death but have been unsuccessful, Dr Mawby.'

'Forgive me, Sarai, but it is necessary to ask certain questions,' Mawby said, after a pointless pause in the hope the constable would speak. 'Had he taken any alcohol last evening?'

'Not a drop. He had been abstaining for quite some time.'

'I have to enquire if everything was all right between the two of you?'

'Yes, we spent a pleasant evening together,' she lied, then added more fabrication. 'We spent an hour or two discussing spending a few weeks over Christmas with his family in Sweden. I retired early due to a headache, and left my husband downstairs reading.'

'When did you next see Emil, Sarai?'

'I didn't,' she replied, finding it easy to weep for all the wrong reasons. 'I slept heavily, and only discovered he had not come to bed when someone from the village called to tell me about Caesar being discovered on the cliff.'

'I see,' Mawby said. 'I am sorry to have intruded on you on so sad an occasion, and hesitate to leave you alone.'

'Your concern is very much appreciated, Dr Mawby. However, I will not be alone. Mrs Winchell is aware of the tragedy and has insisted in preparing nourishment for me,' Sarai explained, as Mawby and Coombes prepared to leave.

Travelling across Salisbury Plain in a stagecoach, Lancer found it good to relax after several days of hectic activity. They were days in which he had turned down an offer to return to the army with the rank of major, and had accepted what to him was a vast sum in compensation for having been wrongly accused. His provisional plans were to return to Adamslee. For what purpose he wasn't sure. Lionel Heelan was a murderer but, nevertheless, he was Arabella's husband. That being so, as long as he was not mistreating Arabella, Lancer would stay clear of the couple. That wasn't what he *wanted* to do, but he accepted it was what he *must* do.

With it certain that Emil Edelcantz was still there, Lancer would not be calling at Adamslee House. He was still drawn to Sarai but doubted that they could recapture their earlier relationship after the way she had betrayed him. Even though it transpired that her disloyalty had brought him good fortune, she hadn't known that at the time she had committed her treachery.

Devon had come to mean a lot to him, so he was returning there while leaving his options open. As money was no problem, his favourite, but as yet undecided scheme, was to purchase a property and start some kind of business. Farming was definitely not a possibility. His experience of Euart Owens had put paid to that.

'Are you a military man, may I enquire, sir?'

His fellow passengers were two young girls, obviously sisters, and an older woman who was their chaperon, and an elderly, obese couple who had the drained appearance of having endured a long marriage.

It had been one of the girls who had asked him the question. Around the age of twenty, slightly older than her sister, she frowned in annoyance when the chaperon reprimanded her.

'You know better than to address a gentleman so, Mary-Anne, especially in such a rude manner.'

'There is no harm done, madam,' Lancer assured the older woman prior to answering the question. 'I was an officer in the army but no longer, miss.'

'Then allow me to wish you a happy retirement, sir,' the elderly man said, as he surveyed Lancer through heavy-lidded eyes. 'You richly deserve it after fighting for your country.'

'Thank you,' Lancer acknowledged. 'Were you army, sir?'

'Lamentably, no. I was in administration due to my—'

The old fellow stopped in mid-sentence as outside an order of some kind was harshly given, the coachman uttered a mild expletive, and the coach came to a sudden halt.

A voice outside the coach spoke in a conversational tone. 'Do not be alarmed, ladies and gentlemen. I will take little of your time, but I will require from each of you a substantial contribution toward my venture.'

'A damned highwayman,' the old gentlemen muttered in disgust. 'I'll be damned if I will—'

This time it was his wife who cut his sentence short. 'The miscreant will be armed, Algernon. You will do nothing other than to obey his commands.'

'That is wise advice. May I suggest that all of you leave the coach? I will come out last and do whatever I can to protect yourselves and your property.'

Lancer had said this without knowing what he could do, if anything. Never had he faced a gun or guns in a situation where the safety of women was involved. Relying on quick thinking, he was in the doorway of the coach about to step down, when the highwayman he hadn't yet seen let out an astonished squawk. 'Joby Lancer! As I live and breathe!'

Buckingham Joe was standing there smiling at him, to the puzzlement of the coachman and the other passengers. 'Stand in line with the others, Joby, but rest assured that I will not require any contribution whatsoever from you.'

'No, Joseph,' Lancer shook his head in refusal. 'Walk to one side with me for a moment, old friend.'

'My pleasure, Joby,' Buckingham Joe said as he walked at Lancer's side to a few feet beyond the coach.

'These folk are like us, Joseph,' Lancer explained. 'They are not the arrogant, selfish wealthy type we despise. I ask you to leave them be. Let them continue on their journey.'

'I hear you, and I appreciate that you are a fair man, Joby. That is why I must put my case. As much as I would like to, I cannot comply with your wish as at this moment I am completely without sustenance.'

Smiling, Lancer slapped his friend on the shoulder. 'That is not a problem. I have had a stroke of luck and am now a relatively rich man. I can take care of your needs. Put them back on the coach. I assume that you have a horse nearby?'

'In that thicket over there,' Joe concurred, a doubtful expression on his face. Then he brightened up. 'And I can steal one for you not a half-mile from here, then we can ride together.'

'That's good, Joseph. Now let us get these folk on their way.'

The coachman shook Lancer by the hand before climbing up on to the box, and the two girls and their chaperon said a soft-voiced 'Thank you' as they passed by. The old man was last to get back in the coach, and he paused to say. 'What has just happened puzzles me as to what you really are, sir. But I do know one thing for certain; you are a true gentleman.'

'Coming from a man like you, I take that as a real compliment, sir. Good luck to both your lady and you.'

Lancer stood with Buckingham Joe watching the coach depart. Then he put his hand in his pocket and passed Joe a handful of coins with the instruction, 'Leave this money where you steal the horse. I want to start my new life in a correct manner.'

'You have my word that I will do just that, Joby.'

'If I needed your word I would not have given you the money, Joseph,' Lancer declared truthfully.

Within half-an-hour Buckingham Joe returned leading a fine horse that was harnessed and saddled. A delighted Lancer walked over to pat the horse appreciatively while Joe explained how he had obtained it.

'For the first time ever, Joby, I paid more for a horse and riding gear than the animal and the saddle together was worth.'

'Forgive me for thinking wrongly of you, Joseph,' Lancer apologized. 'I was certain that you had stolen it.'

The highwayman paused on hearing this. Then he elaborated on what he had already said. 'Technically speaking, you are correct, I did steal the horse but in extenuating circumstances.'

'Then who were you bargaining with?'

'My conscience,' Buckingham Joe replied. 'Like that old fellow on the coach said, you are a gentleman. Aware of that and being keenly aware you wanted to do the right thing by the owner of the horse, I imagined my conscience to be a horse-dealer with whom I haggled with for a considerable time before striking a fair deal.'

'I trust that you conscience has come back with you,' an amused Lancer remarked.

'There was not the slightest possibility that it would not, Joby. I have been trying to dispose of the darn pest for most of my life. Here is the proof that I have failed yet again,' he said as he held out several coins in the palm of his hand.

'Keep the money for services rendered, Joseph.' Lancer waved his friend's hand away. 'Let us mount up and head for the fair town of Salisbury. If my memory serves me correctly, there is always a good meal, a decent drink, and good enter-tainment to be had in the Greyhound Inn.'

'I have no wish to impose on your good nature,' Buckingham Joe said humbly, as he swung agilely up into the saddle.

'That would not be possible,' Lancer assured him. 'I still owe you for the drinks you bought me in the Lamb Inn all those years ago.'

With the washing and rinsing over, Arabella wrung out the baby clothes and Ruth's and her own laundry ready to put out on the line. There was no satisfaction in the work for her as there had once been. It wasn't a job well done due to soap now being as scarce as food in her house. Lionel hadn't contacted her in any way since leaving. Not that she had expected him to, resigned from the day he had walked out the door that she would never see him again. That had not worried her particularly, as the Lionel who had abandoned both her and his child was not the Lionel she had known and loved since they were children.

It wasn't his fault. The dull life of drudgery in Adamslee was the cause of all their problems. But there was no escape for her and her little daughter. Both of them were doomed. They were destined to serve a life sentence of hopeless poverty that had destroyed the hearts and souls of Adamslee folk since the beginning of time, as she had heard the Reverend Worther comment during one of his bleaker moments when life in Adamslee seemed to threaten his faith.

Looking out of the window now hoping to see Ruth returning with baby Thelma, she silently prayed that she wouldn't see the rent collector advancing with his accounts book under his arm. There was more than two weeks to go before his scheduled visit but she was many months in arrears. Though she was constantly on edge looking out for the man, she was spared the knowledge that history was about to repeat itself. She had been too young to remember that she had once been playing happily on the floor of this house while her mother had been in the same dire straits as she now was.

Seeing Ruth and Thelma coming back, she was heartened to see that her friend was carrying a small sack in one hand. This meant that Dr Mawby, Reverend Worther, or some other kind person who was aware of their plight, had given Ruth some food. Arabella was thankful for this even though it meant that they would only have something to eat in the next few hours. That wasn't much comfort but she had long ago learned not to look any further forward than half a day.

Having booked a double room for the night in the Greyhound Inn, they sat together eating bread and cheese and drinking ale in the quietest corner of the bar. The place was crowded, mainly by travelling folk. Lancer recognized many of them as those Buckingham Joe and he had passed along the road into Salisbury. Some of them seemed to know the highwayman and exchanged a wave with him. It was plain to Lancer that this recognition pleased his friend greatly. They were a part of a community here that wasn't alienated by the way he earned a living.

That knowledge increased Lancer's regret that, out of necessity, he would have to spoil this evening to some extent for Buckingham Joe. Though he knew that he must do so, Lancer was reluctant to bring up the subject of the very real threat to his friend that he had learned of while in Dorchester Prison. He knew just how dangerous and insecure a highwayman's life was. In addition to having to watch out for the law he was also in danger of being betrayed by fellow robbers. There was no honour among thieves on the by-ways and highways of England. Lancer shrank from burdening his friend with more worry. He decided to postpone mention of the Kentish Hero until after they had finished their food. That way Buckingham Joe would at least be able to enjoy a part of the evening.

When that time came he had to force himself to introduce the topic. At last he made the effort in a conversational way that made what he was saying appear to be small talk. 'I should mention that the Kentish Hero was in Dorchester Prison at the same time as I was, Joseph.'

Hearing this brought a slight but significant change to his friend: a perceptible tensing of Joseph's body. Lancer anxiously awaited a response.

'It seems that you consider this would be of concern to me, Joby,' the highwayman remarked.

'It bothered me that he was making discreet enquiries about you.'

'Do you know what it was about?'

'No, but it seemed to me to be important, Joseph. I suppose it was intuition more than anything.'

'You had it right,' Buckingham Joe admitted. 'I should explain that my financial circumstances at the time, but above all my stupidity, forced me join the Kentish Hero in a robbery down in Devon, even though I knew well that he couldn't be trusted. He went too far and clobbered the mark over the head with an iron bar, killing him. We both went our separate ways afterwards. I got out of the county real quick but I later heard that he lingered in Devon for a while. He was pulled in by the law, but told a good tale, backed up by a lying testimony from Nancy Locke, a seller of lace I had once spent some time with. We parted acrimoniously, and no doubt she lied to get back at me.'

'And it worked?' Lancer checked.

'It did. As he was no longer a suspect, the Hero was freed. It is logical that he is planning to set me up and thereby clear himself of the murder completely. This possibility has been haunting me for a very long time, Joby. If he should be successful then I will be facing the long drop.'

'Not necessarily,' Lancer said. 'We are friends, Joseph, and I can now afford to think about setting myself up in business and I could do with an educated, intelligent partner like you.'

'I appreciate your consideration for me, and nothing would give me greater pleasure than joining you in a business; but I am convinced that it is out of the question, Joby.'

'I don't understand.'

'When I took up my career, for want of a more descriptive word, on the road, it was tantamount to joining one of those secret societies, that once you are in, won't let you out.'

'I still don't follow you,' Lancer said, still trying to help his friend.

'It is simple. I have led a dishonest life, just as the wealthy lead dishonest lives assisted by those who run the country, who are also dishonest. They have taken much more than they have a right to from a society that has made laws that favour the haves and mercilessly persecute the have-nots. In my time I have robbed the gentry of a considerable amount of money, and I will never be forgiven. They will hunt me down regardless of how long it takes. One day I would be your business partner, the next I'll be dangling from the gallows on a rope.'

Their conversation had reached an impasse that was relieved for Lancer when a dark-skinned man began squeezing a concertina and another man tucked a violin under his chin and waved the bow. They warmed up by making discordant sounds with their instruments that gradually turned into a pleasant hum. A travelling woman with long, jet-black hair pulled back and tied with a blue ribbon walked over to stand by the musicians. She had a strong-featured face and held herself in a proud stance.

The concertina and violin expertly struck up a melody. The black-haired woman straightened up, waiting for a cue from the music, and then started to sing *Home Sweet Home* in a voice that had angels in it. The rumble of general conversation instantly switched off, leaving the music and the beautifully sung song as the only sounds in the room.

An old woman sitting close to Lancer leaned to her companion to remark, 'That Lucy Hughes has a marvellous voice.'

Lancer couldn't have agreed more. Sitting entranced by the singer and the song, the females of his past romantic liaisons did an abridged and blurred rerun in his head. Then that distant history was replaced vividly by Arabella, Sarai Adams and Nancy Owens drifting separately and tantalizingly through his mind. He was awakened from his half-dream by the concertina player's shout as the vocalist reached the end of her song.

'Now let the dancing begin,' the musician called.

It surprised and delighted Lancer when, as a catchy dance tune was struck up and dancers moved out to the centre of the room, Buckingham Joe suddenly returned to being his usual high-spirited self. Standing up, a wide smile on his face, he patted Lancer on the shoulder.

'Please excuse me for a short while, Joby,' he said politely, 'but there is a lady over there whom I simply must dance with.'

Losing sight of Buckingham Joe as he merged into the crowd, Lancer then saw him smiling happily as he danced with Lucy Hughes. Then his attention was drawn to a man who was standing with his back to a wall watching the dancers. What made him stand out first was his clothing. There was a mediocre sameness about way the rest of the gathering was dressed but he was too smart. The man standing alone was expensively clad in a bronze-coloured coat, burgundy waistcoat, corduroy breeches, earth-yellow stockings and calf-length boots.

Though he tried to give the impression that he had a general interest in watching the dancers, the man couldn't fool Lancer's keen powers of observation. He was in no doubt that the well-dressed man's attention was focused on Buckingham Joe. He had to be a representative of the law, and being able to afford the sort of clothing he was wearing meant that he was of a rank well above a constable.

The dance ended and Buckingham Joe was heading back to Lancer with Lucy Hughes at his side. Lancer divided his observation between Buckingham Joe and the lawman, who furtively kept the highwayman under surveillance. It was a scene that didn't bode well for Buckingham Joe.

'This is Lucy, Joby,' Buckingham Joe introduced his new friend. 'Lucy, this is my good friend, Joby Lancer.'

'I'm pleased to meet you, Lucy,' Lancer said, as he stood to pull a chair across for her. 'I enjoyed your singing.'

'Thank you. It's nice to meet you,' she replied with a charming smile as she sat down.

Compared to most women he had met in his short time on the road, she was a nice-looking, elegant lady. He enquired, 'What would you like to drink?'

'May I have a red-wine?'

'Of course.'

Lancer went to the bar to order Lucy's drink and refill Buckingham Joe and his glasses. Bringing them back through the crowd he made a slight detour to pass close by the man whose presence worried him. This closer look did nothing to diminish his unease about the man. Placing the glasses on the table he got a welcoming smile from both Lucy Hughes and Buckingham Joe.

'Lucy is staying at Mary Blanning's for a few days while she's working this part of Salisbury,' Buckingham Joe said as Lancer sat down.

'What business are you in?' Lancer enquired, not interested but out of politeness.

'This and that. Nankeen mostly, sometimes lace or lavender when it's in season,' Lucy informed Lancer. 'I also do dukkerin.'

'Telling fortunes,' Buckingham Joe translated the Romany word for Lancer.

'I could give you a reading, sir,' Lucy said, as she reached for Lancer's hand.

'I have never really believed in that sort thing.'

'In all modesty, I have a real gift.'

Lancer tried a different deterrent. 'I would have to cross your hand with silver.'

'That isn't so in your case,' she disagreed. Grasping his right wrist she turned the hand palm up.

Studying his hand without speaking for some time, she then began to speak as she slowly traced a line on his palm with and index finger. Uninterested, Lance wasn't listening but was looking around, seeking the well-dressed man. Then he saw him at the far end of the in animated conversation two other men who were obviously colleagues of his and not travellers. Fear for Buckingham Joe gripped him but was defeated by shock as he caught the words Lucy Hughes was saying.

'... this broken line here shows that recently, or perhaps I should say *fairly* recently, you survived death in miraculous circumstances. Since that time the line has become stronger, which means that you will live a long and healthy life.'

Shaken by her knowledge of him, and deciding that Buckingham Joe must have told her about him while they were dancing, Lancer tried to catch her out by saying, 'That can't be right. I had a medical examination not long ago and was warned that I was suffering from an incurable illness.'

'That isn't correct. You must get another opinion,' she informed him confidently. Then she continued, frightening him with the accuracy of what she said. 'Just a moment ... that was an army doctor who examined you, and he told you nothing of the sort. If you have it in mind to lie to me again, then I will go no further.'

'I apologize, and promise not to doubt you again,' Lancer declared.

Lucy accepted his assurance with a nod before going on, 'You were examined by an army doctor because you were then in the army but are no longer so. You served and faced great danger in many foreign countries. Before what has been described as your incredible escape from death you were wrongly accused of desertion or something like that. However, that is all behind you now.'

'Everything you have said so far is behind him, Lucy,' Buckingham Joe pointed out. 'Joby would rather learn his future.'

'Please don't interrupt, Joseph,' she chided the highwayman. 'Much of the future is determined by the past.' She returned to studying Lancer's hand. 'You have been something of a lady's man in the distant past, Joby. But since you avoided death you have matured and now there are only three women in your life, two or them were your lovers, but one of them is now dead to the world but not to you.'

'Your knowledge of my life has more than impressed me, especially your reference to my women companions. In fact, with you sitting so close and holding my hand, I have the urge to add you to the remaining short list,' Lancer remarked jokingly to hide the fact that he was serious. But she raised her eyes to look into his, a serious expression on her face.

'I know that,' she told him. 'I warn you that you would be unwise to do so.'

'You have just spoiled my evening, Lucy,' Lancer complained.

'Which must be preferable to spoiling your life, Joby?'

'Let us discuss that some other time. What of these two women?'

'You want to know which one is the right one for you.'

'That would be useful.'

'You have been out of touch with both of them for some time, the younger one longer than the older, so at this time the choice is yours. You will be in contact with them both soon. Come to see me then and I will be able to help you make your choice.'

'Where will I find you?'

'Along the road somewhere,' was the vague and disappointing answer that she gave him.

Buckingham Joe broke the spell that Lucy had cast on Lancer by saying, 'It's my turn now.'

He presented his hand palm upwards to Lucy. 'Don't go into my past, it's too sordid. Just concentrate on my future.'

Free to look around now, Lancer searched the crowd for the three men without success. Concerned by what their disappearance might mean to Buckingham Joe's safety, he was startled suddenly to hear a distressed exclamation from Lucy Hughes.

'I can't. I'm sorry.'

As she had spoken, Lucy had released the hand of Buckingham Joe, who asked, 'Why not?'

Lucy struggled with a reply. 'I don't know … it's just that … it's just… At times like this I suddenly just lose the ability to read a palm.'

Lancer didn't accept this garbled answer as genuine. He noticed that Buckingham Joe appeared to be as mystified as he was. In fact, the highwayman seemed distressed by Lucy's failure to read his palm.

Passing his friend some coins, careful to ensure that Lucy didn't see the transaction, Lancer said. 'Go and get us some more drinks, Joseph. Maybe Lucy's powers will have returned by the time you get back.'

'I wish you hadn't said that, Joby,' Lucy said sadly when Buckingham Joe was out of earshot.

'Why, Lucy? Surely it's possible that whatever is stopping you from doing Joseph's reading is only temporary.'

Close to tears, Lucy moaned, 'You don't understand, Joby. It's not that I can't read his hand. I have good reason not to want to.'

What was happening came together in Lancer's mind. Lucy's refusal to tell Buckingham Joe's fortune, the menace that was the Kentish Hero, linked up with the three men who had earlier been loitering in the Inn. Recognizing the connection plunged Lancer into a depressed state that he had to fight to conceal from Buckingham Joe when he returned with the drinks.

Apparently having forgotten his disappointment over the failed hand reading, Joseph was his usual sociable self. The possibility that he had diagnosed the problem and was overcoming it seemed very real to Lancer.

Twelve

T HOUGH NEITHER BUCKINGHAM Joe nor Lancer had shown any outward sign of being affected by the distress caused Lucy by the sight of the highwayman's palm, the evening didn't end as pleasantly as it had begun. There was tension between Lucy and them from the moment she had turned down Buckingham Joe's request for her to tell his fortune. There was no animosity in the atmosphere between them, just an uncomfortable awkwardness. When her friends called to her that they were leaving, Lucy welcomed the chance to get away.

'I wouldn't like you to leave without seeing you both again,' she said to Joseph and Lancer before she left. 'Would it be possible for us to meet in the morning?'

'We would like that,' Lancer replied although having serious doubts that Joseph and he would still be in Salisbury at daybreak.

'Shall we say at the Red Lion coffee-house at ten o'clock?'

'That will suit us fine,' Buckingham Joe agreed.

Giving both him and Lancer a kiss on the cheek, Lucy hurried away.

They watched her go with Lancer sure that Joseph was experiencing the same sense of loss as he was. Though always self-sufficient, in the kind of life that the highwayman and he had led, it was comforting to be in the company of someone who was friendly without any strings attached.

Commenting on Lucy's hurried departure shortly afterwards when they were upstairs in their room, Buckingham Joe said, 'There was something really worrying Lucy when she rushed off.'

Welcoming the chance to discuss what had happened in the bar, Lancer had tried to open up the subject by asking, 'Don't you know?'

'I am not a fool, Joby. I do, of course, know, and I am certain that it didn't go unnoticed by you. Nevertheless, it isn't something that I want to talk about.'

Accepting this, Lancer half changed the subject by advising, 'I wouldn't take off anything but your boots when you get into bed, Joseph.'

Grinning at him, Buckingham Joe responded, 'I knew that you saw them, too. That flashily dressed gent standing by the wall and then joined by the other two. The one standing by the wall was watching me the whole time, even though he thought that he was clever enough to do so without me noticing.'

'It worried me to see him and the two others plotting together,' Lancer mused. 'Do you think they will make their move tonight?'

'It's possible, but it would be easier for them to jump me along the road somewhere. I have weighed up the situation here, Joby. Should they come here, at the far end of the landing there's a small window that opens on a sliding roof that goes down to an alleyway. That's the way I'll go out, but you have no reason to run. They won't be interested in you.'

'Maybe not, but I will do everything I can to assist you.'

'We'll see about that if and when it becomes necessary. Right now, let's get some sleep, Joby.'

Lancer discovered that he was too much on edge about the possibility of an attempt to arrest Joseph to relax. But the sound of regular breathing coming from Buckingham Joe's bed told him that sleep had not eluded him. When he judged about half an hour had passed, he was alerted by a scuffling sound in the back yard of the inn. Quietly leaving his bed, he went to the window and looked down on the movements of what were either two or three shadowy figures.

Going to Buckingham Joe's bed he shook him awake. 'I think they are here, Joseph.'

Instinct and experience of similar incidents had Buckingham Joe react by instantly leaping out of bed. He was putting on his boots at the same time as Lancer was lacing up his own boots.

'They will be on their way up the stairs by now, Joseph,' Lancer said. 'There is a door at the top of the stairs that opens inwards. You get out of the window while I hold them off.'

'Come with me, Joby.'

'No. Get moving.'

'I'll wait for you in the alley,' Buckingham Joe said, as he went out of the door too fast for Lancer to object.

Going out on to the landing Lancer turned left, relieved to see that the door was still shut. Moving close to it, he could hear stealthy footsteps ascending the stairs. He waited, poised for action. The door latch was lifted slowly to avoid noise. Then the door gradually opened. Timing his move with precision, Lancer waited until the door was about one-third open. Backlit by light from an oil lamp he could see most of the body of a man pressed up against the door as he gradually pushed it open. Then Lancer took one quick step forwards, lifting his right leg as he went and kicking the door hard with the flat of his booted foot. The door closed rapidly, colliding hard with the man standing behind it. There was a squeal of pain followed by the sound of bodies crashing down the stairs.

Opening the door wide, Lancer could see a man at the foot of the stairs holding an oil lamp and looking down on two men who had been sent tumbling down the stairs when he had kicked the door. One of the men lay head facing downwards at the bottom on the stairs while the second man had landed on him head and face upwards. The face of that man had been hit by the door when Lancer had kicked it was a bloody sight of pulverized flesh and shattered nose and cheek bones.

Looking up at Lancer, the man holding the lantern released a roar of rage and, clambering over the unconscious bodies of his two comrades, came rushing up the stairs waving a truncheon in his free hand.

He wasn't a young man and Lancer caught the sour stench of his belaboured breathing. Waiting until the panting man reached the third stair from the top, Lancer grasped the banister running up the stairs on his right with both hands. Anchored by his grip on the banister he swung his body up and around, kicking out backwards with both feet to catch his would-be attacker full in the face with the soles of both his boots.

With a cry of either pain or fright, probably both, the man was sent flying down the stairs, preceded by the lantern that he had let go of on his way down. Waiting for a moment to witness the man crashing with a mighty thud to the floor at the foot of the stairs, Lancer saw the lantern smash against the wall and flaming oil splash out to ignite the wood panelling that covered the lower part of the walls.

Slamming the door closed he ran along the landing to climb out through the window that Buckingham Joe had left open. Sliding down the sloping roof, he braced himself as he reached the edge to plummet downwards. Landing in the alley on his feet jolted him painfully. He was prevented from falling by Buckingham Joe who ran up to steady him.

'You shouldn't have waited for me, Joseph,' he breathlessly complained.

'I'm glad that I did. You set the whole bloody place on fire,' his friend chuckled. 'Save your breath now, we have to run to the stables and fetch our mounts.'

'Do you think they'll have some men waiting there for you to arrive at the stables?' Lancer enquired as they ran out into the street.

'Not a chance, Joby. They are not that well organized.'

He was proved right when they reached the stables and had harnessed and saddled their horses without interference. Mounting up they headed out of Salisbury passing the Greyhound Inn, the rear end of which was ablaze.

It was two o'clock in the morning in Adamslee and Arabella Heelan lay in her bed wide awake and weeping. She smothered her sobbing so as not to awaken Ruth, who had put in sixteen hours of hard work waist deep in the sea the previous day. Selling the most seaweed she had ever collected in one day, she arrived home exhausted but overjoyed at being able to pass the money from her sale to Arabella.

Though she had hugged and praised the crippled girl out of love and appreciation of her gallant efforts, Arabella had been starkly aware that the money would do no more than keep them and baby Thelma in food for a few days. It would do nothing to forestall the looming inevitable catastrophe when the demand for the rent arrears was made.

She had considered all possible sources of financial help. Though she hadn't been up to Adamslee House, the gossip all around Adamslee was that the once beautiful and proud Sarai Adams was now nought but a shambling alcoholic wreck. It was difficult for Arabella to imagine the sophisticated and eye-catching Sarai fitting the description of her that was now rumoured. What she did realize was that any approach she might make to Sarai for assistance would not only be pointless but also a terribly upsetting experience. The Reverend Worther was a gentle, caring person who would be all too ready to help her, but Arabella was aware that he existed on a meagre stipend that would mean he would starve if he gave to her the amount of money she needed. Her final hope would be Dr Mawby who had become increasingly infirm of late and there was talk that he would soon retire and hand his practice over to a younger doctor. What money he had made in a far from financially viable surgery would barely be enough to support him in retirement.

With the possibility of outside help non-existent, Arabelle recognized that her only chance was to plead for more time to pay. That was a hopeless idea because the rent collector would know, just as well as she did, that the time when she could pay her rent, regardless of making a contribution to paying off the arrears, would never come.

Drying her tears with a handkerchief made from a piece of threadbare and unserviceable bed sheet, the hope of getting to sleep was useless. Within minutes her body was convulsed with deeper sobbing.

They reined up just before entering a village just outside Somersetshire. It was a peaceful countryside community and it puzzled Lancer as to why they had stopped. Occasionally villagers in this sort settlement were wary of and often hostile toward strangers, but the majority welcomed outsiders.

He looked uncertainly at Buckingham Joe. 'What's the problem, Joseph?'

'No problem. But this is where we must part company, Joby. I beg you not to dismiss what I am going to say now as nothing more than a presentiment. From my years on the road I know for sure that somewhere in that village ahead they are waiting for me.'

'Then let's skirt it,' Lancer strongly suggested.

With a negative shake of his head, Buckingham Joe said, 'All that would do would bring me to the next place where they will be waiting. Lucy Hughes saw my future last night, and I know that she was right. It is set in stone, Joby.'

'There is no reason why we should split up. I am staying with you to the end of the road wherever that may be, Joseph. As you said yourself, I am not wanted by the law.'

'Your loyalty is commendable but mistaken. One or all of the three men you knocked down the stairs last night may well have perished in the fire. If you are seen with me even the dimwits awaiting me will manage to think logically that you were with me last night in the Greyhound. Get away while you can. I am the only one who could involve you, and you know that I would never do that.'

This made sense to Lancer, but he was still very reluctant to ride away from his good friend. He pleaded, 'At least allow me to give you some money to help you on your way, Joseph.'

The highwayman managed a sad smile as he replied. 'You are a good man, Joby. But where I am heading neither goods nor money will be any use. Ride away now. Remember that our friendship will survive into eternity. Goodbye, my friend.'

'Goodbye, and may God bless you, Joseph,' Lancer said, a tremor in his voice as he reined his horse about. As he rode away he heard what he feared would be the last words he would ever hear from Buckingham Joe.

'I doubt that will happen, Joby.'

Everything was very ordinary when Buckingham Joe rode his horse into the village at a walking pace. Two women standing talking at the door of a house didn't even afford him a cursory glance. A group of children playing a game of chase paused for a moment to study him, then resumed their energetic game. An elderly man tending some flowers outside of a cottage called 'Good morning' to him and he politely replied 'Good morning, sir', as he passed by.

He was nearing the end of the street when a tall, well-built man stepped out in front of him. An alert, authoritative figure, the man held up a hand in a signal for him to rein in his horse.

'Would you be Thomas Oliver, alias Joseph Infield, alias Buckingham Joe?'

'The choice is yours, sir. I am whichever of those three that you prefer,' the highwayman volunteered genially. 'My personal preference is Buckingham Joe but I have no authority to impose my predilections on you or on any other person for that matter.'

'I am Constable Anton Rawlings.' The big man's facial expression showed his dislike of the highwayman's idle chatter as he introduced himself. 'Permit me to caution you that at this very moment Constable Meakin has a musket aimed directly at you.'

'Thank you for the warning, Constable,' Buckingham Joe said. 'But please advise Constable Meakin that if he should discharge his weapon he will face a charge of murder, as I am unarmed.'

'Dismount slowly from the right side of your horse and I will discover if what you say is true, Oliver.'

Obeying, Buckingham Joe was aware from the careful manner the constable positioned himself to search him for weapons that there was indeed a firearm aimed at him. Glancing around he was satisfied that the man with the musket had to be in a small gap between a cottage and a wood shed.

'Constable Meakin must be really uncomfortable squeezed up against that wooden shack,' Buckingham Joe remarked in a friendly fashion.

'I was told that you talked a lot, Oliver,' an annoyed Constable Rawlings said through clenched teeth. 'Now just keep your mouth shut and let me speak. You are wanted for the murder of one Alexander Moorfield, a Gloucestershire animal feed supplier who was in the County of Devon at the time of his demise. Constable Meakin and myself are taking you in.'

Constable Meakin, a tall thin man, came out from the gap beside the shed, smiling an unpleasant smile at Buckingham Joe as he walked slowly across the street.

'Stay where you are, Oswald, and keep the musket trained on him while I tie his hands.'

'I would be riding on to Exeter to give myself up had I not encountered you, Constable Rawlings,' Buckingham Joe stated. 'That being so, there is no need whatsoever to secure my wrists.'

'You talk too much, Oliver,' Rawlings said, as he secured the highwayman's wrists tightly.

'You are fortunate that you are not facing further murder charges, Oliver.' Meakin spoke for the first time.

Shrugging, Buckingham Joe said dismissively, 'What difference would that make? They can hang me only once.'

'We understand that you stayed at the Greyhound Inn in Salisbury last night, and the place was damaged by fire when you left. Three constables suffered only minor burns, but they could have died in the blaze,' Rawlings informed him.

'I am very sorry about that,' Buckingham Joe said, aware that they were wondering whether he was sorry that the three had suffered burns, or because they hadn't died.

As they helped him up on his horse and secured his ankles together with rope under the animal, Buckingham Joe was rejoicing at having learned that Joby Lancer was not in danger of being arrested.

After leaving Joe near the village, a worried Lancer rode back in the direction of Salisbury. Not knowing what to expect he entered the city cautiously. Securing the horse in a back street he walked to stand among a number of people viewing the rear of the Greyhound Inn. Seeing the extent of the damage immensely increased his worries over the fate of the policemen he had brutally dealt with in the night.

'Shame, ain't it? It'll cost a lot to put it back like it was,' a man standing near him remarked.

'When I heard about it I didn't think it would be this bad,' Lancer agreed, pushing himself to ask a question then steeling himself in preparation for the answer. 'Did everyone get safely out?'

'Yes, thank the good Lord,' his incidental companion replied. 'Three men, probably boarders I imagine, were slightly hurt, and Stan Whittle, the landlord, burnt his hands a bit trying to put out the fire.'

Relieved beyond measure by the good news, Lancer walked back to where he had tethered the horse, mounted up and rode out of Salisbury. Although intent on finding Buckingham Joe as soon as possible, about a mile out of the city he came across a paddock containing a number of horses. Although good fortune had just miraculously cleared him of murder, he couldn't now take the risk of being discovered on a stolen horse, so he dismounted. Pleased that there was nobody around, he removed the saddle from the horse and threw it into some long grass before leading the horse to the gate of the paddock. Opening the gate he led the horse partly in before taking off the bridle. Pushing the horse into the paddock he closed the gate. Walking away, he threw the bridle into the same long grass where he had deposited the saddle.

Stepping back out on the road he drew in a deep breath, exhaled and then walked away a free man again.

As the result of a valiant effort, Sarai Edelcantz had spent the last twenty-four hours without drinking. Now, as she groomed Caesar in late afternoon, she was enjoying being in the world more than she been able to for many weeks. Contrarily, she now felt more ill than she had during the long period of living in a drunken haze. Doctor Mawby, who had supported her as much as she allowed him to, had constantly told her that the only one who could save her was herself.

'The decision must be yours, Sarai,' he repeatedly told her. 'You must decide never to take another drink. I will not be far away if you need me, but I must warn you that it will be far from easy.'

On the last occasion the old doctor had said this she had casually, far too casually, replied, 'It would be much easier for me to keep on drinking.'

'I don't doubt that, and dying will be just as easy,' Rupert Mawby had told her bluntly.

This was the first time he had coupled her excessive use of alcohol with death. It had achieved his intention by terrifying her. She had asked shakily, 'How long have I got if I carry on drinking, Dr Mawby?'

His terse answer had been, 'Less than six months.'

That had been yesterday. She had then immediately promised him, 'I will start tomorrow, Doctor.'

He had shaken his head. 'The time to stop is not tomorrow but this very moment, Sarai.'

'Then I won't take another drink from now on,' she had decided, changing her earlier promise and intending to keep it.

The last day had been hell, and right now she didn't think that she could hold out much longer. Seeing a horseman approaching down the hill she tried to take an interest in who it was. She had to concentrate to do so because people had irritated her terribly in recent weeks. Now she didn't want to have to face anyone. Even poor Mrs Winchell stayed distant as much as possible to avoid her foul moods.

As the rider neared she recognized Kendall Harrison. Kendall the vulture, Sarai said inside of her head, come not to pick the bones of the dead Emil Edelcantz but the hope of sampling the flesh of his widow.

When he reined up his horse beside her, and Ben Morely who had been working nearby had discreetly disappeared, the first thing she noticed was the valise fastened behind Harrison's saddle.

He beamed a too friendly smile at her, saying, 'Good day to you, Sarai.'

'To what do I owe this doubtful honour, Kendall?'

'Now, now, Sarai,' he reproached her. 'Is that any way to greet an old close friend, an extremely *close* old friend if I may say so?'

'Shouldn't you be in Dorchester right now overseeing the next issue of your newspaper before going home to your lady wife?'

'There have been many changes since we were last together, Sarai. I have sold the newspaper; for a considerable sum of money I would add. As for the wife, things haven't been right between us for some time. She has now left me and gone back to stay with her parents in Cheshire.'

That explained the valise he had brought with him, Sarai realized angrily. She berated him, 'What made you think for one moment that I would allow you to stay here in Adamslee House?'

'It would be just a short stay of a few days, Sarai. I have no recollection of you ever rejecting me before.'

'There is always a first time,' she snapped, her wrath having accentuated the sick feeling caused by her short abstention from alcohol.

'I have no wish to upset you, my dear Sarai,' he said soothingly. Tilting his head back he surveyed the hills around them. Catching hold of her hand to pull her nearer to him, he half-whispered, 'Dusk is such a romantic time of day, don't you think? Might I suggest that I saddle that magnificent stallion of yours and we ride together into the hills to discuss this?'

Though her head was muddled, Sarai tried to think logically. To be alone for the evening and the night, yearning for the relaxation that one drink would provide, would be impossible for her to face. She had recognized that long before Kendall Harrison had ridden in. Had he not arrived she would quite probably have opened a bottle by now.

She spoke while wagging a finger at him. 'I will join you, Kendall, but all we will do is to discuss why you are here and whether I should, fool that I am, let you stay.'

'Nothing other than that had crossed my mind, Sarai,' he pledged.

As he turned away to walk to the stables to fetch her saddle, Sarai thought, but couldn't be sure, that there was the trace of a smug smile on his face.

Perturbed by Buckingham Joe's strange behaviour the last time they had been together had for some reason convinced Lancer that his friend was heading for Exeter. Whether his decision had been brought about by Lucy Hughes's refusal to read his palm, or if Lucy had simply given life to something already latent in Joseph's mind, Lancer felt sure that he was desperate to carry out what religion referred to as an act of contrition. In Joseph's case it was likely that he aimed to atone for his wayward life as a highwayman by handing himself in for a murder he hadn't committed.

The fact that it had taken several weeks for Lancer to reach Honiton on foot had greatly troubled him in fear that he wouldn't reach Exeter in time to help his friend. He was walking out of Honiton on the Exeter road when a carter pulled up and called out to him, 'Where are you headed for, friend?'

'Exeter.'

'Well come on board,' the carter invited, patting the seat beside him on the cart. 'I always say that a third-class ride is better than a first class walk.'

'Thank you kindly,' Lancer said, as he climbed up on to the seat.

'I am not prying, just making conversation. Are you an Exeter person, friend, or going there on business?' the carter enquired as he moved the cart on.

'I've arranged to meet a friend there.'

'Best if you find him tomorrow, as the city will be crowded the next day.'

'What is it, some big celebratory annual event?'

'Nothing of the sort, friend. It isn't something to be celebrated but many will be doing so. It's a public execution.'

The blood coursing through Lancer's veins suddenly turned icy cold. He asked, 'A local person?'

'No. You might have heard of him, a highwayman they calls Buckingham Joe. He was tried and convicted of murder some weeks back.'

'I've heard of him,' Lancer said.

'I don't care whether he did it or not,' the carter said vehemently, 'but I don't hold with hanging.'

'I certainly don't,' Lancer said quietly.

'Having said that,' the carter uttered the words thoughtfully, 'we do have a lot of that sort of crime in these parts, and I supposes something has to be done. Have you come across them sort of people in your travels, friend?'

'I can't say that I have.'

''Course you ain't, being a gentleman.'

As they reached the outskirts of Exeter, the carter said, 'Anyway, friend, I hope you enjoy your time in the city. Are you able to stay with this friend of yours?'

'No, that isn't possible,' Lancer replied, the question being a stark reminder that he wished hadn't occurred.

'If you are interested I can give you the address of Mrs Williams who owns a boarding house. It's a very respectable, clean place?'

'I would welcome that. Thank you,' Lancer said gratefully.

It was shortly after dawn when Sarai stepped out of Adamslee House and, out of habit, stood and looked up at the sky. There was a deep red glow on the eastern horizon where the incipient sun of that day was about to rise. Another day she thought, but not in the helpless and hopeless way as she had in recent months. On the plus side was the fact that she had not touched alcohol since giving her word to Dr Mawby. Another possible plus was the arrival of Kendall Harrison at Adamslee House. However there was a big question mark hanging over this. When they had ridden out together the previous evening and had dismounted in a leafy glade, things between them had gone further than she had planned for them to but not so far as Kendall had wanted.

Walking away from the house to open the top halves of the stable doors to save the ageing groom Morely one chore when he rose from his bed, she weighed the pros and cons of Kendall being there against each other. On the plus side was that Kendall was a man, a palpably attractive man, and a rich one. Since the death of Emil Edelcantz her financial status had for the first time in her life been uncertain. Apart from the money factor she had need of a man about the place, but last night she had sent Kendall to a room far along the first landing from her room, and had bolted her bedroom door securely. In Kendall's favour was the fact that she had abstained from drink since he had been there. She was sure that she would have surrendered to her urge for alcohol had she been alone all of last evening. That to her seemed to her to put the stamp of approval on Kendall Harrison.

With the sun now up and shining in all its glory, she went back into the house just as he was coming down the stairs. They exchanged polite guest and visitor 'Good mornings.'

Then she said, 'I am about to tell Mrs Winchell that I want eggs, sausages and bacon for breakfast. Would you care for something different, Kendall?'

'Not at all. I am content and most grateful to have the same as you, Sarai,' he rejoined.

When breakfast was served they both kept the conversation light, although Sarai was aware that he was every bit as keen as she was to discuss the possibility of him staying at Adamslee House. But doubts whether it would be a wise move prevented her from introducing the subject. Though she accepted that it didn't make sense, she felt it would help her to make a decision if he was the one to mention it first. She didn't have long to wait.

With his plate empty he expressed his thanks for the meal, sat back in his chair and came straight to the point. 'Well, Sarai, I believe that we both want to settle the uncertainty as to whether I was just an overnight visitor or am I moving in?'

'Your use of the terminology *moving in* has puzzled me, Kendall,' Sarai said hesitantly to gain thinking time. 'You told me that your wife had left, but your home is in Dorchester.'

'I am selling my house, which means there is nothing to keep me in that town,' he explained, adding, 'The decision is yours, Sarai, and I will abide by whatever you decide.'

'I believe that we should give it a trial run,' she declared. 'That way we can test the idea to see if it works. A rider to that arrangement is that it allows either of us to end it at any time if necessary.'

'That suits me fine. I am sure that it will be to our mutual benefit, Sarai.'

Sarai was about to agree when Agnes, the maid, came in to ask if she could clear the breakfast table.

Epilogue

'GOOD MORNING,' LANCER addressed Reverend Herring who answered his knock to the door. 'My name is Joby Lancer.'

'Good morning,' the tubby little clergyman greeted him, but fell silent for a few moments, frowning. 'Forgive me. Your name means something to me but I just can't recall what. Another positive sign of old age no doubt.'

'I have been to the Bridewell hoping to see the condemned man who is a friend of mine,' Lancer enlightened him. 'I couldn't obtain permission, but the governor suggested that I called on you.'

'Of course!' Herring came close to shouting the two words as he slapped his thigh. 'I have been visiting Thomas Oliver regularly who told me that you were his closest friend. Please, do come in.'

Invited into the small house, Lancer was brought a cup of coffee by an elderly housekeeper. Seated in a large, comfortable armchair, he listened with interest and some sorrow as the clergyman told him that he had seen Thomas Oliver, the name under which Buckingham Joe had been tried and convicted.

'Your friend has found the peace of God and will face tomorrow unafraid, Mr Lancer. He spoke to me a lot about you, and believed that you would arrive in Exeter at some time. He instructed Walter Cole, the prison governor, that he didn't want you to visit him. He told me that his ardent wish was for you both to have a memory of when you were together on the road as free as the Almighty intended men to be. That would not be possible, Thomas said, if your last memory was of visiting him in the condemned cell.'

Able to envisage Joseph saying this, Lancer changed his mind about asking the clergyman to arrange a visit to his friend before he was put to death.

'You say he is at peace now, Reverend?' he asked, needing to double-check.

'You have my word on that, Mr Lancer. In the weeks that he has awaited execution he has found the Lord and is now a devout Christian. As you will know, Thomas is a truthful man. This very morning when I visited he assured me that he will go to the gallows tomorrow happier than he has ever been in his life.'

Lancer would not have been able to accept that about anyone other than Joseph. On the day when they had parted when leaving Salisbury he had sensed that his friend was regretting the life that he had lived.

'Did he tell you that it was not him but another man who committed the murder that he has been found guilty of?'

'He did,' the clergyman nodded. 'However, Thomas is aware that vengeance would make him lower than the person known as the Kentish Hero, but forgiveness would raise him above that man. He also instructed me that if you came to Exeter you must not be here when he faces the hangman. As you know the execution will be held in public. He prays day and night that you will grant him that fervent wish. He also asked that if I should see you I should tell you to return to Adamslee. He says that when you do it will be absolutely clear to you which of the two choices you must make. I expect that you understand his meaning, Mr Lancer.'

'I do,' Lancer confirmed. 'You will be seeing him in the morning?'

'It is my sad duty to be with him right to the end, Mr Lancer.'

'Then please tell him that it would have been hard for me to be here tomorrow, but it will be worse to leave. Nevertheless, I shall do as he wishes. You will have the right words to tell him how my thoughts are with him now and forever more.'

'I will tell him, my son,' the Reverend Herring promised in hushed tones.

Already grieving over his friend, Lancer was further upset when he noticed the tears in the old clergyman's eyes.

Now in a close relationship with Kendall Harrison, Sarai gave thanks to providence for guiding him to her. She had come to realize that she had misjudged him in the past, for he was a far more thoughtful and caring man than Emil Edelcantz had ever been, even in his most affectionate moments. Kendall had spoken of his desire to marry her when the situation with his wife was resolved. Sober and clear-headed for many weeks now, Sarai told him that was what she wanted, too. He was out riding that morning and, finding lately that she hated being parted from him, she hoped that he would have returned as she made her way back to the house after a pleasant walk in the garden.

As she reached the front of the house her heart pounded as she saw a horse tethered to a post near to the door. Then she was disappointed to see that it was not Kendall's fine chestnut but a pony. The rider was standing at the door talking to Agnes. When the maid saw her approaching she pointed her out to the rider, who hurried to her. She found herself dreading whatever it was that brought the stranger here.

Little more than a boy, nervousness caused him to stutter when he got to her, he held up a folded piece of paper he was carrying in his hand. 'Mr Trevor Bolland, the Governor of Dorchester Pris—'

'I know who he is, boy,' she cut his stammering short, wondering why she was treating the lad so rudely.

Then, as the blushing lad handed her the paper, she recognized that the same feeling of dread was still with her. She unfolded the paper and began to read.

My dear Sarai
I am writing to you because Kendall Harrison has left Dorchester and I fear that he may be heading your way. He is in trouble, Sarai. His newspaper business has collapsed and he is destitute, with no wife, no business premises, no home, no money, and massive debts. Having known Kendall for a long time I am familiar with the way his scheming mind works. It is likely that he will see you as widowed and vulnerable but financially sound.
  My advice is that he is smooth-tongued so should he come to you must not listen to a word that he says. Send him on his way.
  With kindest regards
  Yours
  Trevor Bolland

Sarai spoke to the lad as she folded the letter. 'Thank you for bringing me this. Please thank Mr Bolland for me. What is your name?'

'Robin, mistress.'

'Well go back to the door and knock, Robin. When the maid opens the door tell her to give you a nice meal of whatever you fancy.'

'Thank you kindly, mistress,' the boy said, pleased to get away.

Sarai turned facing the hill that Harrison would come down when he returned. She would wait for him and wouldn't have permitted him to dismount were it not for the fact that he would have to pack his belongings before leaving. She would make certain that he would not remain at Adamslee House for one minute longer than necessary, even if it meant using the shotgun on the rack in the hall to drive him away.

*

It was exactly eight o'clock in the morning when Lancer, riding a horse he had purchased in Exeter the previous day, topped a hill above Adamslee. He had planned to get here at this time in the belief that a once familiar view would ease his anguish over what Buckingham Joe would be going through at that very moment. There was nothing that could lessen his sorrow or alter the horrific picture he had in his mind of his friend's last moments on earth. He had an impulse to dismount and kneel in prayer, but resisted the urge thinking that it would be sinful, because of the time that had elapsed since he had last prayed.

He found himself watching as a sparrow taught a youngster to fly while a tiny rabbit, totally entranced by the demonstration, tried it itself. The furred, panicky catastrophe that resulted caused the feathered student to crash-dive, while the adult sparrow, screaming abuse, chased the rabbit through hawthorn bushes.

Guilt overwhelmed him then as he realized that Joseph had died during the brief time he had been distracted by the display of nature. Then it occurred to him that the diversion had been a miracle sent to comfort him at that terrible time. Thinking that was an excuse for being too cowardly to share the suffering of his friend, he reprimanded himself as he rode off in the direction of Adamslee House.

Unsure of how Sarai would greet him, as well as wondering whether he should be here at all, Lancer dismounted and walked to the door of the house.

'The mistress is poorly, sir,' the maid who came to the door informed him.

'Is it possible for me to see her for just a few minutes?'

About to reply, the maid remained silent as Sarai's voice came from behind her.

'Let him in, Agnes. I saw him riding up.'

The way the words were slurred should have warned Lancer. Even then he wouldn't have been prepared for the sight of Sarai as she appeared behind the maid. Her hair was unwashed, loose and straggling. Her eyes were puffy and bloodshot, while her normally strong-featured face was swollen.

'Go on about your duties, Agnes,' she mumbled, before opening her arms in invitation to Lancer. 'Come on in, Joby dear. Welcome home.'

When he made no move towards her she came at him with her arms still open wide and a crooked smile on her face. Revolted by both the way she looked and the odour that came from her, he swiftly turned and hurried to his horse.

'Joby, darling. Joby, please do not leave me.' She was crying, running towards him as he swung up into the saddle. She stumbled and fell to her knees. Staying down on her hands and knees she raised her head, matted hair falling about her now tear-stained face as she called to him, 'Don't leave me all alone. Please, Joby. It was Emil Edelcantz who betrayed you, not me.' She screamed out more words. 'It wasn't me who betrayed you, Joby. I can't live without you. I can't live … I can't live….'

He voice faded away. She was such a pathetic creature that he was moved so strongly by pity that he was about to get down from his horse and go to her. But his good sense clicked in and he pulled the horse's head round, kicked his heels into its flanks and rode away.

Don't look back, he instructed himself. A few feet further on and his conscience gained the upper hand. Rising up in the saddle he half turned to see her lying face down in the dirt with her arms stretched out in front of her body. Agnes and Mrs Winchell had come out of the house and were running towards her.

Be strong, he commanded himself as he kicked his horse into a trot and rode away.

A short while afterwards he was riding along the cliff and saw Ruth Heelan wading through the sea with the large basket on her back. Going further along the cliff he came to the path and guided his horse down to the beach. There he dismounted and walked to the water's edge.

'Ruth,' he called, but she ignored him.

'Ruth. It's me, Joby Lancer.'

This time she turned her head in his direction. After a slight hesitation she started wading to the shore. As she came limping out of the water she said, 'I am sorry, I didn't recognize you. What are you doing here?'

'Just paying a visit.'

'Will you be going to see Arabella?'

'Is she well and happy?' Lancer enquired.

'She is well but not happy. My mum died and I am living with Arabella now. She can't find work and I don't make enough to keep Bella, her baby and me.'

'What about her husband?'

'Lionel, my brother, deserted her ages ago. I know she is not your responsibility, but it would mean a lot to her if you paid her a visit. She is really unhappy today as the rent collector is due.'

From the way she said this Lancer gathered that Arabella lacked the rent money. He put an arm around Ruth's thin shoulders, telling her, 'It was great seeing you again, Ruth. I won't keep you from your work any longer, and I promise that I will go to see Arabella now.'

Hearing the door latch being lifted struck terror through Arabella. A few hours earlier the rent collector had called. When she told him that she still had no money, then tried to come up with a lie that her husband had written that he would be home soon, he hadn't believed her. Staring at her, undressing her with his eyes, he had told her menacingly that he would be coming back later in the day. He had left her in no doubt what he was coming back for.

Willing herself not to look at the door as she heard it opening, she gazed lovingly down at her little girl who was sitting on the floor playing with a rag doll that Ruth's mother had made for her. She heard the door close and had the urge to pick up her child and flee. But that was impossible. Not only was there nowhere for her to run to, but she couldn't even get out of the house.

Unable to stand the strain, she held her head high as she looked towards the door. Then a strangled almost incoherent whimper came from her. 'Joby Lancer.'

It was him. As handsome as ever he stood there smiling at her. Unable to believe her eyes she blinked twice before exclaiming. 'It is you, Joby Lancer.'

'It's me, Arabella,' he assured her. 'I have money now and I have come to take you away from here.'

Unable to move, she stood looking at him afraid to believe that this was really happening and not some mental breakdown caused by near-starvation and worry. Then she saw that Thelma was looking up at Lancer with one of her special smiles. If her child could see him then it was Lancer standing there. What she was experiencing was real. Yet she still decided to test the reality of it by asking a question, knowing full well what the Lancer she had known would answer.

'Can we take Ruth with us?'

'We most certainly can.'

That was proof enough for Arabella and she ran to him. He took her in his arms and she heard him quietly say, 'Joseph was right.'

'Who is Joseph?'

'He was a very good friend of mine, Arabella,' he answered. Then he kissed her. Clinging to him Arabella shed tears of relief. The terrible dread of the rent collector's return faded away as she was held in Joby Lancer's arms. At last she had a future, the secure and happy future she had longed for ever since she was a girl. The dark cloud that seemed to have settled on the house many years ago had suddenly been lifted.